The Shikari 2:

The Evil Headmaster

DORA BLUME

Dora Blume

Visit my website

www.DoraBlume.com

https://www.facebook.com/Do
raBlumeAuthor

Printed in the United States of
America

First Printing: January 2019

ISBN: 978-1-5136-4254-3

For my students, who have changed my life
in so many ways.

You remind me every day to be better. Thank you!

I love each and every one of you.

Table of Contents

Chapter 1

"Ugh, I hate flying. So, what the hell are we doing now that we're in Denver?" Sloane bent to the right of the exit, brushing off her pants.

Erik shook his head and smirked. "I'm sure that kid didn't mean to spill on you, it was an accident."

"Yeah, yeah. So, where are we going?" Sloane stood up, checking her dark spiky hair.

"We've got to meet Magnus in baggage claim. He's our contact in Denver. He'll fill us in on the missing girl." Erik shifted, waiting for her to finish. He brushed his blonde hair back out of his eyes.

"Do we know anything beyond her being a high school student?"

"That's why we're meeting Magnus; he'll fill us in on the details. He has the reports from the investigation here in Denver. Her father was a high-ranking official in the order."

"Well, in that case, lead the way." Sloane reached to grab the handle of her carry-on.

Erik hurried and took the escalators down to baggage claim. They had to wait for a few minutes before the loud buzz announced their luggage was coming down the chute. Sloane had been leaning against the wall texting. Her hand seemed to be glued to her phone. He couldn't imagine what she was texting that couldn't wait until they got settled, or at least until they found Magnus. Erik only knew they were to meet Magnus, and he would fill them in when they got here. Bryant, Jessie, and Mike had driven because they had to make a few stops along the way. Bryant wanted them to get here quickly and start doing some recon work. Erik wouldn't have minded the drive, but with his ability to hear people's thoughts, Bryant thought he should get here as soon as possible. Bryant was also hoping that Sloane would get a vision of the future. Erik was truly doubtful she would. He didn't see her being much help.

Sloane walked over to retrieve her bag. "Hello, Earth to Erik. I thought you were going to get our bags?" She waved her hand a few inches from his face, and he grabbed it before she could move back.

"Don't do that; I hate that," he growled.

"I know, that's why I did it. Where did you go just now? Did you hear anything interesting?"

"I was just thinking about what we're supposed to be doing here. I'm not entirely sure it was necessary for us to get here sooner than the rest." He shrugged his shoulders and turned back to the carousel. His bag was coming around the corner. He grabbed it off the carousel and placed it next to him.

"Oh, I see, you wanted to drive with them. Maybe get some time with Jessie? I noticed you two getting close. Want to share the history there? A few days in the car with her could bring you closer together." She winked and laughed at the smirk he was giving her.

"Our history is none of your business, and I wasn't thinking about that since we'd be in the car with our father." He ran a hand through his hair, pushing it out of his eyes.

"Whatever, I'm glad we flew. Although, I hate it. I like that it's so much faster. I have better things to do than spending a few days in a car." She looked down at her phone.

"Seriously, would you put that away for a minute. We need to go find Magnus." He turned toward the exit and found the guys in suits holding signs. He glanced down the line until he saw a short man wearing a Hawaiian button-up shirt and khaki shorts. The old man's face was wrinkled with two jowls loosening his round face. He smiled, the old man had long gray hair swept to the side to hide his hair loss. His welcoming round face turned to look at the tall man in a suit standing next to him. He smiled up at the man and shrugged, then looked to the other man in a suit, towering over him. He shrugged again and looked forward, plastering a wide smile on his face. Erik knew that was Magnus; he was exactly as his father described. Bryant even made a point to say you would know him when you saw him. "He's a little different," were his exact words, and Erik could see why.

"Hey Sloane, Magnus is over here." Erik pointed over to the men standing in one area holding various white signs. Most of the men were in black, tailored suits. Magnus stood out like a sore thumb.

"Oh good, we're going in style. Which one is Magnus?"

Erik smiled, knowing she hadn't looked at the men. "Follow the line to the right until you find the one guy that looks out of place."

"Out of place? What do you mean, out of place?" She glanced down the line of men until she stopped on the one guy not wearing a suit. "Oh perfect, just perfect, is this Bryant's idea of a joke or something? Couldn't we have a decent guide? He had to find the wackiest person he could to show us around the city. Just perfect." Sloane slammed her phone into her pocket and grabbed the handle of her suitcase. She trudged toward Magnus.

Erik laughed, "I thought you weren't the prima donna type, Sloane?"

"Shut up; I like to travel in style." She dropped the handle of her suitcase, huffed, then picked it up again.

"Can you see anyone more stylish than him?" he motioned his open hand toward Magnus.

"Whatever, that wasn't the style I had in mind."

"Be nice; you don't even know him." Erik reached out his hand, stepping in front of Magnus.

"Hi, I'm Erik, and this is Sloane." He motioned to his sister standing next to him. He looked over, and she had put on an award-winning smile just in time.

"Well hello, nice to finally meet you. I think I got the time wrong. I've been here a little while. Oh well, let's get you two kids on home, shall we?" Magus headed to the parking lot.

"Wait, home what do you mean home? I thought we were staying in a nice hotel or something?"

"Oh no, my wife wouldn't hear of it. You will be staying with us. We have plenty of room. There's something like, seven bedrooms in our house. I'm just doing what I'm told. I'll let you know; she's the one calling the shots here. It's certainly not me." Then under his breath, he said, "it's never me."

Erik couldn't help but laugh. "Lead the way, Magnus. Don't mind my sister; sometimes she forgets how to be nice, or to thank others for their generous hospitality."

Sloane rolled her eyes at him. "Yes, of course, lead the way." She glared at Erik.

Magnus walked them to a plum PT Cruiser, and Erik smiled again. "This your car, Magnus?"

"Yeah, my wife picked it out for me." He opened the back to put their bags in.

"Stylish," he responded and swung his bag into the back. He grabbed Sloane's and did the same. Magnus shut the door and moved to get into the driver's seat. Sloane got in the back, slamming the door. Erik looked through the window. Sloane had crossed her arms over her chest with a pout. Erik shook his head and got in the passenger seat.

Magnus looked in all of his mirrors, he double checked the height of the steering wheel and moved it down slightly. He checked all the mirrors again and adjusted the rear-view mirror no more than a quarter of an inch. He seemed like he was nervous and overly thorough in his check. Erik had never seen anyone check to make sure all their blinkers were working before even leaving the parking space. When he was done with his inspection, he looked to both Erik and Sloane "Okay I think we're ready to go."

"Are you sure?" Sloane asked, her tone biting.

"Yes, I believe we're ready," he boasted.

Erik shot a glance back to Sloane, waiting to catch her eye before turning back around.

Magnus put the car in reverse and very slowly began to back out of the space, suddenly he hit the break. Then he eased on the gas slightly, then suddenly the break again. He went to the gas, then the break again. Erik couldn't believe it. They hadn't even gotten out of the space yet. Sloane moved quickly to buckle her seat belt. The same thing happened a few more times before Magnus put it into drive. He then eased on the gas pedal, but as soon as he did, he hit the break. He did it again, the same thing a little on the gas, then on the break.

"My God, are you driving with both feet?" Sloane said from the backseat. She already had her hand on the handle above her head and was shaking her head. "At this rate, I will have a severe case of whiplash before we even get out of the parking lot."

"Oh, I'm sorry this is how I drive." Magnus put on the break again.

Erik couldn't take it; they couldn't drive through Denver like this. They wouldn't get anywhere. "Do you mind terribly if I drive?" Erik asked trying to be as nice as possible.

"Well I don't know, I usually don't let just anyone drive my car," he hesitated.

"Oh, you don't have to worry about Erik, he's a great driver."

Erik couldn't believe his ears, "Oh yeah, I am a good driver. I promise I will take good care of your car. How about we switch spots?"

"I'm not sure about that; you don't even know where we're going." He gripped the wheel tighter turning his hands in a circle.

"You can give him directions from the passenger seat." Sloane sat forward in her seat.

Magnus looked over to Erik and shrugged. "Well, I guess it'll be okay." He moved to go back in the spot but hit the break as he hit the gas pedal.

"It's fine, let's switch here. We'll be quick," Erik said. He couldn't imagine continuing to watch Magnus try to park again. Plus, he wasn't sure his neck could take much more of the whiplash.

"Are you sure? I don't think we should just switch here." Magnus turned his head looking out both windows, then in the rear-view mirror.

"It'll be fine, let's make it quick. Throw it in park and let's switch." Erik opened his door hoping that would make it final.

"Okay, okay." Magnus put it in park and got out of the car. By the time he opened the door, Erik was standing next to his door, waiting.

Magnus got out of the car and sluggishly moved to the other side.

Before he could open the car door, Sloane sat forward. "Do you think he moves quickly at anything?"

"Doubt it," Erik said, as Magnus opened the door. He sat to buckle his seat belt, pulling it out as far as his arm would reach, before pulling it well across his body and finally clicking it into place.

"So, you need to head out onto Highway seventy." Magnus pointed toward the signs showing the way to the highway.

Erik decided to read Magnus' thoughts to get the directions instead of waiting for Magnus to actually give them to him. When he did, he caught a glimpse of the house Magnus was talking about. He wasn't kidding; it's a big house. Shikari members always had money. He received a monthly payment for his service in Minneapolis. He knew he would get more depending on the job and his age. He knew his father was making more than him because he was the liaison for Minneapolis.

After some light traffic, they made it to Magnus' house. Erik parked in front and got out to grab their bags. "You have a nice place here, Magnus."

"Thanks, it's all my wife's doing. She picked it out and designed everything in it." Magnus grunted a minute and glanced over hoping they hadn't heard him.

Sloane took in the house, "Your wife has good taste, I can't wait to meet her."

"She's inside. She'll be waiting for us, I'm sure," Magnus grumbled.

Magnus walked up the steps, hunched forward and opened the door. He shouted, "Honey, I'm home." His tone was acidic.

"A classic," Erik looked sideways at Magnus as he set his bag down in the entryway.

"Hmph," Sloane said as she set her bag next to where Erik left his.

A very boisterous woman glided down the stairs. Her auburn hair was in tight ringlets that framed her face. She wore a cream-colored pantsuit with a gold necklace around her neck. When she reached the landing, she moved in to greet her guests. "Oh, how wonderful, you've arrived. I'm Jolene. I trust you had a comfortable flight. Magnus showed you the best hospitality I'm certain. Oh, how wonderful to meet you." She reached out to hold both of Erik's hands and then went to kiss him on both cheeks. Erik was surprised but reciprocated the kisses.

"Oh well, aren't you just the sweetest thing ever, and so handsome." She looked over to Sloane and dropped Erik's hands. "Oh, and look at you, aren't you just the most beautiful little darling I've ever seen." She grasped both of Sloane's hands and moved to kiss her on both cheeks.

She dropped Sloane's hands and stepped back. "Why Magnus, have you ever seen someone quite so beautiful. I can tell you both have good genes, yes, very good genes indeed. But of course, you do, Bryant's your father and aren't you just the spitting image of him." She looked in Erik's direction. Sloane baulked, but she closed her mouth quickly.

Erik looked over to Sloane before mumbling, "Ah, thanks, I guess." He wasn't all that happy about being compared to his father. He didn't look anything like him.

"So, can you show us where our rooms are? It would be nice to get settled and figure out our next move." Sloane looked to the stairway.

"Oh yes, of course, of course. I'm sure you could use some decompression time. Dear, would you be so kind as to show Erik where his room is, and I'll take our dear Sloane, here."

"Wait, are we staying on different floors or something?" Sloane asked her tone sharp.

"Well, of course, dear, men are on the lower floors and ladies stay upstairs. Is there a problem with that?" Jolene asked.

Erik spoke up quickly before Sloane could be rude "No, there's no problem." He glanced in Sloane's direction, meeting her eyes, hoping she would agree.

"I guess that will be fine." She receded.

"Well, alright then, let's head up the stairs. Don't worry about your bag dear; I'll have Magnus take it up to you later." She nodded toward Magnus.

"Oh yes, I would love to take your bag up for you," he said, sarcastically.

"Oh no, I'd rather take my own things. Besides, I'd like to get settled in right away." She lifted her bag and turned toward Jolene.

"Okay dear, well then, we'll be heading right up these stairs." She turned back to the stairs. Sloane followed. They passed by three rooms, then Jolene went to open the third door on the left. She walked gracefully into the room and held out her arms.

"This is where you will be staying." She walked over to a door on the left side of the room. She opened the door and stood against it, her hand still on the handle. "This is your private bathroom. I know how us girls need our own space in the bathroom." She closed the door and moved over to another door on the other side of the gold four poster bed. "And here is your closet." She stood again against the door with her hand still on the handle.

Sloane peeked her head around the bed to see in the closet; she couldn't believe how large it was. She could easily fit ten different wardrobes in there. She couldn't help but smile at the thought. Yes, she could get used to this.

"I can tell you like it, of course, we girls need plenty of space for our clothes. Well, now you've seen your room, would you like a tour of the house?" Jolene walked toward the door expecting Sloane to follow her out.

"Um, if you don't mind, I could use a few minutes to relax after the flight. Can I come down in a little while to see the rest of the house?" Jolene had been so nice she didn't want to hurt her feelings, but she wanted a few minutes to herself. She also wanted to text Mike to see how far they'd made it, and when they would be arriving in Colorado.

"Well, of course, dear, I can imagine how you must be feeling with everything that's happened. You sure can have all the time you need, dear. Just head down the stairs and to the left. Dinner will be served at six sharp, and the dining room is just down the hall from the entryway." She smiled one last time before she moved to the door and closed it behind her.

Sloane moved over and fell backward onto the gold, four post bed. "I always wanted to do that, in a bed exactly like this." She grabbed her phone out to text Mike. She wanted to take a nap after the flight, but she knew she should try to get a vision while they were here. Maybe, she could figure out what the hell the demons wanted in Colorado besides good weed. She had to admit; she wouldn't mind a little right now, get her in the right mood for all this. On the other hand, being high in the midst of who knows what would be a very bad idea. She tried to concentrate and moved into a sitting position. She closed her eyes and tried to listen to what the universe had to tell her.

Magnus waited until his wife had reached the top of the stairs then turned to Erik. "Follow me, us men get the lower floors. Wouldn't want us staying on the same floor as the ladies. Damn, traditional southern values." Magnus continued to grumble as he walked.

Erik couldn't help but laugh, "Yeah, women, right?"

"Tell me about it, that woman has me so tied up, I can't even take a shit without asking her permission." He shrugged and continued down the hall.

Erik followed shaking his head; he couldn't believe that someone as powerful as Magnus was taking orders from a woman. Magnus showed him the stairs to the basement.

"Wow, you weren't kidding. We get the basement, huh?" Erik smirked toward Magnus.

"Yep, we get the basement. Don't worry; it's as nice down here as it is upstairs. She wanted to make sure I had a nice man cave.

She'd never let a guest stay in anything but luxury." Magnus grumbled, "I, on the other hand, get to sleep on the couch when she decides. Tons of rooms in this house and I get the couch."

He showed Erik into the first room on the right. He wasn't kidding about the man cave. He could see down the hall into a billiard room. "Is that a pool table down the hall?" Erik couldn't help but ask.

"Yep," Magnus responded quickly, then went back to showing him the room. He walked in and opened another door. "Here you have your bathroom." He pointed to the other door, "and a closet if you need it." He looked down at Erik's bag. "Okay, that about covers it. I'll be upstairs if you need me. We eat at six, sharp." He moved out of the room quickly. Erik could tell he didn't like having to be the host, especially with his wife around.

Erik grabbed up his bag and set it on the bed. He kicked his shoes in the corner and sat in the chair behind the large mahogany desk. He couldn't believe the inlaid of the desk. It was beautiful; he knew there weren't too many desks like this one. He pulled out his phone to message Jessie to see where they were, and when they would arrive. He finished and set the phone on the desk. He was relieved that Sloane asked for some alone time because he was beat. The flight wore him out, and he was going to catch a nap before they had to get back to work. He knew that once Bryant was here, they'd be on a mad dash to figure everything out. He wanted to rest before they were on the hunt again. He hoped Sloane was doing the same, so that they could find out about the missing teens.

Chapter 2

After a few hours, Erik woke to a start. He heard something crash in the adjacent room. He got out of bed quickly and opened his door. Magnus was bent over in front of a bookshelf. Books lay scattered and opened at his feet. He bent to retrieve two, closed them and placed them back on the shelf. He muttered to himself, "Damn, stupid, god-forsaken shelf."

"Do you need any help?" Erik asked.

"Oh no, I'm just a little clumsy sometimes." Magnus waved his hand and went back to picking up the books. His short, sausage-like fingers couldn't hold more than two books at a time.

Erik bent next to Magnus and picked up a pile of books, stacking them on his knee. "It's alright; I needed to get up anyway."

"Did you sleep well?" Magnus asked after he stacked the last novel on the shelf.

"Yes, I did, thank you." Erik took a step toward the office door. "If you'll excuse me, a second." He headed back into the room to check his phone. He wanted to know how far away Bryant and the rest were. Erik looked to his phone; there was a message from Jessie. They, made it to Nebraska. Bryant is checking with a friend then they'll be on the road again.

Erik knew that Bryant planned to talk with a few other members before getting to Colorado, but he couldn't imagine who was living in Lincoln Nebraska.

Erik headed back to Magnus. He found him sitting at a desk with papers scattered across the top; some lay on the floor next to the desk. Magnus had one hand splayed over one stack while his other hand held another. He was frantically looking from one to the other. "So, it sounds like they've made it to Lincoln Nebraska where they're stopping and talking to a few people, before continuing to us."

"Ah yes, of course, they're most likely stopping to talk with Alex before they head here. He'll know anything going on in his area. It wouldn't surprise me if some demons were hiding out in such an inconspicuous place. There's also a lot of power hiding out in Lincoln." Magnus nodded to himself "Very smart stop indeed," he said again to himself as he grabbed another stack of papers and set it on top of the one directly in front of him.

These papers are a little chaotic, Erik thought.

"Yes, I work well with Chaos," Magnus answered.

Erik's mouth dropped, and his eyes were wide. "What?"

"It can be annoying. I certainly didn't want to know what my wife was thinking, but suddenly there it was." He looked up to Erik. "I suppose I should explain; I can copy other powers from those who are near me. I can read minds right now because you can. I guess you could call it a sort of transference.

I haven't gotten anything from Sloane, but yours was pretty easy to pick up and copy." He smiled.

"Oh, that's interesting. Bryant said you were very powerful." Erik sat in the chair in front of the desk. His father had been right, being able to copy anyone's powers made Magnus powerful and interesting indeed.

"So, is Jolene powerful too, or is she normal, so to speak?" Erik was curious. Shikari married other Shikari, always. Other people weren't allowed to know about them. It was a rule; if you were to marry, you had to marry another Shikari hunter. Erik had never been serious enough with anyone to even think about it, but since he had Jess, he hadn't needed to. Amy shouldn't have even known about them, but that was on Sloane, not him. He wondered for a moment if Sloane had even talked to her since Minneapolis. She didn't have a place in their life, but he thought it would be rude if she cut her out entirely.

"Yes, she's one of us. She can blow shit up if she wants to. Don't make her angry, trust me. She lit the damn couch on fire when she was angry with me." Magnus shook his head remembering.

"So, if she can blow things up, can't you do it, too?" Erik was curious as to how far his power extended, and how it worked.

"Yes, I can copy her power. I haven't needed to, and I sure as hell am not going to use it back on her. She's fucking crazy." His eyes darted to the door then back to Erik, then to the ceiling.

"So, what's Sloane's power? I haven't gotten a read on her, yet."

"She can see the future, but it doesn't always work." He knew firsthand how Sloane's power wasn't as helpful as Bryant and everyone thought.

"Ah, yes powers like that can be temperamental," he smiled.

"Speaking of Sloane, I might go up and let her know what's going on. We need to talk to the girl who was kidnapped by the demons." He started for the door. "Ah, so where is she staying?" he asked.

"She's up the stairs, in the third room on the left. She may be sleeping. You both seemed exhausted when you arrived." Magnus shrugged.

He took two steps toward the door, turned, and said, "Thanks." He bounded up the stairs and knocked on Sloane's door.

"Come in," she called.

He opened the door and popped his head in first.

"Hey, ah Jessie, Mike, and Bryant made it to Lincoln, and are stopping to talk to a few people before they continue here. Magnus said there's someone there named Alex that's head of the area." Erik sat in the chair near the window. Sloane sat on her bed with her laptop opened in front of her.

"Yeah, they'll probably stay the night before they head out. Alex, huh? I wonder who that is." She looked up from her computer, staring into space then went right back to it.

"What are you doing exactly?" Erik asked.

"Checking the local scene. I want an idea of where we should start." She looked up from her computer. "Do you have any idea where we should start?"

"Ah, not really I thought we should talk to the girl who was kidnapped, first."

"Oh, Jolene gave me the report from her questioning, already. Not much there to help. She was out with some friends, the next thing she knew, she was in a strange house. Her father found her and dispossessed her. She didn't have much to share. Here, see for yourself." She handed the report to Erik.

"Were the friends Shikari members?"

"No, just some regular kids from school. Her father kept her in a public school in Denver, Mullen, I guess. The friends said she was meeting up with some guy. It wasn't all that strange for her to meet up with new guys." Sloane typed a few keys on the keyboard before focusing on the screen again.

"One friend said he was a college guy. They'd met near campus a week before her disappearance. She gave the description in the report, but she didn't know much beyond that."

"Yeah, I think the college may be a good place to start."

"What's the deal with college students?"

"No idea, I'm doing some research to see where we want to go." She focused back on her computer.

"What have you discovered?" Erik asked. He perched behind her to see the computer screen.

"I think we should start tonight in Lodo. It seems to be the best spot for nightlife. Tomorrow we can head out to the U of Colorado and check out the campus." She closed her computer.

"Sounds good to me. When do you want to start?"

She looked him up and down "Um, you need to go shower and change before you're going to any club with me." Her voice was filled with both annoyance and authority.

He glanced down at himself. "Oh yeah, okay, so, what maybe in an hour?"

"Do you even know what time it is?" she asked.

"Well no, I don't," he admitted.

"We'll be joining our hosts for dinner in about thirty minutes, so you should probably go get ready for that first. I don't think it's a good idea to show up at the club at seven We'll do some more research and maybe check out any other reports before going to the club." She continued her authoritative tone which Erik found to be annoying. He'd forgotten his sister's desire to be in charge of things. He'd always been the leader, making leadership decisions as his father had. Now, Sloane was leading him. It felt strange to him to be doing what someone else had planned.

"Oh yeah, I didn't even realize. Alright, I'll go get ready for dinner." He turned and left the room.

Sloane stared at the blank screen on her phone. She was waiting for a text from Mike. She hit the messages app and saw her messages had been delivered. Why wasn't he answering back? She thought as she stared at the screen. She clicked on his name and began typing. Where are you guys? Why aren't you answering me? She stared at the words, Do I sound desperate? She wasn't sure why Mike wasn't answering her. It was obvious he'd read all her messages. Was a ninth message too many? She felt a knot settle into her stomach. The only reason he wouldn't be answering, was if he was mad at her. Was he mad enough to end a relationship? She sighed and set her phone face down next to her laptop. She needed to focus. She took a deep breath.

She opened her laptop back up and began researching Denver. She typed into Google, hot spots in Denver for college students. Shit, there were over two million results. She needed to narrow that down. It seemed like lower Denver was popular so they would start there. She was hoping it would be as easy as last time, and they'd find them on a college campus. The only problem was there were like twenty-two colleges in the Denver area. Bryant's informant said they were in Denver. She wasn't one hundred percent sure about Bryant's informant either, since he wasn't exactly giving up who the person was or anything. It was convenient to have Erik around.

She glanced to the clock in the corner of her screen. Shit, dinner was in five minutes. She needed to get downstairs. She reached the dining room, which had been elegantly set for a dinner of four. The pearl plates had gold rims, which matched the wine glasses. Cloth napkins were held by gold rings. In the center was a long glass vase with long-stemmed white lilies. Sloane ran her finger along the petal of a lily, caressing the soft silkiness. She sighed and went into the kitchen to find Jolene. She wanted to tell her how beautiful the table looked.

"Hello?" Sloane called before catching sight of the woman at the stove.

The woman was short and hunched over the stove. Her back looked as if she'd been hunched in that position, holding the weight of service on her shoulders for decades. She jumped when Sloane called and almost dropped the spoon she was holding onto the floor.

"I'm sorry, I didn't mean to frighten you." Sloane couldn't help but move toward the woman.

"Oh, It's okay. You must be Jolene's guest. Hi, I'm Penelope. I do the cooking and some of the cleaning here." Her tone was warm and welcoming.

"Nice to meet you. I'm Sloane. Any idea where Jolene went?" Sloane looked to the other door in the kitchen. She wasn't sure where everything was in the house.

"Um, I believe she went to go talk to Magnus downstairs, but I wouldn't disturb them. You can take a seat in the main living quarters, and I can fetch you when dinner is served. It will only be a few minutes." She smiled and turned back to the skillet. The aroma of garlic and onions wafted to her nostrils. She inhaled heavily, savoring in it before her stomach grumbled in answer.

"It smells so good, Penelope. I'll be in the main room, thank you." Sloane turned and headed back to the living room. She thought about heading back to her room but figured she could check her phone down here just as easily. She wished she would have asked where Erik's room was so she could find him. She figured he was downstairs, but she was going to heed Penelope's warning not to look for them. She figured there was a reason, or she would have told her where the room was located.

It wasn't too long before Jolene had come to find her.

"Oh dear, I am so dreadfully sorry. I hope you haven't been waiting long." Jolene came right up to Sloane and stood in front of her. She was wearing a black pencil skirt and plum, ruffled blouse.

"Oh no, it's fine," Sloane said, standing quickly.

"Oh good, good, Dinner is ready in the dining room. Penelope said that you came looking for me. She is such an amazing cook; you'll love her." She waited for Sloane to stand, then walked into the dining room.

Erik and Magnus entered through the kitchen door just as we entered. Sloane gave Erik a look. He wore dark gray button-up collared shirt and black slacks. The silver belt buckle reflected in the light from the chandelier. Sloane smiled, nodding her head in approval. His hair was slicked back from his face, but a few strands fell over his forehead in rebellion. His bright blue eyes stood out in stark contrast to his dark clothing.

"I do hope you were able to rest well." Jolene looked to both of them.

"Oh yes, your beds are amazing," Sloane answered.

"Ah yes, I do enjoy my comforts. A good bed is one of them," Jolene glanced momentarily toward Magnus, then twisted the wedding ring on her finger.

Magnus looked down to his lap, a sly smile spread across his face. Sloane looked to Erik, and one side of his mouth was lifted. Sloane wanted to ask but thought better of it.

"So, what's the plan for you two this evening?" Magnus asked.

"Oh, we're heading to lower Denver tonight to check out some clubs. Tomorrow we'll head to the university campus to see if we can find anything out about the college guy who may be involved with luring our victim." Sloane explained.

"Oh yes, that sounds like a good place to start." Magnus nodded and turned to his wife. "Don't you think so, dear?" Magnus focused on his wife, and for a moment, Sloane wondered if there was something more to that comment, something she may be missing.

"Yes, Magnus, it sounds like a good plan. These two are as beautiful as they are smart, I can see." She held Magnus' gaze, then reached for her wine glass. Realizing a moment late, it was still empty she rose from her chair. "I'm going to see what's taking Penelope. If you'll excuse me a moment."

Sloane looked to Magnus, "You know most of what goes on here correct? Has anything else happened that you would consider out of the ordinary, especially with demons or the order?"

"Well, since the legalization of Marijuana happened, weird is every day here." He chuckled.

"Okay, besides that, anything with the Shikari? I mean, it's not like they're all getting stoned before hunting demons. Unless they have some kind of death wish." Sloane was concerned with Magnus' evasiveness. He was avoiding her question which she found suspicious.

"They better not be getting stoned before hunting," Magnus grumbled.

Erik looked to Sloane and moved his finger to tap his temple twice. She narrowed one eye for a minute; then she looked to her plate as she inhaled sharply. Erik was letting her know that one of them could hear thoughts, too. Clearing her mind as best she could, she took another deep breath. It always felt like an intrusion when she knew someone could hear what she was thinking. She liked that her brother didn't intrude on her thoughts. At least, he claimed he didn't. She wouldn't be able to control herself if she could hear everyone's thoughts. On the other hand, there were some things you couldn't unknow once you heard them. She figured his rule of not listening in on friends and family was probably for his sanity as much as anyone else's privacy.

Jolene returned with Penelope and a bottle of white wine. She took her place at the table and poured herself a glass before handing the bottle over to Penelope. "Would anyone else like a glass of Bella Sera Pinot Grigio? It's one of my favorites; it has a rich body with a hint of citrus and peach."

"I'd love some." Erik answered, "Sloane, I bet, would too. She's a big wine connoisseur."

"I would love a glass, thank you," she side-eyed her brother.

Penelope moved to pour them both a glass and served all of them. The angel hair pasta was covered in fresh bruschetta and a light vodka sauce. The garlic, tomato, and onions smelled delicious. Sloane had to stop herself from shoveling it into her mouth like a ravenous beast.

"So, what do you two do for fun in Minnesota? I hear it gets so cold there. I couldn't imagine going out in such cold weather all the time." Jolene looked between the two.

"Oh, it's not so bad. You get used to it. I hear you get more snow here than us, right?" Erik responded then scooped another forkful of pasta into his mouth wiping away the dripping sauce with his napkin.

"Oh, yes, I believe we do, but it usually melts right away," Jolene said

"Thank God for that, sometimes I don't even have to shovel," Magnus said quickly.

"Oh please, like you do any shoveling." Jolene shook her head at him.

"Oh, I do plenty of shoveling all right," Magnus said but looked down at his food when his wife gave him a stern look.

Sloane downed the last of the wine in her glass. She hated small talk. She wasn't sure if she trusted these two. They should be discussing what they knew about the girl who'd been kidnapped or anything suspicious going on.

"So, you two had quite the scuffle in Minnesota I hear," Jolene said.

"Yeah, we sure did. Didn't Bryant tell you all about it before we came here?" Erik asked.

"He told us a little about why you were coming. We only heard about the battle through the grapevine. Bryant didn't say too much about it. That man has trust issues when it comes to telephones, I swear." Jolene shook her head.

Sloane stared at Erik, narrowing her eye slightly. She tried to clear her mind of thoughts again before she thought about the implications of what Jolene said. There would be a reason Bryant hadn't filled these two in, and Sloane thought they should know what it was before telling them anything.

"Yeah, it was quite the battle. The demons have been possessing college students. We took care of the ones in Minneapolis, but they have a bigger plan, we just don't know what it is yet. The demons lead us here." Erik explained.

"Oh, a battle, it's been years since we've been involved in any real battle. Can you tell us what it was like? It's been so long." She smiled at Magnus. "We must be getting too old, dear."

"The battle was hell." Sloane responded, "But we made it." She sighed heavily.

"I bet," Magnus said, watching her as she spoke.

Sloane finished eating and wanted to excuse herself, but knew it was rude to leave the table before everyone was finished. She tapped her foot on the floor and tried to think of something to say to change the subject.

"So, how long have you lived in this house?" Erik asked.

"Oh, what has it been now?" Jolene looked to Magnus.

"A very long time," he responded.

Penelope came into the room with more wine. "Would anyone care for more wine?"

"Oh, none for me thanks," Sloane responded.

Erik shook his head.

"I'd love another glass, please. These two have serious business to attend to. I have no such business, so I believe I will indulge." She smiled wide as Penelope poured her another glass. "Why don't you just leave the bottle here by me, dear? I don't believe anyone else will need anymore." She lifted her glass to her lips and took a small sip, "So, I presume you two will be off to your work tonight then."

"Yes, we need to get ready. We're heading to Lodo tonight to see what we can find out about what's going on here." Erik moved his chair back.

"Yeah, it seemed like a good place to start. Well, if you two don't mind, we will be getting to it." Sloane stood "Thank you for dinner; it was lovely."

"It was our pleasure, dear," Jolene said. "Let us know if you need our assistance with anything." She smiled wide then, rose her glass to her lips to take another drink of her wine.

"Will do," Erik said and walked out the door. Sloane followed.

"So, do I get to see where your room is?" Sloane asked.

"Oh yeah, sure, follow me." He walked toward the basement.

They passed through the kitchen and Penelope was busy at the sink filling it with water.

"Thank you for dinner tonight, it was delicious," Sloane said.

"Thank you, dear," she responded and returned to the sink.

Erik continued through the kitchen into another hallway that led down to the basement.

"This is such a big place," Sloane said. "I wish I could afford something this extravagant. The two-bedroom apartment that I was living in is lacking compared to this place."

"I wouldn't know, I stayed living at home." Erik ran his hand through his hair.

"Yeah well," Sloane wasn't sure what to say. She didn't want to dredge up the past, but his comment bothered her. "Some of us couldn't stay in the same place after what happened," she sneered.

"Seriously, it wasn't the house." Erik shot back.

"It was all of the memories associated with it. I just needed to get away." She took a deep breath.

"Maybe I wanted to get away too, but someone had to stay behind and pick up what was left." Erik couldn't believe they were talking about this now. "Can we just get on with what we're here to do."

"Yes, we absolutely can." Sloane huffed out a breath. She wasn't sure if he would ever get over her leaving. She had hurt both Erik and Mike when she left, but she couldn't stay at the time. It was too hard, too many things reminded her of her mother. She cried all the time back then. If she had stayed in the house, it would've been worse. Leaving seemed like the right thing to do. She blamed Bryant for everything. She couldn't live there when she thought he was responsible. She knew she had been a coward for running, but she couldn't change it now. She tried to clear her mind. She needed to be clear-headed for tonight.

Erik opened the door to his room and moved to the side so that Sloane could step in. There was a large bed with four mahogany posts in the middle of the room. Sloane could see that Jolene had spent time meticulously designing the entire house. This room was meant for a male guest. On top, the bed was dark blue comforter with matching shams. To the right was a mahogany desk with a brown leather chair. On the opposite side was a brown leather chair with matching ottoman. Every detail was meticulous, down to the carvings on the headboard and the dark Reconstructive era painting that hung above it.

"So," Sloane plopped in the brown leather chair. "What now?"

"We still have a few hours, let's check social media to see if anything suspicious is happening." Erik sat at the desk and opened his computer.

Sloane took her phone out of her pocket. She sighed looking at the screen — no new messages. She would have to see what the deal was with Mike when he got here. She typed a message to Jess instead.

"I'm running up to get my computer." She got up quickly and left the room.

Chapter 3

E rik was on his computer researching when he realized Sloane was taking a long time. He glanced at the clock. She'd been gone for over an hour. She said she'd be right back. In fifteen minutes, he'd find her. He hadn't had much luck finding out anything on any social media. He thought he'd find something. Everything is always documented on social media, even things that you never wanted to know.

Fifteen minutes had passed, time to find Sloane. He headed up the stairs. He ran into Magnus as soon as he reached the landing.

"Have you seen Sloane?" he asked.

"Not lately, she went upstairs a while ago." He shrugged. He looked like this conversation was keeping him. His mouth seemed to be muttering things, but no words came out.

"Oh, before I forget. Do you have a car we can use to get to town tonight?"

"Oh yes, of course, ask Penelope where the keys are. She will show you to the car, as well. I'm afraid I have business to attend to." He launched down the stairs with more speed than someone his age should have.

Erik wanted to ask about what business he had to get to but knew by the way Magnus took off down the stairs; it wasn't something he was willing to share. They were strangers, after all. Just because they were both Shikari, didn't mean they automatically trusted each other. Trust had to be earned.

He headed up the stairs to find Sloane, maybe she knew about what was going on with their host. He reached the door to her room and knocked. He waited outside the door, but after a few moments of tapping his foot on the floor, he knocked again. The door flew open, nearly nailing him in the face.

"What?" she demanded.

"What, nothing. You were supposed to be coming right back with your computer."

"Oh yeah, I forgot." She waved a hand dismissively and walked over to sit on the bed.

"So, why do you look so distracted?" Erik asked.

"Um, nothing really. So, are you ready to go?" Sloane asked.

"I guess since you're not going to talk about what's going on." Erik studied her for a moment.

She stared back at him in defiance. "Wasn't planning on it."

"Fine, I asked Magnus about a car. He said Penelope would give us the keys and show us to the car. He had important business to attend. He didn't feel like sharing. The way he bolted down the steps made me think it was important, though." Erik ran his hand through his hair.

"Great, let's get to it." She grabbed her purse off the desk. Erik studied her as she turned.

"Come on already." She strode out the door. Erik followed behind her closing the door.

"So, where is Penelope?" Sloane asked when she reached the bottom of the stairs.

"Kitchen," Erik responded.

They reached the kitchen and Penelope was sitting at the table reading, a glass of wine in her hand. Sloane noticed her feet didn't reach the ground. She swung them under the table as she read. She was so engrossed she hadn't noticed them enter the room.

"Hello Penelope," Erik interrupted. "Magnus mentioned you'd have a car that we can use."

Penelope looked up from her reading. "Oh yes, of course." She moved to the key rack and removed one of the square black keys. "Here, I'll show you out to the garage." She motioned her hand for them to follow her out of the kitchen and into the back entranceway. She slid on a pair of shoes and walked out the door. She hit a button on the key chain, and the garage door opened to reveal a black Dodge Challenger. She looked back to Erik, "Here's the key." She pointed to the small button on the connected key chain. "This opens the garage door; I think you can figure out the rest." She smiled and headed back into the house.

"Not too bad for a borrowed car." Sloane went around to get into the passenger seat.

"I'm surprised you're letting me drive." Erik got into the driver's seat.

"Yeah well, sometimes I like to be driven around." She smiled as she clicked her seatbelt.

Erik headed toward lower downtown Denver. He planned to park and walk around, listening.

"So, what's our first stop?" she asked.

"I figured we'd head to Howl at the Moon first. Seemed like a fitting name for our purposes." He smiled and winked at Sloane. She shook her head at him.

"Why that place, other than the name?" she asked hoping that he had another reason other than the namesake for going there. She didn't want to waste time when they needed to figure out what was going on here. She wanted answers, especially since they had no problem possessing another Shikari member. She was young, but still. The idea bothered Sloane. If they could possess Shikari members, they'd all be in trouble. Imagine if they possessed a member with a unique power. It was the one thing hunters had against the demons. Their powers allowed them to fight. Without that advantage, they'd be ripe for the picking. Sloane shook her head at those thoughts. There was no way they could possess grown Shikari members. They were too strong and would fight against demons. Besides, Sloane had always been taught that their angel blood protected them against demons. What if it didn't? Was everything she'd been taught wrong? What else could be wrong? Her string of thoughts had her worried.

"The names not enough?" He looked to Sloane, and she scowled at him. "It's popular among college students. They have two pianos at the front and take requests. It's a hit on campus."

"Okay good. Do you know where you're going?" she asked.

"Yeah, I do." He looked over to her, and a look of doubt was planted on her face. "What? I do."

"Have you been to Denver before?" She wasn't sure how he would know his way around.

"I have," he said and hoped she would leave it at that.

"Oh really? When did you have time to travel to Denver?" Her eyebrow shot up in peaked interest.

"After I graduated, I came here to check out the schools." He looked to his lap then back at the road. He brushed his hair back from his face and chanced a glance over at Sloane. She was staring at him; her mouth parted slightly.

"What? You wanted to go to school here why?"

"I don't know, at the time I wanted to get away from home. I wanted to at least consider a college for myself rather than what I've been told I have to do. I wanted to make some choice for myself." He clenched the wheel with his hands. He looked from the side mirror to the back. He stole a glance at Sloane, and she was studying him.

"So, why didn't you go?"

"I was needed to fight demons. I didn't get much of a chance to do anything else. There aren't enough of us in Minneapolis, and I needed to do my duty as a Shikari." Erik looked down.

"Oh, I see, Bryant guilted you into staying." She sighed. "You've always followed what he wanted you to do, no matter what you wanted, huh? You should have said fuck it; if you wanted to go to college, you should have gone to college." She placed her hand over Erik's on the wheel.

Erik looked to her hand then back to her. "Bryant didn't guilt me into staying; I'm the one who decided what was more important. What we do, killing demons, saving people, it's important. I realize how important it is. Do you?" He was annoyed with her. He still hated how easy it was for her to walk away from her family, her duty to save people as Shikari. Part of him envied her, but he was angry he didn't have the same opportunity.

"What? Of course, I know what we do is important. I wouldn't be here otherwise." She turned her head to look out the window, crossing her arms over her chest. Erik focused back on the road.

"The only reason you're here is because we came and found you. If it weren't for me, you would still be in your two-bedroom apartment with Amy, discussing the upcoming party. Let's be real. You couldn't care less about the Shikari or helping us." Erik studied Sloane for a minute before focusing back on driving.

"That's not true. I could've told you to go to hell when you found me. Don't fool yourself; I'm here because I want to be here."

"You can tell me to go to hell if you like. I could never do that; I'm in this till death. I doubt you have the same loyalty. I believe in the Shikari, and all that we stand for, even though, right now, it's corrupt. It's my mission, and my life to bring us back to the values we've held for millennia. Can you say the same?" He glanced over to her again.

"No, I can't. They killed our mother. Where is your loyalty to her? Where is your compassion for her? I can't pledge my loyalty as long as they're the murderers of our mother. They can burn in hell for all I care." Erik watched her clench her hands into fists. She continued to stare out of the window. She didn't want to admit how much Erik's words bothered her. She couldn't believe he was so trusting, even now.

"You know that was because of a few corrupt members. The entire order isn't to blame." Erik shook his head.

"Well, as we're finding out, there are more than just a few corrupt Shikari. I believe we should question them first. I don't trust any of them right now."

They had made it to downtown Denver, and Erik was pulling into a ramp. He parked and looked to Sloane. "I know that Mom's death hurt you. It hurt me too, but we need to put that behind us if we're going to succeed. We need to keep our head in the game. I agree we need to question them. You're right about the corruption being deeper than we first thought. We also shouldn't judge them all for the actions of the few. That's not right either. Do you blame, Jessie, Mike, Bryant, and myself for mom's death? Because we are part of the Shikari. I just want you to place your blame where it belongs, and I promise we will find the people responsible. We need to end the corruption even to have a chance of continuing the order and all the good that we have done. Don't forget that, the Shikari have done some great things, too. Right now, we need to focus, can you do that?" Erik had turned to study Sloane's reactions as he spoke. She could feel the weight of his gaze on her. She knew he was right. He usually was, but she'd never tell him that. His ego was big enough. A tear rolled down Sloane's cheek.

"I don't blame any of you for mom's death. I know it's the few who have corrupted the entire Shikari. It's hard not to blame them all. They didn't stop the corruption. They let it happen when it could have been stopped. I know I need to be focused on stopping what's happening here. I'm here to help end the corruption."

"You never believe those closest to you could ever betray you. That's why no one saw a betrayal from the inside coming. Now, we need to end it and make sure it doesn't happen again." He looked to Sloane; her hands were still clenched at her sides.

"So, are you ready or do you need a minute?"

"I'm ready, let's go party." She winked at Erik, and he shook his head.

"We're not here to party." Erik's tone was serious.

"You may not be here to party, but I definitely am," she smirked at him and wiggled her brows.

They left the ramp and headed down the street toward the bar. When they reached the street in front of the Denver Chophouse Brewery, they saw a line heading down to Howl at the Moon. "Shit, of course, there's a line," Erik put his hands in his pockets and rocked back on his heels, straining to see the end of the line.

Sloane moved her finger along her neckline smiling, "Please, lines don't stop me." She swaggered along the outside of the line with Erik in tow. At the front, she paused in front of the bouncer and winked, running her finger along her low-cut hem. "Hey honey, do you think my brother and I could get through?" she smiled, blinking at him through her long lashes.

"You and your brother, huh?" his eyes evaluated Erik from head to toe then looked to Sloane. "Yeah, go on in." She ran her finger down his cheek. "Thanks, hun, hope to see you later." Her hips rolled as she struts into the club. Erik shook his head and followed.

"Does anything stop you?" he asked.

"From getting into clubs? No, not that I can think of." She was scanning the room to see if anyone stood out to her. "Do you hear anything?" she asked Erik.

"Other than everyone talking at once and the piano in the corner no, not really." He shouted into her ear.

"Okay, well, let's head to the bar to get a drink. Does this crowd seem a little older than college students to you?" She scanned the crowd. They seemed older. Men with beards and flannel filled the room. The women had messy updos and long maxi skirts. It wasn't like the scene in Minneapolis at all.

"Now that you mention it, they do seem older, but maybe that's the abundance of beards throwing me off. Online it seemed to be a hotspot, but I guess it could've been wrong." The band was playing a cover of, The Boxer, as they made their way to the bar.

"It's still early; maybe the college students will be around later." She motioned to the bartender and ordered two beers. She handed one to Erik. "I thought we should start light." She smiled and held up her glass to cheers. "Here's to our success." He clinked his glass with Sloane's. "Let's go find a seat."

"Could we find one on the fringe of the crowd? I need to be able to concentrate on their thoughts" he said as he followed her to the corner where there was one free table.

"Well, that was lucky," he said as he set his beer on the table. He looked around the room to scan the scene looking for anything out of the ordinary.

Sloane looked to him. "How about you scan their heads, I'll worry about scanning the crowd? It's not like they're going to stand out or anything. You're the only one with the advantage here."

He moved, placing his elbow on the table, resting his hand atop his fist. He closed his eyes to focus on their thoughts. He didn't want to be the weird guy with his eyes closed in the middle of the crowded room.

"I got nothing, I think we struck out here." Erik closed his eyes one last time to double check. He wanted to make sure he wasn't missing anything.

"Nothing, huh?"

"Nope, nada, there isn't a single demon in the place. Lots of thoughts about sex though." Erik stood and moved away from the table.

"Sex, huh? Not surprising in a bar. I guess we can go, since there are no demons here, well not the possessing kind, anyway." Her lip jutted out in a pout. Erik was curious as to what had her distracted, so he quickly scanned her thoughts and regretted it immediately. Her thoughts matched many others at the bar. She was thinking about sex.

"Forget about Mike that easily, huh?" Erik shook his head at her.

"No, stay the hell out of my mind brother." She stomped out of the bar and burst through the door onto the street. When Erik caught up, her hands were clenched in fists against her thighs.

"So, where to next?" Sloane asked.

"I think Herb's is going to be our best bet." Erik walked down the street.

"So, how far is it from here?" Sloane asked.

"It's a little bit of a hike, why?" Erik responded.

"Oh, no reason. These shoes are more stylish than comfortable."

"Whose fault is that? You knew we were looking for demons. Should have prepared better." Erik stopped in front of Herb's and lit a cigarette.

"Yeah, yeah. I thought you stopped smoking those." She stopped alongside him and pointed toward the cigarette.

"I cut back but haven't quit, yet. We've been busy." He inhaled deeply, enjoying the moment. He was also searching the surrounding minds. He closed his eyes to concentrate on people's thoughts, both in and outside the bar. He opened his eyes quickly, he heard a demon inside Herb's, but it wasn't a college student.

"Sloane, there's a demon in there, but it's not who you'd think." His tone rose in surprise.

"Oh yeah, not a college student, I take it?" Sloane waited.

"Nope, it's the bartender. The older lady." He jerked his head to the side in the direction of the bar. Sloane looked through the window.

"Hmm, well at least she's a hip, older lady. Must've been a hippy at one time."

"I think it's still weird," Erik said.

"Yeah but think about it. Who is the one person everyone will share their deepest, darkest secrets? The bartender, she's a perfect plant for them. She gets all the dirt and passes it on to the other demons. Look around; it's popular around here. The place is packed, overflowing out the door. It's perfect." Sloane was looking around the block. "How close do you need to be to hear her?" she asked.

"I don't want her to be suspicious of us, which could happen if we go in."

"I can hear her from about a block away, maybe more. Why?" Erik said looking around and seeing a patio across the street.

Sloane pointed up to the roof patio, "Will that work?"

"Yeah, I should be able to hear her from there," he responded.

Sloane headed across the street. She went to the host and asked for a table on the patio. He nodded and said, "Follow me."

Erik followed, and Sloane smiled at the host before he left.

"We'll need to order some food, but we should be able to stay here until they close." Sloane moved her chair slightly to scan the room.

"This works, I can hear her from here." He scanned the bar and listened to those around them. He didn't want to be surprised by another demon. It seemed all clear, so he focused back on the woman.

"Incoming," Sloane said a moment before the waiter came to take their drink order.

Erik's head snapped up a second before the waiter reached their table. Sloane ordered a Crispin, and I asked for a Red Rock IPA.

"So, hear anything interesting?' Sloane asked.

"Not yet, she doesn't seem to be thinking about much beyond the crowded bar, and the drinks she's making. It might be awhile." Erik took a drink before attempting to refocus.

The waiter came to take their order. He was tall and lean with spiky blonde hair. He dropped his pen when he jostled his notepad, trying to flip to a clean page. Sloane bent to retrieve it. She fluttered her lashes when she held the pen out to him. Erik shook his head; he wondered if she even noticed she was flirting, or if it just came naturally in everything she did. After their order was placed, Erik turned his attention back to the thoughts around him.

"So, have you heard anything from Jess as to when they'll be here?" Sloane asked.

"Yeah, she said tomorrow. They got information from whoever they saw in Nebraska. Why anyone would live in Nebraska is beyond me." He took a drink of his beer.

"It's nice they're at least answering you." She took a long pull from her bottle and clasped her hands tightly in front of her.

"Yeah, I guess." Erik went back to listening. He didn't want to hear Sloane complain about whatever problem she was having with Mike.

Erik sat upright in his seat quickly, "I think I got something. She thought about a meeting she has tomorrow with other demons. It sounds like it'll be at the local university. Some professor is heading up the meeting. Older guy, brownish gray hair, and a full beard. Typical professor type, suit and all." Erik looked over to Sloane.

"Any idea which campus?" Sloane asked.

"Yeah, the professor is in the ECS building, fifth floor, room five-ten. Hold on; she hasn't thought about when other than tomorrow." He rested his head on his hand, listening.

"Okay, anything else?"

"She's thinking about how early the meeting is, and how late it's getting. She has to close the bar, so she isn't happy about the early meeting. She's trying to think up an excuse for not going but isn't coming up with any. She knows she needs to be there."

"So, early tomorrow ECS building. Do we need to stick around here longer, or can we take off?" She glanced around the patio. The waiter had already dropped off their check and was glancing over to the table periodically.

"I think we can take off. Unless we want to check out other places. See if there are any other demons around, we should know about." Erik felt energized. He loved the hunt; he drummed his fingers on the table in anticipation.

"I'm not sure; I'm up to heading to any more bars tonight. I think the action of the last few days is catching up to me. I'm beat." She yawned. "I'd like to take some time to see if I can get a vision tonight. I haven't been able to wind down since Minneapolis, and I would like to try."

"We should go then, catch some sleep before the meeting in the morning. We'll get some leads at a demon meeting. I still can't believe how much things have changed. Demon meetings are becoming a regular thing. What next, demon cocktail parties? At least that would make sense since they're demons. This whole college campus thing is throwing me off." Erik threw his hands up before standing. He dropped a twenty on the table for a tip and walked toward the front door. Sloane followed close behind.

Erik reached the car and got in quickly. He agreed with Sloane; he was beat. It had been a long few days between the hunting and battle a few days ago. The last few weeks felt like months. He could use a good night's rest and, suspected Sloane could too. Erik could see the dark circles under Sloane's eyes, indicating she hadn't rested enough either. They could both use a good night's sleep. He knew neither of them would get the rest they needed until this was all over, but he was determined to try.

Chapter 4

Sloane walked down to the kitchen looking for coffee, lots of coffee. Erik said they needed to leave for the campus by eight. Sloane didn't like her good night's sleep being reduced to four short hours. She swore she'd catch a nap after all this was over. She deserved a pajama day as far as she was concerned. Then the thought occurred to her; she may never get a pajama day again. She shook her head to clear that awful thought.

"Morning sunshine," Erik smiled from the kitchen table.

"Seriously? Go to hell, Erik. How are you so chipper, right now?" Sloane moved to grab a mug and the coffee pot.

"Well, aren't you just a ray of sunshine?" He took a drink from his mug.

"I already told you to go to hell. Do you want me to put you there?" she threatened.

"Keep dreaming sis; you couldn't send me to hell. You love me." He cocked his head in a defiant gesture and crooked the corner of his mouth up.

"Not right now, I don't." She sat at the table, cradling her coffee cup in both hands.

"You got about ten minutes to wake up before we have to leave." He got up to pour himself another cup of coffee.

"Seriously, ten minutes?" Sloane took another long drink from the cup. She closed her eyes as the coffee slid down her throat.

Erik finished his coffee and went for the keys. "I'm running down to grab my phone; then we can go."

"Okay, I'll run up and get my purse. What weapons are you grabbing?" she asked.

"Magnus gave me access to the stash downstairs, just a few guns, and knives. Things I can hide on my body. You want me to grab you something?"

"Yeah, could you?" she headed toward the stairs.

"No problem," Erik emerged from the basement holding a duffel bag and keys. Sloane was standing by the back door for him, hand on her hip.

"Ready?" Erik asked.

"Let's do this." She was preparing herself mentally for the possible fight.

They both headed to the car, Erik opened the trunk to dump off the duffle, then headed for the driver's seat. They were off to campus. "Could you get directions to the campus?" Erik asked.

Sloane took out her phone and searched the address. She hit the navigate button, and the voice of the navigator filled the air.

Sloane was silent for the ride. She was still trying to wake up before they jumped into whatever role she would need to play today. She rested back in the seat and closed her eyes. She tried to focus her energy on a vision of what was to come. She wanted to see what they were getting into before they arrived at the college. She didn't want to be blindsided again. Last time they went to check out a college campus; they sent Amy in to find out the building was filled with demons.

Sloane felt Erik's tap on her arm, "Did you fall asleep?" he asked.

"No, just trying to have a vision of what we're walking into before we walk into it."

"Any luck?" he asked.

"No, not really. Just a few quick flashes. It's like the universe hasn't decided the future, so I can't see it." She shook her head. She felt useless when she couldn't get a vision. She thought that the potion Shaundra gave her would help her get visions when she wanted, but she knew her power didn't exactly work like that.

"That's weird, I wonder what the universe is waiting for?" he asked, mockingly.

"That's not funny. Remember last time? Amy walked into a building full of demons. I don't want to be surprised like that again." Sloane opened the door and got out of the car.

"Yeah, I remember. I will hear it if the building is full of demons." He tapped his finger to his temple.

"That's good because I feel useless." Sloane closed the door behind her.

"So, are you going to let me get to the weapons, or are you keeping them all to yourself?"

"Keeping them." He rolled his eyes and went to open the trunk. "Remember, we're here to get leads, not kill them."

"Yeah, I know, but we still need a few weapons just in case." She bent to see what she could fit in her purse or on her person. "Aren't you grabbing any?"

"No, I already have what I need on me. Some of us like to be prepared before we reach our destination. You know, just in case something happens on the way." His tone was mocking.

Sloane grabbed one last gun, and slipped it in the back of her pants, pulling her shirt down over it. "You can be such an ass sometimes. Speaking of being prepared, are we trying to look like college students cause neither of us has a backpack?"

"I hadn't thought about it. I'm sure there are others on campus without backpacks."

"Sure, Let's go with that." She rolled her eyes.

"Whatever, no sense worrying about it now. Let's go."

"Lead the way, little brother." She smirked and squared her shoulders.

"You know I hate that, right?"

"Yep, that's exactly why I do it."

Finding a bench outside the ECS building, Erik lit a cigarette and sat down. Sloane sat next to him. "Anything yet?" she asked.

"Nope, but I know she'll be here soon." He sat back and inhaled a long drag from his cigarette. Sloane watched him slowly release the smoke from his mouth. She rolled her eyes at his casual appearance. Sloane scanned the approaching students, trying to recognize the bartender, she'd never seen. Closing her eyes, she tried to focus on her powers, searching for the tell-tale sign of demons.

"Why don't you text Jess or Mike to see where they're at?"

"Yeah, I would like to know what time they're coming." Sloane focused on her phone and sent a text to Jess. She knew Mike wouldn't answer her. Thoughts of Mike filled her head. Taking a deep breath, she stared at her phone. Mike still hadn't answered her messages. He hadn't forgiven her, despite her apology. She didn't get what the big deal was, one mistake shouldn't ruin what they have. Taking another breath, she typed in, *Hey, what time are you guys arriving? We're on a lead right now and could use your help. Lmk.* After a few moments, Sloane's phone dinged signaling a message.

"So, where are they?" Erik asked.

"They're a couple of hours north. It sounds like they're heading straight here. She said the information they found out isn't good news, and they need to get here quickly." Sloane sent a text back about where they were, and what they found out the night before.

Erik sat bolt upright as he felt the hair on his arms stand up. "There's a demon close by, I can feel it," he said looking around, trying not to be noticed.

"You didn't hear their thoughts?" she asked as she scanned around them.

"No, apparently not, but I'm searching." Erik became still before he spoke. "She's walking up to the building with another demon. She's talking about how tired she is from working at the bar. They're both headed to the building."

Sloane slid her hand in her bag, wrapping her fingers around the grip of the gun. Erik touched her hand. "We're only looking for information, remember?"

"Sorry, instinct," she said.

Erik stood, and Sloane rose a moment after he did. Feeling the familiar tingling up her spine, she knew another demon was near. She turned to Erik, "Ha Ha Ha Ha Ha." She tried to fake laugh but sounded a little too on edge to pull it off.

"What are you doing?" he asked.

"I realize that you're focused, but some people are staring at us. I thought I would pretend you said something funny, so they'd stop staring. It worked." She looked to the two, and their attention was back on each other. She didn't think they were the demons she felt, but it was good to keep up appearances.

"Oh good," Erik lead her into the building. As soon as she saw the coffeehouse, she grabbed his arm and led him in the direction of the coffee shop. She loved that they could both work and grab a coffee.

"Can you hear where she went?" Sloane asked as she joined the line.

"Yes, they're upstairs."

"Any chance they'll be out of your range if we stay here?"

"I'll be able to hear what's going on as long as we're in the building."

"Perfect, I can enjoy my coffee and maybe a little breakfast since I only had ten minutes before we left this morning." She smiled, her arm still wrapped in Erik's

"You're unbelievable," he shook his head.

"What? We get to blend in and enjoy some food while you listen to what's going on. I personally think I'm a genius. Plus, aren't you the one yammering on about needing breakfast to function or some such nonsense." She punched his arm playfully and smiled.

"I do love me some breakfast." He focused on what they were thinking upstairs. "Holy shit," Erik said under his breath.

Sloane looked over to him concerned, but she didn't want to say too much. They were still in line and the woman ahead of them had already turned around to roll her eyes at Erik. Sloane grabbed Erik's hand and looked into his eyes, warning him of saying anything out loud.

Sloane walked up and ordered for both of them. Erik followed her to wait for their drinks. Sloane could tell by his blank expressions that he was concentrating hard on what was going on upstairs. When they finally got their drinks and reached a table, Sloane leaned forward, getting closer to Erik before she spoke. "What's going on?"

"They have a school here. They're possessing high school students. One of the kid's parents is possessed. I can hear her thoughts along with the demons. She's screaming, not my child, in her head." He explained, then his eyes glazed over, focusing.

"Are you fucking serious? They're going after high school kids. That's insane." Sloane said in disgust and shock.

"Yes, now please wait, so I can get all of the details I've seen a picture of the inside, but I'm hoping one of them will give me more about the school and where's it's located."

"Okay," Sloane sat back and sipped her latte. She poured her granola into the yogurt and began stirring. She was happy to be eating something. She didn't like the news that Erik shared, but she knew she needed to let him listen. He needed to learn all that he could if the demons were going after kids. She questioned how in the hell they would be able to do that, weren't the parents noticing? Then she thought about her teenage years. She left home at sixteen after a traitor killed her mother. Her father didn't know anything about her when she was a teenager. Many parents are in the same boat, teenagers are volatile and transitioning. Maybe their parents chalked any weird behavior up to being a teenager and hormones. She could see how that could be explained.

"It sounds like they are leaving," Erik said.

"Did you find out any more?" she asked.

"Yeah, apparently the school isn't in Denver it's in Colorado Springs. I'm not sure where exactly and none of them thought about it. We need to follow them. We need to dispossess the one woman who is still present inside the demon's mind. That's not typical for a possession. Usually, the demon completely drowns out the host's mind. This woman is screaming in its head. I think we need to figure out why that is. It's bothering the demon as well, and they may do tests on her if the other demons find out. Plus, they're after her daughter because she's a leader at her school. If we save the woman, they may not be able to get her daughter. She plays a major role in their current plan." He got up from the chair as the three women were walking by the coffee shop.

Sloane accompanied Erik as he followed the woman. They split off when they got out of the building. Erik stayed a safe distance behind the woman with the daughter. Sloane followed the woman from the bar. She figured Erik would be able to dispossess the one woman while she could work on one of the others. When the woman got to the parking lot, Sloane came up beside the woman and matched her stride to hers.

Looking over to the woman she said, "Hey do you think you could help me with something?" The woman glanced over and shrugged. Sloane led her behind a large van. When she turned, Sloane hit her in the side of the head, and she slumped down quickly. Sloane said the incantation and then sat the woman on the ground against the van. She knew that she shouldn't leave her there when she didn't know how long she would be out for, but at least a demon did not possess her. She wouldn't know what had happened and would be confused. She thought that would be perfect for the current situation.

Sloane looked around to make sure there weren't any cameras around in the lot. There weren't, and there weren't any people in the immediate area. She walked quickly back in the direction of their car. She liked that she'd gotten rid of one demon today. She wanted to dispossess all three of the women but knew at the moment it wasn't possible because they all headed in different directions. She was surprised the demon hadn't sensed she was Shikari. It was too easy to take the woman out. They were usually better than that. She couldn't help but look around. She felt like she was being watched. She quickened her pace. She had a feeling another demon was watching her, and they were aware of what she'd done. She smiled wide sending a message. She stopped at the railing before the next stairway. She leaned against the railing and looked around her with her cocky smile. She wanted to send the message that she was ready for them and to challenge whoever was watching her.

Sloane waited a few minutes to see if the demon planned on challenging her. When she was finished waiting, she headed back toward the car. She took the steps two at a time, figuring that Erik was most likely finished with his demon. The third demon must've been the one to see her. She knew that they shouldn't have left one alone and should've tried to go for all three. Now the third one would go and tell the others of their presence. They no longer had the element of surprise, but the demons had to know there were hunters in Denver. There were hunters everywhere. They would need to be a little more careful in the future, now that they knew what she looked like. She didn't know if the demon had seen Erik, but she figured she had seen both of them.

Sloane got to the car, and Erik was leaning against it. "Did you take care of the other woman?"

"Yeah, you?" she responded.

"Yep, we need to go the other woman saw us both," he said

"Damn, I was hoping she only saw me," Sloane said.

"Nope, she's up there." Erik pointed to the top of the parking ramp across the street.

"Oh shit," Sloane said.

"Yeah, she called reinforcements, and they're headed here now. We should be going." he moved to the driver's door and opened it. Sloane followed his lead and quickly got in the car.

"So, do you think Magnus will loan us another car now that they know this one?"

"Maybe, do you think they'll be able to trace where this car came from?" Sloane asked.

"Probably, they seem to be into everything including hacking or possessing people to help them with what they need. Considering the people who work at the DMV, I wouldn't doubt if they were all demons."

Sloane laughed, "Ain't that the truth."

"I'll call Magnus and let him know." He grabbed his phone from the council and dialed Magnus.

"Hey, just so you know we've been spotted, and they may trace your car," Erik spoke into the phone.

"Okay, we'll go to the address, here Sloane can you punch this address into your phone," he handed her the phone so that she could type in the address.

"Mmmhmm," she said a few times, "Got it. Thanks, Magnus." She hung up the phone.

"So, follow the navigation. Magnus has a few other properties here in Denver."

"Yeah, makes sense, you don't want demons showing up to your actual residence." Erik made the next turn sending Sloane against the door.

"Do you think we need to be in this big of a hurry? I mean, do you think they were able to follow us that quickly?" Sloane reached for the handle above her head before Erik took another turn.

"No, not really, but I like to drive fast," he shrugged.

"Awesome, I'd like to not have bruises on my arms from your driving. Slow down taking turns okay, bro."

"Did Magnus have any other instructions for us when we got to the house?"

"Yeah, he said to change cars there, then head back to the house. He wants to know what happened," Sloane said and stared out the window at the passing city.

"They're going after kids, huh?" she said.

"Yeah, at first, I thought they were going after young kids, but it's high schoolers. It seems that they are looking at other schools, too. We need to figure out where, so we can take care of that as well," Erik explained.

"I still can't believe it. It seems so crazy, I mean before what happened in Minneapolis, I thought that the demons were so sporadic and that they didn't organize. There were only ever single attacks, and small organizations among them as far as we knew. Now there seems to be a grand design among them all. They are well organized and making things happen all over the place. I don't get how that happened, and no one noticed before this. It just doesn't make sense. Something had to have happened to change the demons. I don't get any of this." Sloane huffed.

"Yeah, I know. Some new things were changing, but there was a group covering it up. Mom dying was the beginning for us. Someone in the Shikari helped them. They killed off anyone who found out about the traitor group. It surprised us all, after all of the years of devotion we've all been taught, that one of our own would turn on us and begin this war. We need to eliminate the traitors in the order, which could mean killing our people. I'm not sure how we're going to accomplish that. How do we ask others to kill people they love? This is going to get a lot worse before it gets better." Erik rested one hand in his lap and clenched the other around the wheel. He let out a heavy breath.

"I'm going to message Jess and let them know what's going on. We need to regroup asap." She started typing quickly on her phone. After the news about them targeting high schoolers, she felt a renewed energy and focus. They had an idea about what the demons were doing here. They had direction and some idea of what to do next.

"Jess responded, shit and said they'd be there in forty-five minutes." Sloane looked to Erik; he was pulling into the driveway of another house. The garage door opened and Erik drove in.

A tall, dark-haired man walked toward them from the house. Erik and Sloane got out of the car once they parked. Erik moved to the trunk to grab out his duffle.

"Hi, I'm Scott, I hear you're in need of a new car." He smiled at the two. He was a tall, robust man with dark brown hair. His eyes were soft when he glanced at Sloane.

"Yeah, we ran into a few demons that are probably tracking the car as we speak," Erik said.

"No worries, they won't find it here, and we'll have new plates on the car in a few minutes. For now," he tossed Erik a set of keys and started walking to another stall in the garage. He hit a button, and the door opened. An Audi A8 was in the garage. "I think this will do for you two," he smirked.

"Yeah, that'll do," Erik said in shock.

"I figured you two might need the tint since they saw you as well," Scott said. "It's all yours; you better get on to Magnus. He'll be waiting for a report. He may not seem like it, but he is the head of Denver. If you need anything, I am always here in service of the order." He winked at Sloane and headed back toward the house.

"Well, that was nice of him," Sloane said.

"Yeah, I'm surprised he didn't ask what was going on. You'd think if he were part of the order he'd want to know." Erik said.

"Maybe he will find out from Magnus, anyway. Let's listen and get back to tell Magnus about what we learned. Considering this is all going on in his city, he should know. We may also need to relocate to Colorado Springs, if they are attending a school there, we need to go check out the school."

"Yeah, but we also need to stop them from getting the students here in Denver, too. We may need to split off or elicit some assistance from local Shikari like Scott here," Erik said. He walked to the car and got in the driver's seat. Sloane watched as he rubbed his hands along the steering wheel and whispered, "Nice," before starting the car.

"Having a cargasm over there?" Sloane joked.

"It is a very nice car," he responded.

"Yes, but we have to get going. So, let's see what she can do." She smiled.

"Yes, lets," he smiled and threw the car in reverse to back out of the garage.

He began speeding down the streets toward where Magnus lived. They arrived quickly and sped toward the house with a new determination in their step. Erik didn't even bother to knock, he walked right in and headed toward the basement where Magnus' man cave was located. Sloane followed, she was surprised that Magnus was the leader of this area. He certainly didn't seem like he'd be the leader.

"Magnus?" Erik called as soon as he reached the bottom of the stairs. He hadn't ventured too far past his room, so he wasn't sure what was all down here.

"Hey, come on back," Magnus yelled from down the hall.

They continued down the hall until they reached the last room which had a desk and several bookcases filled with old books.

"Hey, so I hear you had some interesting encounters at our university," he said lightly.

"You could say that," Sloane responded quickly and Erik gave her a sharp glance.

"Yeah, um, they are going after high school kids now. There's a boarding school in Colorado Springs, they're focusing on but have possessed students in Denver, too. I'm not sure what's so special about this school in Colorado Springs, though." Erik explained.

"We need to split up, some heading to Colorado Springs to find out about the school, and some to head off the operation here before they recruit more kids," Sloane said quickly. She didn't like how Erik was leaving her out of the mix.

"So, how many Shikari members are in the area? We have to have a group in Colorado Springs already, right?" Erik asked. "I mean, we are everywhere."

"We have a few members who live there, but I think it may be you, Erik who needs to go."

"Me, really, why?" Erik seemed confused.

"It's because you will be able to locate the school faster than the others will," Sloane said knowing the answer already. "There's no one there with the skill to read others thoughts."

"No, no one around here has that ability. I can copy your power when you are around but not long range. You would be able to find the school faster than anyone," Magnus explained.

"If we joined with Mike and headed there that would be our best bet because he can track the demons once you locate them," Sloane added.

"I can deal with the ones here in Denver, while you guys head down to Colorado Springs."

"That sounds good, but we should check in with the rest when they get here, see what they think," Erik said remembering that Bryant and Jess would be joining them shortly.

"I'm going to run up to my room before the others get here. We can all meet in the main room to decide what we're officially doing." Sloane left the room quickly and took her phone out of her pocket. She wasn't sure if she was ready to see Mike, well she was ready, but she wasn't sure how he would react to seeing her. She figured it'd be easy to be with each other, when they had other things to focus on. She wanted to spend time with him alone, so she could talk to him about what is going on between them. She didn't think the moment in the kitchen was a big deal. She didn't think anything of it until he started distancing himself and freaking out over it. She just reacted at the time. It wasn't a big deal in her eyes, but she needed to talk to him, regardless. She went upstairs and waited. She decided the time for avoiding her was over, and she was going to make him talk to her, in private as soon as he got there.

Chapter 5

She looked outside and saw the car pulling up the driveway. Her heart began pounding in her chest, and her palms became balmy. She wasn't expecting them to be here quite so quickly. She took a deep breath to steady her nerves. Hell, with it, she thought. She was going to talk to him, this avoiding texts and calls bullshit was over. Sloane watched as Jess got out of the driver's seat and stretched her arms over her head and elongated her entire body. Mike got out of the back seat followed slowly by Bryant in the front. Bryant headed straight for the door. He was all business. Sloane held the door open and stepped out into the blazing sun.

"Hello father," she stretched her vowels when she spoke.

He looked at her and asked, "Where are Magnus and Erik? I would like to speak to them immediately."

"They're downstairs; If you follow the house all the way to the back, there is a staircase on the right, then go all the way to the back. It's the last room on the left." She returned her focus to Mike who was staring at her pointedly. Jess looked between the two of them and walked quickly up to the house.

"I think I'll follow Bryant to go find Erik." She walked swiftly into the house.

Sloane watched her go and turned back to look at Mike. He had a pained look on his face but walked toward her slowly, like he was walking to his death.

"Seriously, I just want to talk to you." She stood with her hand on her hip.

"I know, that's the problem," he said.

"Oh yeah, talking to me is a problem? You had no problem talking to me a few days ago in my bedroom; now you won't answer a simple text to let me know where you are. What the fuck, Mike?"

"Talking to you can be a problem, Sloane. You don't listen, you never listen. Besides, your actions the other day made it all too clear. The only discussion you're interested in is the one we have in the bedroom, as you so kindly pointed out. Now that I know where we stand, we can move on, separately." Mike closed his eyes after he spoke. Sloane turned around as she heard Joleen coming up behind her. Sloane sighed heavily.

"We need to take this upstairs," she said when she turned back to Mike.

"This is exactly what I'm talking about. We just began to have a real conversation, and you want to go to your room. No Sloane, I'm not going to be your secret in the night. I'm not that kind of guy. If that is what you are looking for, love, find yourself another bloke."

"No, will you stop? I mean we have company," she said as Jolene reached them.

"Well hello, and who might you be?" Jolene asked.

"Oh, hello love, I'm Mike." He moved forward and shook Jolene's hand.

"Well, it's wonderful to meet you, Mike," she said. "Well, I can see you two have something important to discuss. I'll get Penelope on making lunch for all of us." She flitted toward the kitchen.

"Okay Sloane, she's gone what do you have to say? What could make your actions from the other day okay? Please explain that to me, because as far as I'm concerned, you made your stance very clear." His voice low and hard. Sloane had never heard his anger so clearly before today.

"I'm sorry about the other day. I shouldn't have moved away from you in the kitchen. I was startled, it felt like Jess was intruding on our private moment. It also scared me. We've only been together for a little while. I'm sorry. I'm not trying to hide anything from the others. I just didn't know what to do at the time, so I moved away from you. I didn't even think about it. I'm so sorry if I hurt you, it was just a little thing." She took a step forward and ran her fingers along the scruff on his cheek. She could tell he hadn't shaved in a few days. The dark hairs prickled her hand as she cupped his cheek.

"For me, it wasn't little. You rejected me in front of Jessie. I just don't get why? I understand you being scared, I'm scared too. You left me, remember. I guess I'm afraid you'll do it again. We had been so close when we were younger. Then you take off, and no one knows where you went. Now, we're together again. It feels like we're picking up where we left off, but I'm afraid it won't last. When you moved away from me, it felt like you were ready to run again. You're so good at running away, and I don't want to lose you again." Mike stared into Sloane's eyes and took a deep breath.

"I'm sorry. I know I've hurt you in so many ways. I know I left, but I also know you knew where I was the whole time I was gone. Why didn't you come to find me?" Sloane asked.

"I knew you needed space after your mom. I wasn't sure you wanted me to find you. I figured you'd find me when you were ready, but you never did. I wasn't sure you wanted to be with me anymore." Mike looked to the ground and swallowed hard.

"Oh baby, of course, I want to be with you. We were both young, and I didn't know how to deal with everything. I had to leave to figure out how I felt. But I'm here now, and I'm not going anywhere." Sloane placed her finger under Mike's chin raising it until his eyes met hers.

Mike's eyes glistened as he stared at her. "You want to be with me?" he whispered.

"Yes, what more do I need to say to make you believe, I want to be with you?" Sloane moved a step closer. She wanted to throw herself at him but knew she needed to wait for him. She moved closer. Her lips waited inches from his. She wanted him to go the extra step. She didn't want to force him into it.

She closed her eyes and waited. She could feel him, his heat radiating off his body. It called to her, but she stood firm. He needed to close the distance; she'd never push him.

Before she knew it, he wrapped one arm around her back and pulled her into him. He crushed his lips to hers in an intense meeting of their mouths. She wrapped her arms around his neck and stroked his curls. He responded by pushing her against the house and moving his hands down and hitching up each thigh with both hands. He lifted her, and she wrapped her legs around his waist. He moved one hand to her front, toying with her nipple. He broke their kiss to trail kisses along her chin and down her neck. He moved her shirt aside to nip her collarbone.

"Ahem" Erik stood in the doorway. "Um, I would say get a room, but we have work to do so, get it together." Sloane glared at Erik.

"Hey Erik," Mike said as he stepped away from Sloane, pulling her shirt back in place and smoothing it out.

"Seriously, worst timing ever," she said and glared at Erik.

"Come on Sloane; you know we have work to do. We need to explain what happened and we need to be on our way to Colorado Springs," Erik turned and headed back into the house to meet with the others.

Sloane looked up into Mike's eyes. "Later," she breathed and reached her mouth up to brush his. He responded immediately by grasping her mouth with his and nipping her bottom lip. She let out a little gasp and reached for his hand, interlocking her fingers with his before turning and heading for the house. Later would not come soon enough.

They entered the house, and everyone was seated around the dining room table. Erik had maps spread out across the table. He was pointing to where the bars were that we'd visited earlier. He pulled a map of Colorado Springs out from under the pile.

"The school was large, with a campus of four older stone buildings. It was protected on one side by the mountain. They picked the perfect place from what I could discern from their thoughts. I know it's near the mountain, but it's a little out of the city, so they have little interference with others. Many of the teachers drive in, but the students are there all the time. If the demons decided to possess the teachers as well it really would be the perfect recruitment place."

Magnus nodded to Erik before he began explaining the plan. "Okay, so we are going to need to break off into two groups. Erik, Jessie, Sloane, and Mike will head to Colorado Springs. I have a place there where you can stay, and Caroline will meet you at this address." He scribbled an address on a piece of paper and handed it over to Erik. "You will be comfortable there as long as you are needed. Bryant will stay here and coordinate with me while we try to figure out who is on the inside and helping these demons. We have contacts and can discreetly try to figure out how to stop the traitors. We will also direct others to deal with the problem here in Denver." He looked to Bryant. Bryant nodded once in agreement.

Erik looked back to Sloane, Mike, and Jessie. "We will need to leave as soon as possible."

"I have to head up and get my things before we leave." She turned to leave, she grasped Mike's hand, and he turned to follow her.

"We'll leave in an hour or so, is that enough time?" he asked.

"Plenty," she said as she walked out of the room.

Mike bent to her ear as she walked, "Plenty, huh?" he said before he squeezed her hand.

"Well that depends on you," she smiled and bounded up the stairs with him right on her heel.

She walked through the door and pulled him in behind her, she closed the door and pushed him against it. She reached up to kiss him. His reaction was hungry, he crushed her mouth with his, then backed off running his tongue down the center of her tongue sending a surge through her entire body. He placed his hands on her hips and grasped tightly. She smiled and moved her mouth to trace his jaw and down his neck. He moved his hands up her back and to the clasp of her bra. He set her free with one flick of his hand.

"Hey!" she said, "Can I get my shirt off first?" She reached and pulled her shirt up over her head. She held her arms out, so her bra fell to the floor in front of her. He kissed her along her jawline tracing a trail from her earlobe down her neck, finally suckling her breast. He flicked his tongue across her nipple and nibbled. She gasped and twined her fingers in his hair gripping tightly as he flicked his tongue across her raised nipple. She couldn't take it; she was going to come before they'd even started. She thought back to her fears from earlier. Right now, she couldn't imagine her life without Mike.

As her mind wandered back to the present, Mike moved back to her mouth to kiss her, biting her lip, and kissing her until her mouth was wet and swollen. She tugged on his shirt, lifting it.

He smiled, "Something you want love?"

"Yes, you naked. I want to run my tongue over these hard muscles." She traced the lines on his stomach with her finger causing him to tremble a moment.

"Happy to oblige, my lady." He smirked and raised his hands above his head. She pulled his shirt off and traced the lines of his chest, memorizing every curve. They savored each other, every touch, every kiss. When they were finished Sloane lay, staring into Mike's eyes.

She ran her hand along his face. Gazing into his eyes, she couldn't get enough of him. That thought scared her. She felt like a schoolgirl with butterflies in her stomach. She didn't want to look away.

"Love, although I would like to stay in this bed with you all day. I believe we have to be going." He kissed her lips, nipping her playfully and then moved to get off the bed.

"Do we have to?" she pouted.

"Yes, I'm afraid we do." He held his hand to help her off the bed.

"After that performance, I'm not sure I want to do anything else." She took his hand and let him help her off the bed, but she moved to wrap her arms around him as soon as she was standing. She held him close and reached up to whisper in his ear. "I owe you one," she said and nipped his lobe.

"Try not to keep score, love." He bent to kiss her running his tongue along hers. He bit her lip before he released her mouth. They were both satiated and needed to join the others. She watched as he retrieved his shirt and pants. He tossed her shirt and bra at her. She caught it and bent to retrieve her panties and pants. It felt like they'd been in the room for hours, but it'd only been twenty minutes. She smiled as she looked at her phone and realized she had more time. She walked determined toward him, desire in her eyes. "I believe we'll need to shower before we leave." She grabbed his hand and pulled him toward the bathroom.

"Again?" he said before she crushed her mouth to his. "We're never going to leave if you keep this up."

"Whatever, we'll leave, but I think we should be clean before we head out in a car for an hour." She turned around and walked into the bathroom. She turned on the water, looking to the door as Mike stood there, leaning against it, arms crossed over his chest. *Man, he's hot,* she thought.

She returned her attention to the water, letting it run over her hand and arm while she tested the temperature. She looked up to him, and he moved with determination toward her. She straightened, the water was ready. Mike stepped behind her, running his tongue down her neck to her shoulder.

"Ready to go again I see," she smiled.

"It must be you," he said as he picked her up and deposited her under the running stream of water. "It's good we didn't get dressed," he said as he pressed her body against the wall. He reached down grabbing her thighs. He lifted her, bracing her against the wall. She wrapped her legs around him. Kissing him, she nipped his lip playfully.

She grabbed the soap, smiling up at him as she lathered the soap in her hands. She winked and moved her hands to his chest. She ran her hands all over his body caressing and rubbing every inch of him as he watched. When she was done, she moved him under the stream of water and continued to run her hands over every part of him. He took her chin in his hands and kissed her. She lined her body to his as they kissed under the water.

"Your turn," he said and took the soap from her hand. He began doing the same for her. He kneaded her muscles as he went and she could feel the calluses of his hands as they ran along her skin. She blew out one final breath; she hadn't realized she was holding. He smiled at her and pulled her to him. He kissed her again as they stood under the running water. She pulled away.

"The water's changing," she said as the water went from hot to lukewarm.

"Showers over," he smiled and opened the door for her. She reached and took his hand. She interlaced her fingers with his. She didn't want to stop touching him. She wanted to feel connected to him. He grabbed the towel off the rack and pulled it around her, rubbing his hands on her arms creating and enticing friction. "Oh god, we're never leaving this place," she said.

"Oh yes, we are," he said and stepped back to grab himself a towel to wrap around himself.

"Yeah, like that's going to work," she said.

"It will," he smiled and headed back to the bedroom.

"Okay, that will work," she said as she watched him leave. She dried herself off and joined him in the bedroom. He had already gotten dressed, and she sighed. She didn't want to deal with demons. She wanted to spend all day with him. She looked down to her clothes which she placed on the bed before heading to the bathroom. She picked them up and began dressing. She finished and went to grab her bag. She packed her stuff back into the duffel before turning toward the door. He waited and watched her get her things. He smiled when her eyes met his.

"Ready?" he asked.

"I guess," she said reluctantly.

"You're adorable you know that," he said and reached out to take the bag from her hand.

"Yes, I do know that," she said as she followed him out the door.

"You know I can carry my bag."

"I know, but why would I let you," he winked at her.

She couldn't help but smile back. Jessie and Erik were in the kitchen talking when they entered.

Jessie looked from Mike to Sloane and smiled. "Back together, I see."

"Yep," Sloane said, reaching out to take Mike's hand.

"Whatever, are you two ready because we should have left already?" He moved quickly up from the chair and reached for the keys.

"Lighten up Erik, at least someone here is having a little fun," Jessie smiled at the two again.

"Yeah, whatever," Erik grumbled and moved quickly out of the room.

Jessie watched him leave and shook her head. "He hates when people are having more fun than him. He seems to be all business, right now." She turned and looked at Mike

"I'm happy for you and all, but you both have your head in the game, right? We can't afford any missteps, right now." She looked pointedly at Mike then at Sloane.

"Seriously Jessie, we'll be fine," Sloane said.

"I just want to make sure," she said. "It could be our life on the line."

"We know that," Mike said.

"Okay, well let's go then." She turned and headed out of the door.

Sloane looked up to Mike, and he shrugged, "I guess we're off." They followed behind them out to the car, and Mike went to open the door for Sloane.

Jessie smiled, "Awe, he's even a gentleman." She moved to open her door and got into the front seat.

Sloane stopped at the door and leaned to give Mike a quick kiss before bending to get into the car. Mike closed the door as soon as Sloane was in and went to deposit her bag in the trunk. Erik was putting his bag back there along with another duffle of guns. Erik glared at Mike.

Mike shook his head, "Are we going to have a problem?" he asked looking at Erik.

"My sister, really?"

"Yes! We have a history, Erik. You know it. You of everyone shouldn't be surprised." He said it so strongly that Erik's mouth dropped involuntarily.

"Oh!" He clapped Mike on the back of the shoulder and said, "Alright then," and headed to the front of the car. Mike shook his head and closed the trunk. He got in the back next to Sloane. Erik started the car and headed to the highway.

Sloane traced a heart on Mike's palm. She clasped his hand in hers and smiled.

Jessie pulled out the map of Colorado Springs and began studying it. "Where do you think the best place to begin looking for this school is?" she asked as she folded the map over to look around the areas closest to the mountains.

"Well, I saw it was on the side of the mountain, but I'm not sure which side exactly. It'll be away from the city, so that narrows our search." He looked over to the map.

"When we get close enough, I'll be able to track any demons in the area," Mike said.

"That will be helpful, how close do you think we need to be for you to be able to track them?"

"We can be a few miles away, and I'll be able to track them. Especially if there are a few together that will help. They give off a kind of buzz that I'm able to pick up. The more there are, the stronger the sensation will be." He looked out the window at the passing road.

Sloane looked to him and closed her eyes. She tried to concentrate on the future. She hadn't been able to see anything lately, but she also hadn't felt this relaxed and happy in a long time. She took Mike's hand in hers to keep her grounded as she searched for the world beyond this one. She let her mind wander and reach for that beyond herself. Suddenly, she saw colors swirling around her, felt light and distant. She clutched Mike's hand as she drifted deeper into the vision. *The world solidified, and there was a teenage girl in front of her. She had dark eyes, chocolate to match her hair which was pulled back into a messy bun. She was talking about Chase, which was some guy she was dating. It took Sloane a minute to catch up.* "Chloe, earth to Chloe are you listening?" *she looked annoyed.*

"Oh yeah, sorry," *she said.*

"So, what do you think I should do?" *the girl asked.*

"About what?" *Chloe responded.*

"Seriously, you weren't listening? Chase, what am I supposed to do about Chase? He's changed, he's different, and I feel like I should let the teachers know. I know him, and something's wrong with him. He's like a different person. He's been going around talking to others. Day trips to Denver and coming back with other students, some of them are girls. We're supposed to be together, and he's going off and getting these new girls to come here from Denver. The weird thing is the headmaster is letting them sign up. They're not even one of us, how can they go to school here? I also think he's changed, turned evil even. The other day he yelled at me for interfering, told me he didn't even remember we were dating. I mean we've been together for over two years, how is it possible he doesn't remember." she stopped to take a deep breath. She was getting worked up.*

"That's weird," *Chloe said.*

"Right," *she responded.* "So, do you think I should tell the teachers?" *She put her nail in her mouth and started chewing a nail that was already well past the wick.*

"I don't know; it's a little weird that the headmaster is taking students that don't belong. Shouldn't there be an application, interview, and waiting until the next semester? It's strange that they're starting at our school in the middle of a semester."

"I know, Colorado Springs Prep is a well-established institution. They have high standards for attending this school. I was on a waiting list until my father made a sizable contribution to the school." She flipped her hair. "I don't understand why, I'm a great student," she sighed.

"Maybe we should wait to tell anyone, see if anything else strange happens. I mean, we don't want to set off any unnecessary alarms."

"Or make anyone suspicious of us. What if it's some kind of conspiracy and they come after us because we've figured it out?" She clutched her binder to her chest.

"I think you've been watching too many spy movies. It's probably nothing but for now, let's keep this to ourselves."

Sloane felt the hand in hers and opened her eyes slowly. She hadn't expected to transport to another's mind. That was strange. She must be doing better than she thought, to be able to go so fully into her vision. Mike rubbed his thumb over her knuckles. She shook her head a minute trying to piece everything together.

"Jessie you got your phone?" she asked.

"Yeah," she held her phone in her hand.

"Search Colorado Springs Prep. That's where we're headed. Start digging into the headmaster, too. He's in on it." She took another deep breath to steady herself. She felt drained after her vision.

Mike looked at her concerned, "Are you okay?" he asked. "You got pale."

"Yeah, we just need to find the school, and a kid named Chase. He's been bringing kids from Denver, and the headmaster has been letting them in without any paperwork. I know these two are in on it for sure. Check them out." She felt light headed. She closed her eyes for a moment and took in a deep breath through her nose. She slumped over to the side nearly hitting her head on the window.

Mike reacted as soon as he felt her hand go limp. He grabbed her and pulled her against himself. He felt for her pulse which was still strong. He stroked her hair back from her forehead and held her against himself.

"She'll be fine," Erik said, "She used to pass out all the time after one of her visions. She'll need to rest before she is ready to go again. It's good she had one before we were in Colorado Springs. We'll dig into the headmaster, the school, and try to search the school records for a Chase,"

"So, it looks like the school is near the mountain as you described." Jessie showed the picture on her phone to Erik then Mike. She pulled up the picture of the headmaster. "This is the guy Sloane was talking about." She showed them both the photo of him. Then she began to read his bio. "An alumnus of Colorado Springs Preparatory School, Jonathan Hall has since received his degree in Social Studies education and Ph.D. in educational leadership. He has been an active member in keeping the traditions of the school alive. Yada Yada Yada," she said. "He's kinda boring."

"Is there anything in there that will be useful to us? Does he have a family we should be checking with?" Erik assumed Sloane was right about this guy, but it would help if they could interview his wife or kids to see if he changed lately. Not that it mattered all that much. They would know as soon as they found the school if he'd been possessed.

Jessie searched the information. "It doesn't say anything about his family on the site, but I can dig more when I have a computer. I can find anyone associated with him. He seems very dedicated according to his accomplishments."

"Think you can get into any school records to find this Chase?" he asked her.

"Not right now, I can't do too much on the phone in the middle of the mountains. When we get to the other house where there's decent internet, I should be able to hack into the system to find out who the kid is. I'll check out where he's from, too. If he's taking off to Denver for the weekend, he's getting help from someone," she said. She continued to learn more about the school. She began digging into the Facebook page photos, and anything else she could find that may be useful to their purposes. They would need to get close to find out how many demons were there, but without being seen by the demons. The last thing they needed was another war they weren't prepared for.

Jessie turned to look at Sloane, resting against Mike. "How's she doing?"

"Sleeping soundly," Mike answered.

"We'll need to wake her soon; we're in the city." Erik followed the navigator through the city. The large stone walled house was nestled into the side of the mountain. He pulled in front of one of the three garage stalls and parked. Cactus' lined the red stone walkway. The mountain framed the back of the house.

"This is amazing," Jessie said as she walked in a circle taking in the view.

Erik knocked on the door, and a petite redhead opened it. Her round face held a glowing smile. She held out her hand. "Erik, I presume." She waited, hand outstretched.

"Caroline," he said taking her hand and shaking it.

"Hi, I'm Jessie." She reached out to take Caroline's hand, as well. "We have a friend in the car who needs to rest can you show me to a room where she can sleep?"

"Oh, of course, come on in. I'll show you where the rooms are." She spun and headed toward a large staircase, Jessie followed.

"The room on the far-right side is mine. Otherwise, you guys can take whichever room you like." Caroline said as she motioned down the hall. "The bathroom is the third door on the left."

"Thank you," Jessie said as she went to the first room. She figured Mike and Sloane would want a room away from everyone else, or at least everyone else would want a room away from them, Jessie could hear Sloane down the stairs when she went to pack her things the last time. She knew Erik would want to be far away from that. Jessie opened the first door to a queen-sized bed and a large armoire. Perfect, she thought and headed to let Mike know where he could bring Sloane.

Chapter 6

Erik waited downstairs for Caroline. "So, what do you know about Colorado Springs Prep?"

"It's a world-renowned training school for Shikari members. Why?"

"Some students are possessed by demons, and we think the headmaster is a part of it."

"Oh dear, that school is an institution here. They teach and train future Shikari that aren't trained by their family. Come let's continue this discussion over a drink or two." She walked toward the kitchen not waiting for Erik.

"What, a drink, really? We still have work to do. How is it, I don't know about this school? Are there other schools like this one?" he asked shaking his head and following her into the kitchen.

"Let's not do this tonight. There's plenty of time for your questions tomorrow. Besides, the school's closed. You can't go there, now. They would see your headlights before you even got up the road. We'll visit them tomorrow."

Erik glanced out the window; it was early yet. Well, it was early evening, but he still figured it would be at least an hour before he would need to use headlights. He was sure they could make it to the school before then. He didn't like that they weren't moving on the school immediately. They were talking about kids; he wanted to take care of this problem as soon as possible.

Caroline grabbed a beer from the fridge and shoved it in front of Erik. "I said, not tonight." She scowled at him.

"What the…" He stared at her. Usually, he was the one reading other thoughts. Suddenly, he realized he hadn't heard anything from her. Usually, he would hear something, even though he tried very hard to tune out those around him, especially other hunters.

"While it is nice of you not to try to hear those around you, the attempt is wasted. You wouldn't be able to hear me. I can hear you just fine though." She smiled and poured herself a glass of wine.

"Okay, now I see why I might annoy some people. I take it you can hear others thoughts, too." He looked to Caroline.

"Something like that," she responded and headed back into the living room.

"What does that mean?" Erik questioned as he followed her.

"It means that, right now, I can read your mind, and you can't read mine. For now, that's all you need to know."

"Wait a minute, so you get full access to my thoughts, but you're not going to tell me how? Magnus said no one had that power here."

"He doesn't know," she said. "Now, if you'll excuse me, I have some things to take care of." She walked briskly up the stairs.

Erik stood there dumbfounded for a few minutes. "What the hell was that?" he muttered.

"What?" Jessie responded. Erik hadn't heard her come in the room. He was preoccupied.

"Our host can read minds, too. I can't read her thoughts, though." He pouted.

"Oh, Caroline? Yeah, she's interesting, isn't she?" Jessie plopped down on the sofa.

"Have you met her before?" Erik asked.

"Oh yeah, a couple of times. My mom used to like to come to Colorado often. She said she always felt home near the mountains. I'm not sure why I always thought she was from Wisconsin, but I never knew for sure." She glanced around the room then patted the spot next to her on the couch. "Why don't you have a seat?" she asked. "I don't bite, hard." She smiled up at him.

He smirked back and sat on the couch next to her. "So, I know I'm supposed to be researching the school, but I felt like just chilling before we race off into the next battle." She scooted back on the couch and tucked her legs under her.

"Yeah, I guess we've been going nonstop for a while," Erik admitted.

"It was also a long drive," she said.

"Oh yeah, I guess you've been in a car for quite a while, too." He looked at her. "How are you not completely exhausted, right now?" he asked after thinking about how they had driven to Colorado. They stopped a few times on the way to get information. Then arrived in Denver only to hop in another car, and head to Colorado Springs. He shook his head after thinking about it.

"I'm not sure, but I feel wired somehow. I know I have to keep going, but I just want to sit here for a minute. Just exist for one minute without everything else." She closed her eyes and took a deep breath.

Erik moved closer to her, "Turn around."

Her eyes snapped open, and she looked to Erik, "What, why?"

"Just do it," he said

She shrugged and turned, so her back was to Erik. He moved his hands to her shoulders and began massaging them. He moved his hands and rubbed down the length of her back, kneading the muscles as he went.

"Oh my God, I love you," she said.

"I know." He continued to work her muscles until she was relaxed.

She turned around on him after he was finished. "What was that for?" she asked. She liked Erik, but he never did anything out of pure kindness before. She knew he was nice, but that was unexpected.

"Nothing, I knew you needed to relax. After a few days in the car, you were very tense." He shrugged.

She smiled and stared into his eyes. He was genuine; he gave her a massage to be nice. That touched her. She didn't know why, but she wanted to kiss him. She stared at him a minute more and leaned forward. She moved her knees under her, so she was on all fours and advanced her lips toward his. She met his mouth and kissed softly, letting her tongue slide along his lower lip until he opened his mouth to welcome her. She slipped her tongue inside his mouth and stroked his tongue with her own. She slid her tongue along his teeth and nipped his lip before beginning to pull away. He moved and wrapped his arm around her waist, pulling her into him. She moved her leg to straddle his waist.

She hadn't expected to like kissing him so much, or the way he responded. He nibbled her lips and deepened the kiss letting her know of his own need. She wanted to taste every inch of his mouth. He moved to kiss her chin, her throat and dipped his tongue between her breasts, visible through her tank. Her nipples hardened, and she pushed herself against him. She placed her hand on his chin and raised his head to meet her eyes. His lips touched hers gingerly, kissing lightly. Their kisses were playful at first but quickly turned to a need. He pulsed against her shorts, and she couldn't help but wish they were both without the restricting clothes. He stopped and placed his forehead on her shoulder,

"Jessie," he breathed and buried his face in her hair inhaling deeply. She placed her hand on the side of his face and looked him in the eye.

"I think we need to take this upstairs," she said.

Erik looked around the room forgetting entirely where they were. "Are you sure?" he breathed staring into her eyes, worry crossing his face. He tried hard to hide his emotions, but she saw it.

"Yes, Erik. Let's go upstairs." She placed her hands on his chest and pushed herself up. She held her hand out for him. He took it and followed her up the stairs. When he closed the door, she stalked toward him, determination in her eyes.

When they finished, he moved his hand to her hair and brushed a curl back from her face. He smiled and looked into her eyes. "I've wanted to do that for quite some time now." He stroked his thumb over her temple.

"Well if I would've known it was going to be that good, I would've jumped you sooner." She relaxed back against the pillow. He moved to lay next to her. He still toyed with a curl in his hands. She turned her head to face him.

"Why haven't we done this sooner?" she asked.

"You mean since we left Minnesota? I was at your house a few days ago. You deciding to drive with Bryant and Mike might have something to do with it."

"Oh yeah, there's that. When we were together before we always found time for other things."

"By other things do you mean sex?'

"Well, yes, of course, I mean sex. I know you haven't gone without it." She looked over to him again. "Weren't you with Amy a few weeks ago?" she chided.

"No, I wasn't with Amy."

"Really? You sure had me fooled." She stared up at the ceiling.

"So what? You think I go around banging every girl I meet?" he accused.

"Not every girl," she said. "But you've changed in our time apart."

"Wow, Jess really?" he let go of her hand and moved to sit up in the bed.

"What? You mean to tell me you haven't slept with tons of girls?" She sat up on the bed, sliding to lean against the headboard. "You didn't get that good without practice."

"Well, you better hope that's not the case because you just fucked me without a condom." He rose from the bed and grabbed his pants.

"Oh shit," she said. She hadn't even thought of that at the time.

"Yeah, oh shit. I guess you should think before you have sex with someone you think has had sex with tons of women." He slid his legs through his pants and walked through the door, slamming it behind him.

"Was it something I said?" she looked at the door and cursed.

She knew she hurt him, but she honestly thought he'd been with a lot of girls. He certainly had flirted with plenty around her. She had assumed that when Amy was staying with them, he slept with her as he'd done with her. She didn't think he would freak out. Why would a guy be offended that a girl thought he had "been around" so to speak? She shook her head to clear it. She slid off the bed to find her clothes. She figured she better figure out what the hell was wrong with Erik. She wanted a repeat performance, and if she didn't find him, that was highly unlikely.

She buttoned her shorts and pulled her tank over her head. She didn't bother with the panties or bra; she hoped she wouldn't be wearing them long. She took a deep breath. She couldn't believe she hadn't even thought about the condom. In her defense, she wasn't thinking about it at the time. She usually counted on the guy to think about that sort of thing, and most were prepared. Now she questioned, why in the hell Erik hadn't.

She opened the door and headed down the hall to find him. She wasn't sure which room he'd picked, and she certainly didn't want to interrupt anything Sloane and Mike were doing. She walked to the end of the hall and listened. She thought maybe she could hear him cursing or something.

"Ouch," came from one of the rooms. She knew it was Erik and went for the door handle. She saw him shaking his hand and quickly shut the door behind her. He looked up and glared at her.

"If I wanted to talk, I would've stayed in your room." He turned to open his duffel bag.

"Oh, I got that. What the hell was that back there?" she moved closer to him.

"Apparently, I'm a whore," he said and shuffled a few things around in his bag.

"I never said you were a whore," she crossed her arms over her chest.

"Close enough," he said and found what he was looking for and turned back to the dresser.

"No, not close enough. I just thought you had slept with Amy. You were certainly flirting with her the whole time she was at your house. Sorry, I jumped to conclusions."

"Whatever, can we just go back to doing our jobs?" He looked at her, obvious hurt in his eyes.

"No, not until you tell me what the hell that was all about?" She shifted her weight to one hip.

He moved and sat on the bed. "I just don't like it when people make assumptions that because I look like this." He swept his hands from his head to his waist. "I'm sleeping with everybody. I'm not like that." He stared at the floor.

She sat next to him. "I'm sorry, but I've seen you flirt with other girls, lots of other girls. Are you telling me you haven't been sleeping with any of them? All those times at the pub, when Mike was acting as your wingman, you mean to tell me you didn't hook up with those girls?" she looked to him, he still stared at the floor.

"Nope, not one of them." He stilled realizing he may have admitted more than he wanted to.

"What, you didn't have sex with any of them?" she was shocked. She'd seen him be so smooth with girls, watched him leave with several after Mike's whole, tell her how he saved the world routine. How in the hell had he not slept with them? They were putty in his hands.

"Can I ask why?" she asked, after her few moments of contemplation.

"I could never be myself with them; I always have to hide who I really am. It's hard to be with someone when they don't know you." He looked over to see her face.

She studied his face as he spoke. She couldn't believe what he was saying. She understood this life was hard. You could never let outsiders know about the Shikari. It never bothered her to not tell her lovers; she was a hunter. She hadn't let anyone get close enough to notice, either. She knew about that, the loneliness that accompanied who and what they were. She sat and thought for a few minutes, then the realization hit.

"Wait, have you been with anyone since we separated?" Jess studied Erik as he continued to stare at the floor.

"I've been with a few girls, but none of them were you, Jess. I haven't had a connection with anyone but you." He looked longingly into her eyes. She could accept him completely, and he could do the same.

"Oh," she said, unsure how to respond.

He watched her face and slumped putting his head in his hands. "It's okay; you can go get some sleep. I won't tell anyone about what happened, and we can go back to the way it was before."

"You think that's what I want?' she asked.

"Isn't it?" he looked toward her, a glimmer of hope in his eyes.

"No Erik, I don't. I told you I care about you, too. It was hard after we broke up. I understood why you felt the need to end it, but it still hurt. I want to be your number one, not second to your duty to the Shikari. I'm scared you'll do it again, and I can't bear the heartbreak. I spent a year trying to get over you, and I never did." Her voice came out in a choked whisper. She stared at the floor. She chanced a glance at his face. He'd lifted his head and was gazing at her like she was everything.

"I'm sorry Jess, I don't know what the hell I, was thinking. I should have never let you go." He took her hand in his.

"I'm sorry, too. I didn't mean to assume you've been with a ton of girls. A part of me still wants to lash out at you for the hurt you caused me. Sometimes words just come out without me thinking about them. So, do you think we can try this again?" Her heart fluttered at the thought. She ran her fingers down the side of his cheek. She wanted to be with him again so bad it hurt.

"If you're willing to try, so am I. This time I'll make sure you know how special you are." He placed a kiss on her hand. He cupped her cheek. He bent, slowly moving his lips to hers. Gently, he kissed her, running his tongue along her lip. He brushed a curl back from the side of her face as he drew back.

"So, what do you want to do now?" she raised an eyebrow and licked her lips.

"You." His mouth crushed hers in a sudden, intense need. She opened her mouth welcoming his tongue into hers. She sighed with both relief and pleasure. She gripped him to her tighter in anticipation. She moved herself to straddle his waist. She devoured his mouth with hers. A rush of heat spread through her body, as she gripped her fingers in his hair. The things he could do with his tongue. She felt like every muscle in her body was on fire for him, as he stroked her bottom lip with his tongue. He smiled as he lifted her, turned, and pushed her down on the bed. He slid her shorts off and spread her legs and dipped his head between them.

"What are you doing?" she asked.

He looked up to her and said, "You wanted to see the things I could do with my tongue." He dipped his head lower again.

She stilled as the realization hit. She sat bolt upright moving away from Erik. "What the hell, Erik? You've been reading my thoughts!" she accused.

"Oh shit," he said, realizing his mistake. "Not intentionally," he said hoping she wouldn't be mad.

"What does that mean?" she asked.

"Sometimes when I'm preoccupied, I get glimmers. I can't shut everyone out all the time. I have to work not to hear those around me. I don't mean to, but sometimes when I'm concentrating on something else, I can hear your thoughts." he shrugged, sliding closer to Jessie.

"So, like when you're having sex?" she asked.

"Yeah, like when I'm having sex."

"Well that's just…" she sighed. "I don't know, weird I guess."

"I know, I'm sorry. I actively try not to." He looked into her eyes again. "I wouldn't do anything to hurt you, Jessie, not ever."

Jessie stared back at him; his words were so passionate she couldn't help but believe him. She moved back toward him. She cupped his cheek and kissed him.

"I guess I'll get over it," she said and nipped his lip.

He pushed her back against the bed, "Now, where was I?"

Breathing heavy, she sat against the headboard, staring at him. She had to hand it to him; he was amazing at everything he did.

She waited for him to speak, but instead, he kissed her, lovingly. She'd enjoyed the gentleness of his lips moving with her own.

He put a hand in her hair and played with a curl. He began kissing her cheek, her temple, moving his lips to touch every part of her face. He was still nestled next to her, and she didn't want to be apart from him. He was so gentle; she could feel his calloused hands as he traced them down her spine. Memorizing every line and muscle. She didn't want this to end.

"Oh Jessie," he breathed and brushed her lips with his own.

She reached her hands up and placed them on both sides of his face. Making him look her in the eye. "Where did you learn all that?" she asked as she held him in place.

"Nowhere, I just knew what you wanted; it made it easy to please you." He winked.

"Dammit Erik, you were reading my thoughts the whole time?" she accused.

"Well did you mind?" he teased, nipping at her collarbone

She looked at him and let out an exasperated breath. "I guess not."

"Good," he moved to kiss her again.

"I've never done that," she said.

"I know," he said. "I wanted to see how many you could have." He smiled widely at her.

"Dammit, Erik."

"That's not what you were saying a few minutes ago." He reached a hand down, flicked her and stroked a moment before he kissed her again.

She let out another breath. "Nothing is ever going to be easy with you, is it?"

"Nope, probably not. But I promise that I won't read your thoughts outside of the bedroom. I can't help it when we're together. I can't think beyond the pleasure and you." He smiled again.

She closed her eyes and wrapped her hands around him hugging him closer, so their bodies were completely connected. He held her tightly for a few minutes. He reached down to grab the sheets and blankets to wrap around them both.

"We both need to sleep before tomorrow." He pulled the blankets up. He tucked one side around her as she scooted back to lay her head on the pillow. He kissed the tip of her nose, and she turned her back to him. He wrapped his hands around her waist and pulled her flush with him. In moments, he could hear her breath slow to a steady lull, and he was quick to follow. Before he drifted, he thought about the things they would do tomorrow. He moved his head to kiss her shoulder. He thought right now; he could face anything. He closed his eyes and drifted off to sleep.

Chapter 7

When Sloane reached the kitchen in the morning, Caroline had started a fresh pot of coffee and had a platter cinnamon rolls on the counter.

"Good morning," she said as she turned from the coffee pot.

"Morning," Sloane said. "Where are the mugs?"

Caroline turned and grabbed one down from the cabinet. She handed it to Sloane.

"Thank you," she moved to pour herself coffee. She noticed that Caroline had set out the cream and sugar next to the coffee. She was so grateful for the hot coffee. It was her lifeline every morning.

"So, how did you sleep?" Caroline asked.

"Fine, I guess. Is that really what you want to talk about?" Sloane asked.

"No, just making small talk. I find it helps when under such stressful conditions." She moved to sit at the counter with her coffee.

"Ah well, we are checking out the school today. I haven't talked with Jessie or Erik about what they found out, yet. I hope we can get there and scope it out."

"I can help you with that. I know this area well. I have a tour for my daughter arranged and a meeting with the headmaster." Caroline straightened the paper in front of her and began reading.

"I didn't know you had a daughter," Sloane said.

"She doesn't live here with me, but I do. We need a cover for talking to him, and he will want to recruit more students. I already have someone fortifying documents and sending them to the school to review before the meeting."

"How were you able to get a meeting that fast?" Sloane asked. They found out about the school yesterday.

"I called a friend of mine that works at the school. She's the office manager, I asked a favor of her." Caroline said.

"Oh wow, that's great. I wasn't sure how we were going to get into the school, but considering Erik can read minds, I figured we'd just listen from afar. Now, he can join you for the meeting and find out everything we need to know." Sloane was excited at the prospect of this being over with quickly. She wouldn't mind going back to small moments of normalcy.

"I'm not sure I want him to join me, considering I can read minds as well. I was thinking I would take Mike, since he was the tracker. He could get a lead on all the demons there."

"Oh," was all Sloane could respond. She didn't like the idea of Mike going with her. The part where she could read minds had been left out of anything she'd known, so far. The lack of information, and her being with Mike, acting like her husband made her uncomfortable.

"I know you're leery, but you have nothing to worry about, trust me," Caroline said.

"Oh yeah, that reading minds thing can be annoying. I forgot because Erik usually does us the courtesy of not sharing our own thoughts back to us." She was annoyed because she didn't hesitate at all to read what she was thinking. Erik would block out others thoughts, or at least she thought he did. Now, she was suspicious. What if he didn't actually block them? Maybe he just didn't let her know he was reading her thoughts.

"No, he does actually block you guys out." She answered her thoughts. "I don't," she finished without shame.

"Oh, that's good. So…" Sloane wasn't sure what to say. It was disheartening to know that she could read her thoughts, which she felt made conversation unnecessary. "I'm going to go find Jessie and Erik to see what they dug up on the people from my vision. We may also still check out the school anyway, before your visit. From a distance."

"That sounds good," she said as she moved to pour herself another cup of coffee.

Sloane walked to find Erik and Jessie. She didn't want to spend any more time in the kitchen with Caroline. She was worried about what she would think in her presence, and she would be mortified if her thoughts drifted toward her time with Mike.

Erik was coming down the stairs, his tousled hair was dripping onto his indigo t-shirt.

"Hey," he said as he reached the bottom step.

"Morning," she returned.

"Is there coffee? I could really use some." He glanced down at the cup in her hand.

"Yeah, if you want to brave the kitchen," Sloane responded.

"Brave the kitchen? What's that supposed to mean?"

"Well, were you aware Caroline can hear our thoughts?"

"Yes, I was aware. So, can I. What's the big deal?"

"You don't read our thoughts all the time," she emphasized.

"No, I don't. You're my sister, I don't want to know what you're thinking all the time. I really don't want to relive whatever sexual encounter you've had recently, Ugh." He shuddered at the thought.

"Well, that's reassuring, I guess. I don't like the idea of someone having full access to my brain." She shook her head, "But go on in, there's coffee. When you're done, I'll be waiting in here." She moved to sit on the nearby sofa.

Erik went in the kitchen. He began thinking of his time with Jessie the night before. If she was going to read his thoughts, at least he'd give her a show. He smiled before he pushed the door open. Caroline was seated at the table, eyes focused on the newspaper laid out before her. She glanced up and smirked at him then went back to reading.

"Morning," he said as he reached to grab down two cups from the cupboard.

"Good morning, I see you had a good evening." She smiled up at him and winked.

"I did indeed. Anything interesting going on today?" he indicated the paper in front of her.

"No, not really, but I bet you knew that already." She looked expectantly at him.

"I did, but it seems courteous to have conversation, anyway." He filled both cups.

"Yes, I guess it is. I'm not around too many people who have the same gift as I do. I never thought I would be able to have a conversation without actually saying anything." She pondered a moment.

"I have them all the time." He walked through the kitchen door back to where Sloane was sitting. "I'm going to bring coffee up to Jessie, and I'll be right back down to ask you some questions." He looked at her pointedly and left the room. He bounded up the stairs. He slowly pushed open the door. Jessie was curled in a ball clutching the blanket in her hands. He smiled as he sat on the bed next to her. He set the cups on the nightstand and brushed a piece of hair out of her face. He smiled and bent to kiss her on the lips. She jerked back quickly and shot up smacking her head into Erik's nose. He clutched his nose with his hand.

"Ouch!" he said

Jessie realizing who it was said, "Oh sorry." She cupped Erik's cheek. "Oh baby, I'm so sorry, but you shouldn't scare me awake like that."

"I was trying to wake you with a kiss. I thought it was sweet." He placed his finger and thumb to put pressure on the bridge of his nose.

"I'm sorry, it was sweet." She moved to kiss him lightly on the lips. "Did I hurt you?" she asked.

"No, I'll be fine," he said. "I brought you coffee." He handed her one of the cups.

"Thank you." She took the cup in her hands and took a sip.

"I'm going back downstairs to talk about the plans for today. Come down when you're ready, but there's no rush." He kissed her before heading out the door.

When Erik reached the living room Sloane was gone. He met Caroline back in the kitchen. She sat relaxed at the table, still flipping through the paper. "What do you know about the school?" he asked.

"Well, if you'll have a seat, I will tell you all about it.". Erik sat, and she folded her paper, placing it next to her. She looked up to him and said, "The school is for Shikari members that can't be trained by their families for whatever reason. Many families choose to send their children to the boarding schools to learn from others. Some of the best of our organization strive to become the teachers at said schools. I have several friends who are part of the school staff. The one here in Colorado is the most prestige's in the United States, so it makes sense they would be targeting here first."

"We don't know that they are," Erik interrupted.

"Oh yes, that's true, of course. Well let me continue, then. The school has been around for over fifty years and has trained many Shikari hunters over the years. I'm surprised you don't know of these schools, considering." She paused, looking into Erik's eyes then at the mug in front of her.

"Why would you say that?" he asked.

"Well, didn't your father send you away to school after your mother's passing?"

"No, he didn't. He trained me himself, my entire life my father was always my teacher and trainer." He looked at her, and his mouth moved into a hard line.

"Oh, I just assumed that he would have. There's a school in Duluth. Well, as you know there are hunters who die much too early. When they experience a loss so young, they are brought to one of the schools to be trained. They're provided an advisor upon their entry into the school and they keep the same advisor for the duration of their stay at the school. In their later years, they choose specific roles to train for depending on their skills. The school has many students who have ended up leaders in our organization or top members of the order. It's very prestigious. I've made an appointment for my daughter to check out the school and get information. I'm surprised they were able to infiltrate the school considering, it's all Shikari members. Yet, if they've gotten the headmaster, it does make things much easier for them."

"So, who can we speak to outside of the school? We don't know who's involved. I don't want to take any chances in alerting the demons that we know about them. We need to eliminate them before they have any idea we know."

"I've contacted my friend, who I sent my daughters paperwork to. She doesn't know anything beyond me wanting my daughter to attend the school. I haven't talked to anyone about the real reason I'm going there. I don't know who's affected, and I want to get a lay of the land so to speak. No one knows, beyond those who came with you, and those who you informed in Denver. I know we've had issues with traitors in our group, so I have kept this information tight." She glanced to Erik.

"That's good, I think you're right we should check out the school before talking to anyone else."

"I want to go with Mike to the school. I think he's the best choice." She studied him.

"That's a good idea. You can read them, and he can get a lead on tracking. We can stay within close range of the school if anything happens. You two can go into the school without suspicion to get the information we need. Once we have an idea what's going on inside the school, we can make decisions about how to eliminate the demons."

"My appointment with the dean is at ten thirty this morning. I'm ready, but I would like to learn more about the head of the school and any other prominent members. I'm heading to my study to do some research. When you gather the others, we can make a plan."

"Yeah, I'll let the others know." Erik headed out of the kitchen and up the stairs to see what was taking Jessie so long. When he walked in, he could hear the shower running and the bedroom was empty. He waited a minute in the room, but then headed for the bathroom. They had a few hours before they'd have to be ready. He carefully opened the door and slipped in. He poked his head around the curtain and said, "Would you like some company?'

Jessie jumped and shouted, "Oh God."

"Oh, sorry. I didn't mean to scare you." He held his hand out toward Jessie, an invitation.

"What did you think would happen, surprising someone in the shower like that?" she grabbed his hand and yanked him toward her. He was pulled into the shower clothes and all.

"Hey!" he protested.

"That's for scaring me, you jerk." She crushed her mouth to his. He responded instantly and wrapped his arms around her. She reached her hands down and began unbuttoning his pants. "Let's get rid of these." She pulled his pants off of him and dropped them to the floor. He stepped out and threw them on the other side of the curtain.

"You know I don't have a ton of clothes with me, I kinda needed these."

"You'll get over it." She began lifting his shirt over his head. "Besides, you started it." She threw the shirt on the floor moving the curtain slightly. He lifted her and braced her against the wall. He looked into her eyes and smiled. He loved Jessie for so long he couldn't believe they were together again. He didn't want her to ever leave his side. He shuddered a moment at that thought. He brushed his hand down the side of her wet face. Her hair was plastered to the side, dripping. He watched as her pupils dilated when he stared into her eyes. He nipped her lip and breathed, "Oh Jess," against her mouth. He lapped at the wet skin on her neck, kissing a trail down to her collarbone. He enjoyed the slick feeling of her skin as he hitched his hands under each thigh and braced her against the wall. He savored every swipe of his tongue against her pale skin. Before long, he had her screaming in ecstasy He smirked as he let her legs drop back down to the shower floor.

"What were you thinking about a moment ago?" she traced the lines on the side of his eye. "I could see the tension on your face."

"Oh nothing," Erik looked away, quickly.

"I know you better than that, Erik."

He looked her in the eyes, the fear returning. He wasn't sure he could tell her the truth. Every loss he experienced, felt like a chipping away at his soul. He couldn't lose her, too. "I'm scared of losing you." He confessed, his eyes shimmered with unshed tears.

"Oh babe, you're not going to lose me." She brushed her hand along his cheek and rested it there.

"You don't know that, no one ever knows that." He looked down, unable to meet her eyes. He didn't like to admit weakness ever, people usually used it against him.

Jess wrapped her arms around him clutching him tighter. She rested her head on his chest. "I will do everything in my power to stay with you, I promise."

"I'll hold you to that," he tightened her arms around her and bent to place a kiss on her head.

"We need to get back to the others," she whispered.

"I know, let's just stay here a moment longer." He embraced the feeling of this moment, together. "Caroline's appointment with the dean is at ten thirty, so we need to make a plan," he hesitated. "Although, this is the only place I'd rather be." He leaned down and kissed her. "I'll let you finish your shower." He released her and stepped out of the shower. She turned off the water and stepped out. Erik was standing there holding a towel out for her.

"I thought you were leaving?" she asked.

"I changed my mind." He wrapped the towel around her and leaned to kiss her. "I couldn't resist seeing you naked and dripping wet." He winked at her. "Now, I'm going to go get dressed in new clothes." He turned and headed out of the room. He dressed and waited for Jess in the bedroom.

"You ready?" he asked.

"Yeah, I just have to brush my hair. I can meet you downstairs."

"I'll wait." He sat on the bed to watch her. He enjoyed watching her pull the brush through her long strands of hair. When the brush reached the end, her hair bounced back into curls that wouldn't be tamed. It reminded him so much of who she was. When she was finished, he held out his hand to her before heading downstairs.

Caroline was in her office with Sloane and Mike planning for the meeting.

"So, it looks like we'll be on the sidelines for this one bro," Sloane fluttered her lashes at him.

"Oh yeah?" he smiled. Sloane hated being on the sidelines of anything.

"We'll be parked here," she pointed to the map. "Mike and Caroline will be going into the school for the meeting. We'll be outside the school getting intel on the students and whatever you can hear from those around the school. We need as much information as possible about how deep this goes."

"So, not really the sidelines then," he smirked.

"Well, we are outside. So, still kinda the sidelines," she shrugged.

"Will Jess be with us?" he looked over to her and met her eyes.

"Yes, Mike and Caroline will be posing as a couple interested in having their daughter attend school there."

"Caroline, don't you have friends there? Won't they know?" Jess asked.

"My friend knows I'm divorced. I'm going to introduce him as my current boyfriend," Caroline said.

"Okay," Jess responded.

"So, what time are we leaving?" Erik asked.

"We have about ten minutes before we need to leave for the school" Caroline shifted the gold watch around her wrist.

"Awesome, where are the weapons?" Sloane asked.

"In the next room, here I'll show you our cache." Caroline stopped in front of a thick door, adjacent to the study and typed in a code. In the room there was floor to ceiling weapons hung against the walls, each having their own individual place.

"Nice," Sloane whispered as she appraised the walls.

"You can take whatever you like," Caroline swept her hand toward the room. "I have all that I need for the meeting. I will meet you upstairs when you're done."

She moved toward the door and touched Mike's arm before she exited. He followed behind her. Sloane took a few things off the wall and placed them in her backpack.

"You know this is just recon, right?" Erik asked as she continued to scan the wall.

"Yeah, recon. You never know what could happen, though. I like to be prepared for all options."

"You tend to make those things happen, but yes it's probably good that you're prepared for anything." Erik looked knowingly over to Jessie.

Erik reached up to grab a 9mm down and stuck it in the back of his belt, pulling his shirt over it. Jess smiled and shook her head.

"What?" he asked.

"Nothing, just seems a bit cliché." She shrugged

"Oh, well I like having quick access to a weapon."

"I just think you like having a large gun in your pants." She walked up and brushed herself against his back as she went to grab a few of her own guns to take on the mission.

"Well, you're not wrong," he smirked.

"Are you two ready to go, or do you need a few minutes in the gun room?" she winked at Erik.

"We're ready" Jessie said and walked back out the door.

She shook her head and patted Erik on the shoulder, "Awe, poor Erik."

"I think I'll be fine," he said. "We need to be on our way."

Sloane reached the landing to meet Mike at the door. "Hey, babe," seeing the look on his face she asked. "What's up?"

"I have to go meet, Bryant. There's a situation developing in the city, and I offered my tracking ability to help. Caroline will need to go to the meeting, alone." His eyes stared down into hers.

Erik stepped around the two. "What's going on in the city?"

"I didn't get all the details, but Bryant says it's an emergency. Caroline has offered to let me use one of her cars, so I can head there now." He looked down to Sloane, "I'm not sure when I'll be back, but I'll keep you updated."

"Okay." She reached up to kiss him, wrapping her arms around his neck.

Erik reached back to take Jessie's hand. He walked passed them and into the kitchen to meet Caroline. "So, are you okay to go in by yourself?" Erik asked.

"Yeah, I'll be good." She smiled. "We should be going." She reached for her keys and purse. Erik turned to Jess. "Alright, let's do this." He bent to plant a light kiss on Jessie's lips before following Caroline out the door.

Chapter 8

"It's great to meet you, Mr. Hall," Caroline said and took the headmaster's outstretched hand.

"I'm so pleased to meet you, Mrs. Robinson. I've heard so much about you; I hear you've done some amazing things in our line of work." He smiled wide at her shaking her hand three times and releasing it.

"Oh, thank you," Caroline feigned a wide, appreciative smile.

"So, let's get down to it, shall we? I hear you're interested in having your daughter, Nicole attend our fine school. I've looked over the records you sent, and she looks like a prime candidate for admittance. Would you like a tour of the school before we begin?" He folded his hands in front of him.

"I would love that," She gripped her purse in front of her.

"Okay, Jeanie would you mind giving Caroline a tour of the school?" he turned toward the door.

"Oh, you won't be giving the tour?" she looked to Mr. Hall.

"Jeanie usually gives the tours. She's been here the longest out of everyone here,"

Jeanie reached the door, her smile wide. "Mrs. Robinson, I would be delighted to take you around the school." Her eyes brightened.

"Sounds great," she smiled.

"I'll be here when you get back to talk specifics and to answer any questions you may have for us." He waited, glancing back toward his desk.

"Thank you." she smiled and turned toward Jeanie, "Shall we?"

"Absolutely," Jeanie turned on her heel and walked out of the room. Caroline turned and followed her out of the office and down the stairs.

"We'll start at the main building and work our way to the dorms. This school has been in operation since 1922 and has an amazing campus." She turned her head back to Caroline as she spoke.

"So, does Mr. Hall always send women to do the work, while he stays up in his castle office?"

Jeanie laughed, "Yes, he doesn't do much actual work."

"I bet you do. though." Caroline knew this was the ticket to get information.

"Oh yeah, but I've been here for years, I can tell you all there is to know about this school."

"That's great; I bet this place has changed over the years."

"Oh yes, I remember when this place was the most prestigious school in the United States. It's changed over the last few years.

They've been accepting students from all over without even a thorough application process. I'm surprised they even asked you to come in for a meeting. The last few students didn't even have their parents here when they moved in. Mr. Hall simply said they were his recruits. We've always had the board make decisions about applicants and never had to recruit before. Usually, we have to turn down hundreds of applicants. It's been strange over the last year, I'm worried about the school's future, and reputation if this keeps up." Jeanie put her hand to her mouth, "Oh, I'm so sorry. I shouldn't have spoken, so."

"It's okay. I understand. You sound like you just needed to vent. I understand that, entirely."

She lowered her head, shaking it. "Yeah, I'm worried about the school." Her shoulders sagged.

"That's understandable," Caroline moved her hand to pat her on the back. "You've been here a long time. I'm sure you care very much for the school and the students here."

"Oh yes, I do. Ever since this, Mr. Hall took over two years ago, so much has changed. There aren't even regular board meetings, anymore. Mr. Hall said we didn't need them, now that he was here. The board provided regulations for the school to make sure everything was running as it always had, and as it should according to the order."

"No board? How is he getting away with that? Every school has a board, even public schools. I can't believe he's able to operate a school without the board's input." Caroline moved her hand to her chin, thinking.

"I'm not sure. No one has brought up an issue with him not holding the board meetings. In reality, the board members are too busy to care all that much about the school anymore. Most of them are alumni or were appointed by the order. They have their own lives and jobs and do this on the side. It's hard to get them invested unless one of them has a student attending. Plus, they all trust Mr. Hall. He is a nice guy. You should meet his daughter. She used to be a hellion, skipping class, swearing at the teachers. Since she began attending here, she's a regular saint. It shows how capable he is of helping others when his daughter was able to turn around so quickly. It's rather remarkable." Jeanie smiled and placed her hand over her heart.

"Mr. Hall has a daughter, that's interesting. Can you tell me about when she made this sudden change?" Caroline tapped her finger against her lips in contemplation.

"It was shortly after Mr. Hall took over running the school. His daughter attended for the last five years or so. No one could get a handle on her, and she was facing possible expulsion. Mr. Hall talked with the board and the leaders in the area and asked if he could take over for Mr. Glaspell. He was so exhausted running the school that Mr. Hall's offer was more than welcome at the time. As soon as he took over, so many students that had misbehaved before turned right around. It was remarkable, any student who was sent to the office, came out changed. I've had no office visits since after his first month here. I don't know what he does, but he is a miracle worker with these kids." Jeanie beamed.

Caroline shifted back on her heel and contemplated all Jeanie said. She looked over to Jeanie, studying her. "Should we get back to the tour? I'd love to get a lay of the land, so to speak."

"Of course, I've jabbered on, again haven't I? Oh, I let my passion for the school get the better of me, sometimes. I'll take you straight-away."

Caroline looked around at the four large brownstone buildings which made up the campus. Between the buildings, the grass was split by walkways running from each entrance. Several students sat at picnic tables spread under the trees scattered throughout the campus lawn.

Jeanie led the way to the first building. "This is where many of the classes are held," she announced. She opened the door to the first classroom on the right.

Caroline noticed the musty smell in the air but brushed it off to the age of the buildings. When she walked into the classroom, it felt cozy immediately. The walls were lined with famous quotes from various authors. In the far back corner, there was a reading nook with bean bag chairs and three large bookcases filled to the brim with books. The shag rug on the floor added to the cozy feel. There were tables in the middle of the room, pushed together in groups of two, and pictures of books hung from strings attached to the ceiling with paper clips. Caroline walked around to see the different books the students were reading.

Jeanie noticed her fascination, "The students are in different book club groups, right now for English. They got to choose from various books during a book tasting. It's always so fun to see what they pick each semester. I love the diversity of the books around the coming of age theme."

Caroline reached her hand up to study a book cover, Rooftops of Tehran. She nodded, then moved onto the next, The Hate You

Give. She smiled at the selection. "These are some great choices. The students got to pick these out?"

"Oh yes, Mrs. Olson insists on it. She is firm on students getting to choose to read what they want, and they love her for it." Jeanie walked over to stand beside Caroline who had just reached up to look at the Mexican Whiteboy cover. "I will have to admit; Girl in Translation is one of my favorites that they pick every year."

Caroline turned to face Jeanie, "Although I could spend all day in this room, we should probably move on. Mr. Hall will wonder what is taking so long."

"Why yes, of course. Mr. Hall knows how garrulous I can be. I'm sure you want to see the dorms. Your daughter will be staying with us, I presume?"

"Despite my desire to keep her at home forever, I do believe it will be good for her to stay in the dorms, while she attends school. I'm only a short drive away if she needs anything, but she can also establish her independence, which as you well know, all teenagers need."

"Oh yes, they do. Follow me." Jeanie stood, holding the door for Caroline. She locked the door as soon as they were in the hallway. "We'll head to the dorms, and back to the offices, so you can get all the paperwork squared away with Mr. Hall. Do you have any questions for me about academics or Shikari specializations?"

Caroline narrowed her eyes, "Shikari specializations? Is that the field they will go into when they finish school? Do they get to choose or do you choose for them?"

"They choose their specializations, but we administer various testing scenarios to help them see what each student's skills match regarding their specialization. It's what we're so well known for. No student has ever regretted their decision after out rigorous testing procedures. We want to make sure students have the best fit for their future. As you well know, it benefits us all to have happy members, doing what they enjoy. Our society doesn't have to be all about duty but loving what you can be a big part of our lives. We make sure our students are in the best possible positions to love what they do, while also fulfilling their born duty as Shikari members."

"Sounds great. I want my daughter to be happy."

Jeanie opened the door for Caroline to enter the dorms. "I will show you a dorm room. You have different options for the size and amenities based on your budget. We have three different dorm options. Considering how close you live, you may not need all the amenities available. Some students move across the country to attend our illustrious school, and parents often choose to have more amenities because the student is so far from home." Jeanie opens the door. "This is our medium-sized dorm room." She stepped into the room and moved to the wall so that Caroline could step into the room.

"This is quite the dorm room. It's certainly larger than any I'd seen when touring colleges for myself, all those years ago." The dorm had a full-size bed and dresser as she expected, but it also had a futon with a mini-fridge and television making a cozy sitting area. Behind the door, was a desk with a high-back leather chair and just to the left was a spacious closet.

"As I said, many students come here from all over, and we want to make sure they are as comfortable as possible here."

"If this is the mid-sized dorm, I can only imagine what the large dorm room looks like." Caroline was wide-eyed, as she studied the detail in the room. There was even a Monet painting hung above the futon. A toaster oven sat atop the mini-fridge. She knew her daughter would be quite happy in a dorm this size.

"Oh yes, the larger rooms have two separate rooms, one for the bedroom, and one for the living space. Would you like to take a look?" Jeanie waited at the door.

"No, I think my daughter would be happy in a room this size. Anything bigger could make her jittery. She spends a lot of time in her room because open spaces tend to bother her. I think the mid-size is perfect for my baby." Caroline smiled.

"Perfect, shall we head back to the office to complete the paperwork, and get her enrolled in classes?"

"Absolutely," Caroline followed Jeanie out the building and back to the office. Jeanie knocked on Mr. Hall's door and peeked her head in when he responded. She opened the door. Caroline reached to take both Jeanie's hands in hers. "Thank you for the tour, Jeanie. It was appreciated." She squeezed her hands lightly.

"My pleasure, Mrs. Robinson."

"Caroline, please."

"Caroline."

"Mrs. Robinson, do you have any questions for me?" Mr. Hall asked, turning her attention back to him.

"I would like to know more about the process. How do you deal with problem students who are interrupting others learning? My daughter has issues with that in our public school, which has caused me to look into other more private schools befitting her skills."

"Oh, I believe you will find that we have no issues here whatsoever. All students are attending our interested in learning. You will have no problems here."

"Oh, would you like to speak more about that? Why don't you have any issues?" She sat in a chair across from his desk and clasped her hands together in her lap.

"If any students have misbehaved in class, I have a conference with them. It's amazing what a caring and concerned discussion can do to help students be more successful in class. I'm sure Jeanie can fill you in about our behavior referral statistics are zilch. I promise you, your daughter will get a fine education here." He stared directly into her eyes. Caroline shook her head and had to look away after only a few moments.

"Oh, I'm very glad to hear it. So, what's the next step of enrollment?" She leaned forward slightly in her chair.

"Jeanie will give you the rest of the paperwork to fill out, along with choosing a dorm. She will also send you home with a list of available classes we offer. When you have your classes selected, we can get her enrolled at the beginning of the next semester."

"Oh," Caroline put her hand to her chest. "I was hoping to get her in as soon as possible. I heard that you allowed students to begin in the middle of semesters." She smiled warmly.

"That's not our typical practice. It will be a much better transition for your daughter to begin classes at the beginning of the next semester."

"Oh," she leaned forward. "So, there's no way to get her in sooner?"

"No, I'm sorry that's not how we do things. I promise this is in the best interest of your daughter." He smiled sitting back in his chair.

"Okay, I'm sure you're right. I'm just so worried about her in that public school. It's just not suited for someone of her caliber." She rose from her chair. "It was a pleasure to meet you, Mr. Hall. I will get the necessary materials from Jeanie. I don't want to take up any more of your time." She reached her hand out to shake his.

He rose and walked around the desk. He shook her hand. "The pleasure is all mine. I'm sure your daughter will truly love it here." He smiled and opened the door for her. "Jeanie, if you could get Mrs. Robinson here, the rest of the enrollment paperwork, that would be great."

"Sure thing, Mr. Hall" She reached down into her desk sorting through the files.

Caroline turned, "Thank you. Mr. Hall."

"My pleasure, Mrs. Robinson." He turned back to his office and shut the door behind him.

"Oh, I'm so glad your daughter will be attending. You will be a happy addition to our campus here." She pulled out the paperwork. "I will give you all of this now, but you can fill it out and return it to me at your leisure. You have a few months until the next semester starts." Jeanie held out the papers.

"Thank you, Jeanie. You have been a wealth of knowledge. I can't wait for my daughter to attend." She smiled, took the paperwork, and went out the door. Her spine was still tingling being so close to Mr. Hall. She wondered how the others hadn't noticed. She was curious how Jeanie was able to work that closely with a demon and have no idea. How did he pass right by the board without being detected? She had more questions than answers after her meeting. She rushed to her car and passed the others by the road. She had so much to tell them but wanted to do so in the safety of her own home. She was reeling after being on the campus. She could understand why the students may not have noticed. They may not have sharpened their skills to be able to detect demons, but she certainly had. Mr. Hall was a demon.

She pulled into the driveway and parked. She hurried into the house. Setting the paperwork and her purse on the counter, she turned as the others walked through the door.

"So, we have a lot to discuss our school, here."

Chapter 9

"Mr. Hall has been busy. He took over the school two years ago. Is it possible this has been going on for the last two years, and we didn't know about it?" Caroline asked.

"I'm learning anything is possible at this point." Erik took a seat at the kitchen table.

Jessie sat next to him, "So, what do we need to know about Mr. Hall?"

"Well, Mr. Hall has been recruiting students from all over and letting them into the school without a formal process. He's somehow gotten around the board. They usually make sure the school is running according to Shikari rules. The school has no discipline problems with students because any student who misbehaves is brought to Mr. Hall. They are miraculously wonderful students after the visit, including his daughter. We should probably spend time looking into his family and any other known contacts. Also, I have yet to figure out how he is operating at a school full of other Shikari, and no one is noticing they are demons. What could they possibly have that stops the familiar warning we typically have around demons? I noticed it, but

Jeanie, his assistant isn't possessed, didn't. She's working alongside him every day. She thinks he's the savior of the school. Did you hear anything outside the school?" She turned to face Erik.

"Nothing substantial, there are quite a few students who are possessed. I only get what they are thinking at the time, so it's not always what I want to hear." Erik explained.

"So, basically he's having any misbehaving students possessed by demons? That seems backward. Aren't they supposed to get possessed first, then act like demons? Instead, they act like demons, become possessed, then act like angels. Anyone else catching the irony here?" Sloane shook her head.

"So, what's next?" Jessie asked.

"We need to let Bryant and Magnus know what's going on here. We will need to do some research about what the demons could have access to that would make a school full of Shikari unaware of them," Erik said.

"I want to talk with a few board members. See how this went unnoticed. See if they are demons as well," Caroline said.

"Where do you keep your books? I can start the research. You know it'd be nice if they'd uploaded everything online in a database, rather than having to search through books to find the information we need." Sloane sighed.

"Yeah, that'd be great. So, the demons could hack into the database and find out everything they need to know." Sarcasm was thick in Jessie's tone.

"They are already getting the information, so it's not as secure as we think it is. People are fallible, just like computers. We are the ones who are supposed to know better though." Sloane glanced to Erik.

"My study is down the hall. It has some books, but most are stored at the main hub. My house isn't big enough to have an entire library housed here. I should have what we need though."

"Jess, you want to come help me while Erik makes the calls?"

"Yeah, sounds good." She glanced back to Erik. "Do you need me for anything?"

"Nah, I'll meet you guys there when I talk to Bryant and see what's going on in Denver."

"Oh yeah, you think Mike is there, yet?"

"I'm sure he is. I'll fill you in on what's going on as soon as I know, okay?"

"Okay, come on Jess." Sloane turned on her heel and went down the hall.

Jessie followed behind Sloane toward Caroline's study. When Sloane reached the door, she opened it and walked directly to the bookshelves. "So, where should we start?"

Jessie walked and scanned the titles. Sloane pulled one from the shelf. "I don't remember learning anything about blocking our awareness of demons, but there seems to be a potion for everything."

"Yeah, I can't recall anything either. It's not like we would be taught anything to help demons. Our education focused on what we would need to battle and defeat demons, not how to mask demons from our presence. I'm sure it's in one of the grimoires."

"Great we can start there." Sloane pulled out a book and sat in one of the reading chairs. For not having a true library, Caroline's study sure felt like one. There are three large reading chairs, a corner desk and three shelves filled with books. It certainly felt like a library. Sloane began skimming through the pages to see what she could find.

"Is it weird I feel like so much information was left out when we were learning this stuff?" Sloane flipped another page, studying the description of demon essences. "For example, do you remember reading about demon essences? There's an entire history here for the different realms and types of demon essences. I didn't realize there were types of demons. I always thought they came from the same hell, not levels or realms as this discusses."

"I remember stumbling across something like that in your dad's library. I guess I didn't pay much attention to it. Mike is the only one of us that actually spent time learning the history of demons. We always focused on destroying and hunting. You and Erik always were focused on weapons and training. You didn't do much reading unless it had to do with weapons."

"That's true. We had similar tastes in that regard." Sloane flipped another page.

"I focused more on potions and spells. I focused on channeling my power. I had to learn how to control my power when it changed. I couldn't exactly keep blowing things up when I got angry."

"Yeah, that was hell. I remember when you first found out. Erik's brilliant idea was to put oven mitts over your hands." Sloane laughed at the memory. She remembered him holding the mits out to Jessie. He seriously thought they would help.

"Your mom got so mad because he duct taped them on my hands. It's not like he duct taped my arms or anything. He just used it on the cloth part. She still freaked out on us." She laughed at the memory.

"I remember, she grounded him for a week. She was so worried about you."

"I know, she was amazing like that. She always treated me as her daughter, whenever I stayed with you guys. She always made me feel like family." Jessie looked down to the book in her lap and cleared her throat.

"Yeah, she was pretty great." Sloane's voice cracked as she spoke.

"I'm sorry Sloane. I know it's still hard to talk about her." Jessie moved to sit next to Sloane, placing her hand on her knee.

"She was pretty amazing. I can't help but think how all our lives would be different if she hadn't been killed. I know everyone is mad at me for leaving, but at the time I couldn't stay. Everything reminded me of her, and I was so mad, I was mad at The Shikari and everything we stood for, mad at my father for not being able to stop it. I just had to leave everything and start over. No one seems to understand." She huffed out a relieved breath. It felt good to talk to another girl. She missed having her best friend to talk to every day. She knew she needed to leave her old life behind, but she missed the little things. She shared everything

130

with Amy. Now, she couldn't even answer the phone when she called. It was the right thing to do. Amy had no place here, but it still felt awful. Having Jessie to confide in was a relief and a blessing.

"I get why you left. My mom and I took a trip here shortly after the funeral. She needed to get away, too. They had been so close their entire lives. My mom didn't handle her death well. At the time, she didn't know another Shikari member was involved. None of us knew how deep the betrayal went. I still don't think we know." Jessie patted Sloane's leg and leaned back into the chair, resting the open book in her lap.

"Bryant said he took care of her killer, but I'm not so sure. I think this goes a lot deeper. I know he took care of those immediately responsible, but I think there's someone at the head of all of this calling the shots. I don't think we've even scratched the surface of the betrayal, yet. I have a feeling there are a lot more Shikari members that have helped the demons. I know we're trying to play catch up, but I think we need to find someone we can trust in the group of leaders to find out how deep this goes. Shaundra told me when she called the order her call was strange. She mentioned they seemed overwhelmed, and the call didn't seem right. I think there is something bigger going on, and until we have someone in the order, checking out the leaders at headquarters, we're not going to be able to stop this." Sloane spoke with conviction, but she bowed her head slightly.

"I agree, but who do we know that can help us. We don't know who we can trust. I also wouldn't trust everything Shaundra said." A flicker of anxiety darkened her eyes before she looked to the floor.

"Why?" Sloane questioned.

"She was a traitor working with the demons." Jessie blew out a heavy breath. "Erik and I found out after her power boost didn't work as well as it should have in Minneapolis. We stumbled across her and Curtis plotting their next move against the Shikari. We took care of them without telling anyone. I figured Erik would have told you about them. I'm not sure what she was lying about, but I know she was working with them."

Sloane appraised her and cocked her head to the side before she spoke. "Seriously, she seemed so helpful. When did you guys figure that out?"

"Right after the battle, when she offered to call in the cleaners and take care of everything. I tried to tell Mike, but he didn't see any reason to look into her. He thought it was a fluke the potion hadn't worked like before. He said sometimes they don't work like we expect them to, magic being fallible and all. I didn't believe it. I'd taken a power boost made by her before, and it worked better. Then, I started thinking about why she wouldn't want it to work. I went to find you at your dad's place." She tilted her head to look at Sloane.

"Yeah, I'd gone to my apartment," Sloane nodded.

"I figured." A smile curved the edge of her mouth. "I ended up talking to Erik about my concerns. He insisted we talk to her right away. We found her and Curtis at the shop planning their next move. He heard her thoughts about making the potion weaker. He shot them both. We cleaned up so no one would know about them. We wanted to find out how deep this went, considering they were helping us defeat them while also helping the demons.

I'm still not sure how we were successful when traitors knew about it." Jessie furrowed her brow.

"So, they're willing to help, but not enough to hurt an entire group of us. It's got to be hard to betray your family, the group you've sworn loyalty to since birth. I can't fathom how so many are working with demons. We've been raised to fight demons. I just don't get how anyone of us could help them under any circumstances. There has to be something we're missing," Sloane said.

"Yeah, but what? I don't get it, either." Jessie asked.

"Let's keep reading; maybe we'll get some insight by learning more about the history."

"It'd be nice if Mike and Erik were here, right now. Maybe they could shed some insight into this. Mike knows more about the history than any of us." Jessie settled back into her chair and sighed.

"I wouldn't mind Mike being here, right now." Sloane crooked her mouth into a sly smile.

"Yeah, but that's for very different reasons." Jess winked at Sloane.

"True," Sloane stared off into space.

"Then, you wouldn't get any work done." Jessie raised a brow.

"Whatever, we'd still get work done." Sloane focused back on the page in front of her.

"Sure, you would." Jess rolled her eyes. She looked to Sloane, then focused back on her reading.

Sloane flipped the book closed after skimming through the pages. "There's quite the history of demons and spells here, but nothing on being able to hide their presence from us."

"Yeah, I'm not sure Shikari would necessarily have that information. We've only collected information based on what we've been able to learn over the centuries. What if Shikari didn't know they could mask themselves from us? What if this is new information?"

"That makes sense. If none of us have heard of this before, it could be that it hasn't been written, yet. We should ask Bryant and Magnus. See if they've ever heard of that before."

"Wasn't that what Erik was doing?" Jess asked.

"That's what he is supposed to be doing. I wonder what's taking him so long. He said he'd meet us here when he was done." Sloane ran her hand through her hair and set the book on the table next to her. "I'll call Mike and ask what's going on in Denver. Have him ask Bryant and Magnus while he's there. Can you go find out what's taking Erik so long?" Sloane grabbed her phone out of her pocket to call.

"On it." Jess rose and headed out of the room to find Erik.

Sloane dialed Mike, "Hey, babe. How's it going in Denver?"

"Not great, we have two students missing here, too." His voice was serious.

"Oh, that's not good. So, you won't be back anytime soon."

"No, love. I won't be back until we figure out what's going on."

"Awe, are you sure you can't come back sooner?"

"Babe, you know how much I'd like to have my way with you, right now. But, I can't."

"Okay, fine. So, we found out some info on the school. The headmaster is possessed, but not everyone there is, we're trying to figure out how it would be possible for a demon to mask their possession from us, especially from an entire school. Only some of the students have been possessed, as far as we can tell. You got any ideas?" Sloane paused.

"I can't think of anything."

"Okay, can you ask Bryant and Magnus? Check into how that might be possible. We may have you check out some of the board members located in Denver. Since you won't be coming back here." She blew out a heavy breath.

"Miss me that much, aye?" She could almost hear the sly smile over the phone.

"Yes," she breathed.

"Love, you know this is important. I need to track down the missing kids here." He paused. "These disappearances have to be connected. I will keep you informed on what's happening."

"I know this is important." She huffed. "I'll see you, soon. Let me know what you find out from Magnus and Bryant. I miss you, Mike."

"Miss you too, love." Sloane sighed and hit the end button. She stared at the phone in her lap. She wanted to join Mike in Denver but knew they had to do their job. Sloane left the study to find the others.

Jess was sitting on the couch tucked under Erik's arm. "Hey," Sloane sat in the chair adjacent the couch. "I called Mike. There have been two other missing Shikari students taken since the last girl was found by her father. It looks like they will be stuck in Denver for a while. We should be keeping an eye on Mr. Hall to see if he has anything to do with the missing students." Sloane rubbed the leather stitching of the chair as she spoke.

"Yeah, I agree we should be watching Mr. Hall," Jessie said as she stroked the hair on Erik's arm absentmindedly.

"I don't know. Mr. Hall has an entire school of students he could have possessed. Why would he worry about students in Denver? He has a whole school of them right here." Erik said.

"That's a good question. Why were these specific students targeted?" Sloane inquired, moving her hand to her chin, stroking it thinking.

"The only reason I can think of for why students would be targeted is to cripple the next generation of Shikari. If they possess the next generation, they can't hunt them." Erik said.

"That's true, but there could be another reason. Do you remember reading what power the first missing girl had? Maybe they are targeting these students for their special abilities." Sloane suggested.

"Oh, that could be. I know my power would be coveted, and I've been asked to join other divisions when they find out what I can do." Jess sat up.

"Yeah, you and Bryant went looking for me for my ability. We need to find out what the missing students could do."

"Definitely. I'll go grab the file on the missing girl." Erik stood and ran up the stairs. He returned with a file in his hand. He handed it to Jess and sat back on the couch. "Here, you haven't seen this, yet."

She spread the file in their laps. Sloane watched as Erik and Jess shuffled through the papers. "Look for the transcript of the interview. Maybe she talks about her ability."

Erik pulled out a sheet and handed it to Sloane. "Here, you look through this one. We'll look for any notes anywhere else."

Sloane read the interview, but it only talked about where she was taken and the description of the guy who took her. Nothing about her or any speculative reason for taking her. They probably assumed it was because she was Shikari and didn't think too far beyond that. It's what demons do, why question it further. "There's nothing about it here. If she does have a special ability, maybe her father wouldn't want it to be public knowledge." Sloane handed back the paper and Erik tucked it in the folder.

"So, who would know what her power was?"

"Her father, maybe Magnus would know. I'll call Mike. Maybe since he's a tracker, he can find out if the others don't know." Sloane pulled out her phone and hit send. "Hey, Mike do you know what power the girl who was kidnapped had?" She waited, listening.

"No, why?"

"Could you ask Magnus? We think the students may be targeted for their abilities. It would help prove our theory if she had a special ability." She waited.

"That makes sense. I'll find out about all the missing students. You may be on to something."

"Will you call me back when you find out?" She asked.

"You'll be the first call I make, love."

"Thanks, I'll talk to you soon. Bye." Sloane was all business.

"So, did he know about the girl?" Jessie asked.

"No, but he's going to ask Magnus, or find out himself. He agrees that it makes sense. So far, we don't know why these specific students are being targeted."

"I'm going to go find Caroline and let her know what's going on. See if she got any information about the board members." Jessie got up and strode toward Caroline's room.

"We should probably go back to the school and follow Mr. Hall. See what we can find about him, and the students that have been possessed on campus. It would be good to know if they are being targeted for their ability. We also need to figure out what their ultimate goal is. If they are targeting students for their abilities, what powers do they need and why?"

"Sounds like a plan. I'm going to run and grab my duffle upstairs. Can you be ready to go in say, ten minutes?"

Chapter 10

"You ready?" Erik asked, lounging back against the counter.

"Yeah, where's Jessie?" Sloane asked.

"She's with Caroline. She'll be up in a minute."

Jessie reached the landing and stepped next to Erik. "We ready?"

"Yep, just waiting on you." Erik bent to pick up his bag.

They walked to the car, and Sloane threw her bag in the backseat. Erik sat in the driver's seat, and Jessie sat in the passenger seat. Erik reached his hand over to take Jessie's. He wanted to use his senses to see what she was thinking. She'd been quiet after talking to Caroline, and he wasn't sure why. Caroline had a habit of answering to people's thoughts. He wasn't sure if that was the case with Jessie. He moved his thumb to stroke her knuckles and looked over to meet her eyes. He smiled at her, and she returned his smile for a brief moment before staring ahead again. She kept biting her bottom lip. Erik knew she was anxious about something. He wished she would tell him what it was so they could work it out together.

"Everything okay Jess?" he asked in a whisper.

"Yeah, everything's fine." She looked back out the window.

"O....kay," Erik said and focused back on the road. Jessie looked over to Erik and back out the window. She kept fidgeting in her seat as he drove. Erik pulled alongside the school and parked.

"Are you going to listen from here?" Sloane asked.

"It seems like the best plan. We don't want them to know we're here." Erik's sarcastic tone was biting. He didn't mean it, but it was bothering him that Jess wasn't telling him what was bothering her.

"Jeez, what's your deal? I was just asking." Sloane sat back in her seat and huffed out a breath.

"Nothing. Sorry." Erik said. Jessie looked over at him and narrowed her eyes. He shook his head and looked out the window. They sat waiting.

"So, you got anything, because this is killing me? It's not fun when only you, get to know what's going on." Sloane pouted in a whiny tone.

"Not really, I can't hear Mr. Hall, right now. There's not much happening. It must be a break or something." Erik said.

"Can I go in there, please?" Sloane begged.

"No, Sloane, we can't just go into a school with kids, guns blazing. I know that's your style, but you need to chill out. We need to get information."

"You and your damn information. Don't you ever just want to act? I can't just sit here."

"Why did you even come with? We have to just sit here. We're on the side of a mountain. Where else are you going to go?" Erik glanced around the car. There weren't many places to go. The only thing here was the school.

"Whatever, I'm going for a walk." Sloane grabbed the door handle.

"What? No." Erik turned in his seat.

"Oh, don't get your panties in a bunch. I'm just going to walk along the road. I won't go near the school, I promise." Sloane opened the door before Erik could protest. She closed the door and lifted the back of her shirt, showing Erik the gun, before she began her trek up the road.

"What do you think her deal is?" Erik asked.

"Sloane's never been very good at sitting still. You should know that better than anyone."

"Now that we're alone, are you going to tell me what's bothering you? I noticed your agitation after you talked with Caroline. What's going on Jess?" He studied her. She was gripping on hand with the other. She bit her lip.

"It's not my place to share," Jessie said.

"What does that mean? It's me, Jess. You can trust me." He narrowed his eyes. He couldn't believe she would keep something from him.

"I guess. Caroline hasn't been able to reach her daughter, today. It's probably nothing, but I have a bad feeling. Something's going to happen, something bad. I can feel it." Jessie continued to grip her hands in her lap. She was chewing her lip,

"Isn't it Sloane's power to see the future. You don't have that power, Jess. How do you know something bad is going to happen?"

"I don't know." She glanced down to her hands. "It's just a feeling I have like something's coming, and we're not going to see it coming." She continued to chew he lip.

"Jess, that's ridiculous. We'll figure it out. We always do. It's what we've always done." Erik glanced out the window. Looking toward the school, he noticed a student heading in the direction Sloane walked. He sat up in his seat.

"We don't always figure it out, and lately we have no fucking clue what's going on. So, why do you think we'll figure it out. We've been playing catch-up a lot lately, and I don't like it." She glanced out the window. A shiver ran down her spine.

"Are you cold?" Erik asked.

"No, like I said. I have a bad feeling, Erik. A really bad feeling." She rubbed her hands on her pants and clenched her hands into fists. "Will you please listen in on the school? We need to know what the hell is going on."

Sloane wrapped her arms around herself. She didn't think it was cold, but suddenly she felt a chill go down her spine. Her phone vibrated in her pocket, and she fished it out.

"Hey babe, what did you find out?" She answered after seeing Mike's name.

"It's not good, Sloane. The girl, she can manipulate others thoughts. She can put a thought in your head and make you think it was your thought. That's a dangerous power for the demons to have. They also got another boy. He's a tracker. Put the two together, and you've got a volatile pair. You're right about looking for specific skills."

"Okay, have you learned anything actionable? We're at the school trying to get intel, but it's so boring here. I need something to do."

"Babe, where are you right now?" Mike asked.

"Walking outside the school. Why?" She continued to kick at the gravel on the road.

"You need to get back with Erik, right now. They were able to get the girl because she separated from her friends. They are looking for us when we're vulnerable, and if they are at the school, they know you're outside." Mike's voice sounded panicked.

"Wait, what? How would they know?" Sloane stopped walking and glanced around her.

"I got info on Mr. Hall. He can sense the powers of others. He knew Caroline was investigating when she walked in the school. He also knew she could read his thoughts before she even walked in. He probably knows you can see the future, too. Sloane, love, please go back to Erik. Stick together, I beg you." The sincerity in his voice made Sloane turn around.

"Okay, I'll go back." She wasn't afraid of any of these demons, but if Mike was that worried, she figured she could turn around for him.

"Let me know when you're back with them."

"Uh, okay. Mike, what aren't you telling me? You're way too worried."

"Sloane, you'd be a huge get for them. You need to protect yourself. They're looking for powers." Sloane caught a glimpse of something out of the corner of her eye.

"Hold on; I think I see someone."

"Babe, no, go back to Erik. I know you. Don't take anyone on, alone. Please, just get back to the car."

"Ye of little faith. I'll be fine. I was bored anyway." Sloane turned toward the school, but whatever she saw was gone.

"Don't worry so much, babe. Whoever it was is gone now." Suddenly, the hair on the back of her neck prickled. She knew there was a demon. Reaching for the gun in her waistband, she whirled around, but something hit her head. She dropped the phone, and everything went black.

"What do you think's taking Sloane so long?" Erik shifted in his seat. He wouldn't mind going for a walk right now.

"She's probably scouting the entire school. Planning entry points for later. Making some kind of plan to infiltrate the school. You know, Sloane stuff." Jess smirked.

"Sloane doesn't plan. She just runs in, guns blazing."

"That's such a weird saying, guns blazing. I mean do guns blaze? Really? No, so why do people say it like that?" Jess rubs her forearm with her hand.

"Are you cold? I have an extra jacket in the back. I'll grab it if you need it."

"No, I'm fine." She rubbed at the goosebumps again.

The shrill of Erik's phone filled the car. He hit the button. "Hey, Mike, What's up?"

"Sloane, we were talking, and she disappeared. I could hear a gruff male voice in the background; then her phone went dead. I tried calling back but got voicemail. Erik, find her. She's in trouble. I'm running to my car; I'll be there as soon as I can."

'What? She just went for a walk." Erik glanced up the road in the direction Sloane had walked.

"No, Erik. Are you listening? Go find her, now." His voice was commanding.

"Okay, okay. I'm going." He hung up.

"Mike says something happened to Sloane. We better go to her. I'm sure she's fine, but Mike sounded worried." Jess had the door open and flew out of the car before Erik finished. "Jeez, it's Sloane. I'm sure she's fine. She'd kick anyone's ass who even tried anything."

Jessie took off at a dead run up the hill. Erik shook his head but followed. She didn't stop at the top. She ran another quarter-mile before she finally stopped. She bent to pick up something black from the ground.

When Erik reached her, he asked, "What's that?"

Jessie held it up. "Sloane's phone. Still think she's fine, Erik?"

"Oh shit?" He held his hand out to take the phone. He hit a button, and the screen lit up. When he saw her face on the screen, he curled his hands into fists. "Shit? We need to start looking." Jess was bending down to the ground, reaching her hand to touch the pavement. She lifted her fingers to examine them.

She held out her red blotched fingers. "Blood," she said.

"Fuck, Jess we have to find her. Look for a trail. I'm going to listen."

"If they took her, they would've had to go back to the school. We haven't seen any other cars around."

"Shit, I don't know I wasn't paying attention to the road. I was listening to the people in the school."

"I was, there haven't been any other cars. Come on; we need to get up to the school. If we find any demons, you'll hear them, and I'll freeze them."

"Okay, let's go." They sprint toward the school. Erik was jerking his head around frantically at any noise.

Jess reached her hand out to touch his shoulder. "Erik, you need to calm down if we're going to find her." He paused, looked into her eyes, and nodded.

"Jess, they have Sloane. That's my sister." His eyes were wide as he looked at her.

"I know, Erik. We're going to find her, but I need you to focus on doing that." Her voice was reassuring, and she squeezed his shoulder.

Erik took a deep breath. "Okay, you're right." Glancing in the direction of the school, he paused to listen. "Come on, this way."

"What?" Erik pulled Jessie toward where he'd heard a demon. He paused on the side of the brownstone building. Erik glanced around the corner. He held his finger to his lips. He gripped her hand a moment before letting it fall and reaching for the gun in his waistband. He could hear their voices, but it was their thoughts that got his attention. They had known they were coming. They had hoped Sloane would be separated from them but planned to take her, regardless. Erik glanced to their necks; he saw the amulets sparkle against the setting sun. They looked similar to the one Erik had seen on the demon Jessie couldn't freeze and knew immediately their powers wouldn't work on these demons. Not unless they were able to separate them from the amulets. Erik took a deep breath and turned to meet Jessie's curious gaze.

"They have amulets to make our powers useless. Mr. Hall had known we would be back. He knew of Sloane's power. He wanted Sloane, badly." He whispered, eyes wide.

"Okay, how do we separate them from the amulets so that I can blow them up?"

"Jess, they're only students. We need to follow them. They may know where they're taking Sloane." Erik turned his head back toward the boys and lifted his hand, running it through his hair.

"Fine," Jessie grunted. Erik turned to look at her and smiled at her pout. Damn, she could be so cute, he thought.

Erik listened. They were on orders from the headmaster. Erik crept toward the corner again. He wanted an opportunity to take the amulets off the two men. He wasn't sure why he could still hear them, considering they were wearing the amulets. He took a deep breath and checked again to see where they were. The two boys had stopped before the door leading into the building. One of them had a lit cigarette perched between his lips. Erik watched as he inhaled. They were chatting about some incident in class earlier. They'd almost forgotten, not all of the teachers or students were possessed. One of the boys had said, "Wanna bet," to the science teacher before the other boy had placed his hand on his arm, a subtle reminder. They couldn't be exposed this late in the game. Late, shit how far had they taken over? Erik wondered.

Jessie tapped Erik on the shoulder. She had taken her hoodie off and stood with her black tank. His pulse quickened at the sight of her nipples through the thin fabric.

"I have an idea." She smirked raising her eyebrows at him. She glanced down before looking up through her lashes and bit her lip. Erik's pants felt tight at the seductive look she was giving him.

"Shit Jess, I don't know. They're men, but they're also demons." He appraised her as she batted her lashes giving him a mockingly shocked look. Her mouth dropped into the shape of an o and then she smirked at him.

"Why Erik, are you saying I'm not attractive enough to distract some poor little boys outta their necklace?" She blanched. "You're the one who said the demons react the same way boys would. We know the demons can only take as much pain as their human host. So, why wouldn't it be the same with them, other emotions, say maybe, attraction." Jessie fluttered her lashes and bit her bottom lip, slowly letting go. After her teeth, she licked her top lip, slowly eyes gazing into his. She raised her brow at the desire that must have been evident on his face.

Erik wanted to grab her and take her against the building, right now. He closed his eyes, drawing a deep breath through his lips trying to think of anything but Jessie standing before him in her tight tank top and jeans. It took a few minutes for his pulse to go back to normal. When he opened his eyes, she was grinning wide, and her eyes were alighted with accomplishment.

"See, I think this could work. If I can get my arms around one of them to take off the amulet, I can freeze him. You can sneak up behind the other while I have them distracted."

"And if this doesn't work?" he asked, still trying to pull himself together, which was difficult when she continued to look at him with fire in her eyes.

"We fight like always and take them with us." She shrugged. "You know we can take on two pesky demons. Even if we don't have our powers for an advantage. We've trained for this many, many times and it's us. We've done this before, Erik. What has you doubting yourself?" He could feel Jessie's questioning gaze. It was her; he was worried about her.

Erik lowered his head. "They've got Sloane. I don't want to take any chances with her life, Jess. I can't lose her again." His voice wasn't much more than a whisper. He was afraid she'd hear the hysterics and fear in his voice if he spoke beyond a whisper.

She placed her hand on his cheek. "Trust me; we'll get her back."

Erik stared intently into her eyes and took a deep breath. "Okay, let's do it."

Jess nodded then sauntered around the corner toward the boys. She stopped next to the taller boy with sandy brown hair. She batted her eyes and asked, "Can I get a light?" She held a cigarette between her wet lips and smiled. The boy across from her scrambled in his pocket, cursing. When he found it, he held it out to her, almost dropping it in the process. She fluttered her lashes again. "Thanks, handsome. So, what are you two fine gentlemen doing out here? Shouldn't you be inside learning?" Her voice was low and seductive.

Erik crooked up the side of his mouth. God, he loved that girl. She took a drag of her cigarette and let the smoke out smoothly through her parted lips. The boy across from her had his mouth open slightly, mesmerized by the circles she was making in the smoke. Her eyes were locked on his as she crooked her mouth up in a sly smile.

She bit her lip again, taking a step forward resting her hand on the young man's chest. She ran her hand up from his chest to his neck. She gazed into his eyes. Stopping at the amulet, she said, "So, darling, Are you skipping school?" She fluttered her eyes at him. Dropping her voice low she said, "Are you a bad boy?" She toyed with the necklace and stroked her fingers on the back of his neck. "Mmm, such hard muscles." She let her fingertips trail along his neck and arm.

Erik saw his chance and moved steadily behind the other boy who stood transfixed. Jessie moved her mouth to brush her lips lightly against the boys. His lips parted, he let out a breath of pure desire. Her fingers stroked the hairs on the back of his neck, and she unhooked the amulet. It fell into her other hand. She flicked her tongue against the boy's lips causing a swift intake of breath from the entranced boy. He reached his hands around her, gripping hungry. When she heard the thump behind her, she bit the boy's lip causing him to jerk away. She raised her knee to connect with his groin. He doubled over. She jabbed her knee into his face, and he fell to the side still gripping his injured groin with both hands.

Jessie turned toward Erik. "Nicely done."

He put his hand to his heart. "I'm not sure how much more of you kissing another guy I could watch. I know you were doing it for Sloane but damn. Did you have to be so convincing?" He shook his head and leaned over resting his hands on his knees as though he were in physical pain from the experience.

She took a step toward him and patted him on the shoulder. "Knock it off. We have work to do. We need to get these two in the car, or we need to dispossess them now. Which is it?" She put her hand on her hip waiting.

"Let's get them in the car. We need to know what they know about Sloane." Erik straightened. He tossed the keys to Jess. You want to bring the car closer, to the back lot. I'll carry them over. He glanced around. They'd been lucky no one had seen them so far, but he didn't know how long before someone came upon them. He didn't want to explain two knocked out students to anyone. Jess sped toward the car. Erik bent to lift the first boy who was easily one-sixty. He hauled him over and dropped him down near the back parking lot. He looked around again. Jess had turned into the lot. She skidded to a stop next to where he stood and raced around to open the trunk. He lifted the boy and deposited him into the open trunk. Jessie reached down and unfastened the amulet from around his neck.

"You want to go get the other one?" she asked.

"On my way." He turned and sprinted back to where he left the other boy. When he reached the spot, he slowed. The boy had been here, hands still in front of his groin when he left. He turned in a circle. Shit, He thought. The boy was gone. He knelt next to where he was laying and cursed. He should have known something was off when he was supposed to be knocked out but was still gripping his groin in pain. Unconscious people were limp. The boy hadn't been. If he wasn't so distracted by Jess kissing him, and Sloane's disappearance he would've noticed. He sprinted back toward the car. Jess had a puzzled look on her face as he approached.

"The other one's gone. Which means we have to get the hell out of here, now." Erik jumped in the driver's seat. Jessie's eyes were wide as she ran around to get in next to him. He put it in gear and sped off. He drove immediately back to Caroline's house. He hated the idea of leaving when they hadn't found Sloane, but he knew they had to or they would be meeting a lot more demons. Then they would never find her. He glanced toward Jessie as she gripped the door handle. She was perched forward in her seat, muscles tense. She was ready to fight whatever may be coming for them. He reached a hand over and stroked her thigh.

"It's okay. It's going to be okay." He soothed.

"I know, but I'm worried. Why do you think they needed Sloane?" she asked.

"I don't know, but I bet it has something to do with her power. Maybe they need her to see the future for them," he suggested. His hand still rested on Jessie's leg.

"I hope so. Then at least they'd keep her alive. I don't even want to think about the alternative." She stared at Erik her eyes glistening in the light. Her hands were clenched in fists. "We can't lose her, Erik."

"I know, Jess, believe me, I know." He took her hand in his and squeezed.

"Mike was hauling ass from Denver as soon as he got off the phone with her. Maybe he can fill us in on what's going on, and why in the hell they would go after Sloane. So far, they've gone after students. Why would they suddenly go after an older Shikari member? They have to know that'd be dangerous, right?" He rubbed his thumb along Jessie's knuckles needing to comfort both himself and her.

"Going after Sloane was a huge risk. They must've needed her to take the chance." She squeezed Erik's hand.

Chapter 11

The tires squealed as Erik turned into the driveway and hit the button to open the garage. He stopped and closed the door behind them. They didn't need any of Caroline's neighbor's witnessing them pulling a body out of the trunk.

Jessie moved around to the back, ready to freeze as soon as Erik opened the trunk. Erik lifted the lid, and the boy lay, passed out. Erik bent and lifted the guy into his arms. Jessie hurried to open the door to the house.

"Where are we taking him?" Jessie asked.

"Basement, I'm not sure if Caroline has any place in the house to interrogate him. I want to take him to the lowest level, so it's harder for him to escape if he manages to get free."

"Okay, I'll go find Caroline. Smooth everything over with her. You want to secure him down there?"

"Yeah, I got 'em." Erik turned toward the stairs leading to the basement. Jessie went to Caroline's study.

Jessie knocked on the door before slowly swinging it open. Caroline was sitting behind the desk, leaning intently forward looking at her monitor. "Hey, Caroline."

Caroline glanced to the door where Jessie stood. "Hello, my dear, how can I help you?"

"We have a big problem. The demons at the school kidnapped Sloane. We grabbed one of the students we think was involved. Erik is securing him in the basement so that we can question him. Do you have anything we can use to help with his interrogation?" her voice lowered at the end, hoping Caroline would be okay with the interrogation.

"Oh dear, yes, of course, I do. I'll assist Erik in the interrogation. Have you called her father?" Caroline looked concerned as she crossed the room to meet Jessie.

"Ah no, we were a little busy going after her, and the demons who were involved. We grabbed this one, but the other kid got away. We need to work quickly. We don't think they can find us here, but we need to move before anything happens to Sloane." Jessie clenched her hands into fists thinking about Sloane. They needed to get to her. The front door slammed, Jessie turned and hurried to the front room, Caroline on her tail.

Mike stood, eyes wild, head whipping around in search. "Jess, did you find her? Is Sloane safe?" His words were half crazed in his panic.

Jessie looked to the ground. She wasn't sure how she was going to tell him. "Um... We didn't find her, but we grabbed one of the demons who was involved in taking her. At least we think he was involved. He's in the basement with Erik." Her voice was low as she spoke.

Caroline took a step toward Mike. "Come, I'll take you down to him. You can help us interrogate him."

"No, I'm going to the school. I'm a tracker. I'll find her. They're taking specific people for their powers. It's why only certain students were targeted. They're going after us for our abilities. Students were the test to see if they could possess Shikari members. They're going to try to possess Sloane. I need to stop them before that happens. They'll gain everything she knows if they possess her." He looked pointedly at Jessie, then Caroline. "We can't let the demons obtain her knowledge. We have to save her, now." Mike turned and flung open the door.

"Wait, someone should go with you." Jessie looked back toward Caroline. "Will you let Erik know where we're going, and what's happening. Have him call as soon as he knows anything." She turned back toward Mike. "Let's go."

Jessie jumped in Mike's car. He left it idol in the driveway. "If you were planning on going to the school right away, why did you come to the house?" Jessie asked.

'I was hoping you found her before I got here." He gunned it down the street, tires screeching as he accelerated.

"What did you find out in Denver?"

"They are taking kids with certain powers. They also weren't sure if they could possess adults at first. After Mr. Hall, they knew they could possess any Shikari member. Something big is happening in the order, too. All hell is breaking loose." He whipped around a corner, Jessie slammed against the door.

"Jeez Mike, I'd like not to have bruises when we're done today." She reached her hand over to rub her arm. She grabbed the handle to brace herself for any more corners. Mike decided to drive like a crazy person. She glanced over at him, and every muscle in his body was tense. "We're going to find her," she said with conviction.

Mike glanced over and nodded. "I know. I'll kill anyone in our path. Nothing is going to happen to Sloane."

"Okay, can we not kill any children needlessly? You know we can dispossess them without killing them. Let's try that first."

"I'm not making any promises. They've got Sloane. They'll pay for even thinking they could take her." Mike's voice was hard. He gripped the steering wheel until his knuckles turned white. He pulled up to the side of the school. "Where were you guys? I need to know where she may have been taken."

Jessie pointed up the road. "We were parked here, and Sloane walked up over the hill. She wasn't gone long, five minutes, tops. So, she couldn't have walked far."

Mike drove further down the road and parked on the side. He scrambled out of the car, each step with renowned purpose, as he stormed down the road.

"How does your tracking work exactly?" Jessie asked trying to keep up.

"I get a certain feeling when I get a read on what I'm looking for. Then, it's like my mind hones in on my subject, and I feel a pull toward it. When I focus, I can feel all the Shikari in the area. It's like looking at the stars, but I can just feel where they are when I want to. I'm still not entirely sure how it works, but I follow my instincts." He stopped, instantly. "Got her." He closed his eyes to focus.

Jessie took a step toward Mike. "Where is she?"

"Give me a minute," he said, eyes closed in complete concentration. Jessie paced in front of him, the gravel crunching under her feet. When she turned, and the gravel ground louder under her foot, Mike glared at her. "Can you stop? I need to concentrate."

Jessie stood frozen. "Sorry," she whispered.

Mike stood motionless, eyes closed. After a few minutes, his eyes snapped open. "They're moving her now. She's not at the school anymore. She's on the highway toward Denver. We have to go. We need to stop them before they get to Denver." He took off at a dead run toward the car.

Jessie's eyes widened, and in a moment, she was running behind him. She jumped in the car after Mike. He jammed the car into gear easily and whipped around in reverse. "So, why do we need to stop them before they get to Denver?"

"They'll be fewer demons in the car. If they get her to wherever they're stationed in Denver, we'll have to fight more of them. I'd rather not fight a bunch of demons at once, but I will if I have to. If it means saving Sloane, I'll do anything." The last words were said in a whisper. Jessie heard the shakiness and fear he was trying to hide. Jessie watched as the car sped in a blur onto the highway.

"Can you tell how far down the road they are?" she asked.

"Yeah, they've got about fifteen miles on us." Mike gripped the wheel tighter.

"Oh, so how are we going to beat them if they're that far ahead?" Jessie turned her curious gaze on Mike.

"Drive fast," he responded.

"You're kidding, right?" She peeked down at the speedometer and gulped. They were going almost ninety miles an hour, in Colorado, near mountains. Jessie reached her hand to pull the seat belt over her body and secured it. She said a little prayer in her head before focusing back on Mike.

"Nope." Mike's singular focus was the road in front of them.

Jessie gripped the door as Mike raced down the highway, weaving between cars. Sometimes he got so close; she was sure they were going to crash. A few cars honked as he cut them off. He didn't even seem to notice.

Jessie shrugged. "I'm going to call Erik. Let him know what's going on." She pulled out her phone and hit send when she found Erik's number. "Hey, babe. We're headed to Denver. Mike said they have her in a car. We're trying to stop them before they get to Denver. We're about fifteen miles behind them. What's going on with the kid?" She drummed her fingers on her thigh as she spoke.

"He's still out. Caroline's been getting supplies. We're about to wake him up. Do you think you'll make it to Sloane before they get to Denver?" Erik asked.

"Yeah, Mike's pretty damn determined." She peeked over at Mike "I think we'll be taking on all of Denver if we have to. I don't think we'll have to, but I don't put it past him right now. Don't worry; she'll be fine. We'll get her." Jess reassured.

"Damn straight," Mike commented, and Jessie looked over to his rigid form.

"Good, then I'm trusting you to find her, and I'm going to find out what this guy knows."

"Okay, babe. See you later."

"Later," Jess hit the end button.

"Have you talked with him about your mother, yet?" Mike asked in a low voice; eyes still focused on the road in front of him.

"No," Jess whispered.

"Don't you think you should tell him?" Mike asked, glancing over, his mouth pressed into a hard line. She drummed her hands in her lap again and stared out the window.

"No, I'm not ready to tell him, yet. I don't even know enough to tell him. Besides, I told you in confidence, so I hope you will keep it to yourself. We both know how my mom can be. She's probably out gallivanting with another new fling. It's probably nothing." Jessie's words blurred together as she spoke. She was anxious. She hadn't heard from her mother, but she also knew how flaky her mother could be. It was her flakiness that had her concerned.

"And what if it's, nothing?" Mike asked.

"Then, I will tell Erik, and deal with it. Right now, we need to focus on finding Sloane." Jess huffed out a breath. She didn't want to think about her mother. She'd been nothing but trouble. She'd been dropping her off with Sloane and Erik since she'd been young. Every time she met "the one" she disappeared and often left her behind. The few times she chose not to leave her, they'd go on, what her mother called, grand adventures. Which often left them begging for gas or food, in some Podunk town that had nothing in it but hicks and closed- minded housewives. Their trips never lasted long, and eventually, her mom would call someone to wire them money to get back to Wisconsin.

She always liked when she would get to stay with Erik and Sloane. She loved her mom, but her ups and downs were a little much. Especially, when she was younger and didn't understand why, after two or three days on the road, her mother would suddenly snap at her. She'd tell her she was having a bad day. She'd get a hotel room, where you drove up to park in front of your room, and she'd sleep for a day, sometimes two. Jessie would sleep, but when she'd tried to wake her mom up to tell her she was hungry, she'd yell at her. After a few belligerent moments, she'd fall back asleep leaving Jessie hungry and fending for herself. She learned to make friends with people fast. Being the cute blonde girl with spiral curls always helped. People always thought she looked like Shirley Temple. Learning street smarts came early, too. Knowing who to ask for help was important. She didn't want to end up in the hands of the state, either.

When she was a teenager, she stopped going with her mom. She learned they could get money through the order, so she didn't need her mom anymore. It was a relief not to have to live from motel room to motel room for weeks on end. She never understood why her mother got the whim to leave when she could stay in Wisconsin in a house provided by the order. Jessie liked staying in one place. Her mother got a little stir-crazy if she had to stay anywhere long. Jessie liked the idea of settling down, of staying in one place. She knew as a Shikari; she couldn't do that anytime soon. Especially with a power like hers. But someday, she hoped she could live a normal life. Raise kids to be the next

Shikari fighters. She pictured Erik then; he'd be a great father. She sighed.

"Thinking pretty hard over there. Are you okay, love?" Mike's voice was light. He knew her history, and the many secrets she hadn't shared with anyone else.

"Yeah, I'm fine. Just thinking about what life would be like if we could settle down. Maybe even live normal lives even if it's only for a little while." She sighed.

"Oh," Mike said surprised. "I guess I never thought about settling down, but I technically already have. I have my bar, which is the one place I can always go. It's my home. What made you think about all that, love?" She felt his eyes on her.

"I don't know. Just thinking about my mom, and all the traveling we did when I was younger. Then, all the traveling I've done since I started fighting for the Shikari. I have a great offensive and defensive power, so I thought I might never get to settle down." She looked down to her intertwined fingers in her lap.

"Oh, love. I'm sure you'll get to settle down at some point. They can't keep you running forever. Even the Shikari have limits. I'm sure you'll get the normal life you desire."

"I hope you're right. Especially since, right now, we don't know what the hell is going on, and demons seem to have the upper hand." Jessie rested her chin on her hand. She leaned against the door of the car and stared out the window, dreaming of another life.

Chapter 12

Erik looked up after strapping the boy to the chair with zip ties. Caroline strode into the room. She stopped in front of the boy and put her hand on her hip. "Why haven't you woken him up yet?"

"I was waiting on you. Do you have everything?" he walked over to the items she set on the table.

"Yes, I doubt we'll need anything other than a few words, and a good old-fashioned knife. This kid isn't going to take much." She knelt in front of the kid. She snapped a capsule under his nose. The boy's head flew up in an instant. Caroline smiled wide.

"Ah, there he is. I know you want to tell us where they took our friend." The corner of her mouth crooked up as he tried to pull his arms up, then looked down to the restraints.

The boy shook his head, "Friend? What are you talking about?" His eyes dilated realizing where he was.

"Oh? You don't know what I'm talking about. I believe I need to speak to the demon. I challenge the demon to address me." She spoke with such conviction.

Erik walked over to Caroline, "What are you doing?"

"Shush, I know what I'm doing." She waved his hand for him to go away.

Erik narrowed his eyes but nodded. He didn't like stepping back, but she was the leader here and outranked him. Suddenly, a thought entered his mind. *You're too emotional. This is your sister. Trust me.* He looked shocked. Another thought came abruptly. *You block people's thoughts. I don't, and I can send you thoughts.*

Ah... okay, he thought, and she nodded in his direction. She turned her focus to the boy.

"What's your name?" Caroline asked.

"I am the demon, Orzal." The demon cackled. "Did you mean the pesky human, or wait, Shikari? His name is unimportant to me. Are you angry that I wear one of your own?" His eyes stalked Caroline.

"No, because you won't be there for long. So, are you going to tell me what I want to know?" She stared down the demon.

"Ha, that's what you think. I will come back. I have marked this Shikari vessel. I will be able to find him again." His lips curved into a wicked smile.

"I'm going to ask this one last time." She took a knife from the table and ran her finger down the curve of the blade. "Where did they take my friend?"

"Denver, bitch. That's all you're going to get out of me. I hope she's possessed before you get to her. We have plans for all of you worthless humans." He spat through clenched teeth.

Erik reacted instantly. He bolted toward the demon hand outstretched. He wrapped his fingers around the demon's neck and pushed the demon, and the chair against the wall with a loud crack.

"Erik! Stop!" Caroline yelled as a large crack spread up one of the chairs legs leaving the demon hanging from Erik's hand.

"No, I'm done. I want to know where the hell my sister is, now." He looked vehemently at the demon. He tightened his fingers around his neck.

"Fuck you." The demon spat.

Erik squeezed tighter. "I will snap your neck with my hands. I don't care about the boy you are in. We are Shikari, and we are born ready to die for our creed. Can you say the same demon?" Erik's eyes narrowed, and his fingers tightened.

"Put him down Erik," Caroline demanded.

"Not until he tells us what we want to know." Erik held the eyes of the demon.

"Well, let's see what this boy can take, shall we?" Caroline held a small taser in her hand. "I don't think it will take that many volts to make this one talk." She eyed the demon levelly, and Erik dropped the chair back against the wall.

"Bitch do whatever you want I'm not telling you anything," he spat.

She tested the taser in her hands, and her eyes widened at the blue sparks that shot from the end. She held the taser to the demon's neck "What do you think will happen if I touch this button here?" She stroked her finger over the button so the demon could see. The demon's eyes widened momentarily, then narrowed on her.

"Do it, Bitch."

She shrugged, "If you insist." She pressed the taser against the skin of his neck and hit the button. The demon convulsed momentarily and slumped in the chair. "So, are you ready to talk now?".

"Fuck you, Bitch." The demon spat as he straightened his back in the chair.

"Okay, I guess we'll try that again. Maybe I will have to up the juice." She adjusted the taser and touched the demon's skin again, holding a few moments longer than before. The demon screeched as he convulsed. When the shock stopped, he slumped forward, drool dripping from the side of his mouth.

"You ready to talk, yet?" Caroline asked. She peered over to Erik.

"They're taking her to the warehouse district in Denver. Forest Street, 3890 Forest street. Go ahead, Bitch, go get her." he cackled.

She looked to Erik, call them, let them know where she is. I'll take care of the demon. Erik nodded and rushed out of the room.

"Ha, bitch, it's a trap. We'll get even more of you worthless hunters. You think you can stop us, but you'll never stop us." He threw his head back in a villainous laugh.

Caroline stopped, holding the taser in front of the demon. She hit the button, sending sparks from the tip. "What do you mean, it's a trap?" she asked.

"It's a trap, bitch. We are leading you there, all of you. It's why we took the girl. She was a means to get all their powers. Mr. Hall watched the others outside while you were on your tour. He knew the powers they possessed, and he wanted them for himself. Now, he will have them. Master will be proud of me for delivering even more powers to him. I'll be rewarded." He laughed again, eyes alight.

She touched the taser to his neck and hit the button holding it there until she saw liquid pooling on the floor at his feet. He slumped forward again. Eyes closed. Caroline looked at the boy who passed out after the shock and huffed. She ran out into the hallway. "Erik, Erik! It's a trap. They need to know it's a trap." She looked both ways down the hall, but he wasn't there. She sent out a message telepathically. *Erik, It's a trap. You have to tell them it's a trap. They want all of them.* She raced up the stairs to find him.

She stopped in front of Erik who made it to the door. "Hey, what's going on?" his eyes widened at Caroline. She was panting from racing around to find him. She bent with one hand on her thigh to catch her breath.

"It's a trap. You need to call and tell them it's a trap." She raised to stare into his eyes.

"What? A trap? I just got off the phone with Jessie. They are on their way to the warehouse."

"Call them; they can't go in by themselves. They need help. The demon said it's a trap. They saw you guys at the school. They want to possess all of you for your powers. You need to stop them. They can't get either Mike or Jessie. They'll be able to track and freeze us in a battle. They can't get Jessie or Mike. We'll be screwed. Erik, stop them." She looked into his eyes.

"Okay, okay I get it. I'll call." He picked up his cell and dialed Jessie. It went straight to voicemail. "Shit, it's going to voicemail. Her phone must be dead. I'll try Mike." He dialed Mike's number. It rings twice and goes to voicemail. "What the hell. It shouldn't go to voicemail that fast. I'm going to call Bryant. Send in reinforcements. If anything, they can still get Sloane, but not walk into the trap alone." He dialed Bryant.

"Good plan. I'll call a few friends and send them their way. Maybe we can warn them before they go in." Caroline went to her office to get her phone.

Erik turned toward the door. He wanted to be moving, but he needed to warn them. If it's a trap, they're in danger. Bryant picked up. "Hey, Sloane got kidnapped, and Mike and Jessie are about to walk into a trap. You need to stop them."

"What? Sloane was taken? How could you let that happen, son?" Erik could hear the disappointment in his voice.

"Yeah, I can't give you all the details, right now. Jessie and Mike are following the demons who took her. They are about to go to a warehouse at Park Hill, Northeast. You need to stop them before they go in. The demons are trying to get their powers. We absolutely can't let them get Mike or Jessie's powers. We'd have a hell of a time stopping them." Erik explained.

"We need to get your sister away from them as well. If they can see the future, they'll know when we're coming. I'll immobilize everyone here. Will you be coming to Denver, son?"

"Yes, Caroline and I will be on our way. I'm going to keep trying to warn Jessie, but you need to get there. Stop them, Bryant. The address is 3890 Forest street. Bryant, you need to stop them, please." Erik's voice was panicked. He couldn't believe he let this happen.

"It will be done. I will stop them." Bryant hung up the phone.

Erik rushed to find Caroline. He flipped through his contacts to find Jessie again. He hit send on the phone as soon as he got to her name. "Oh God, Jess, please pick up." He strode through the door of Caroline's office. The phone kept going to voicemail. "Shit, Jess, what the hell?" He huffed a frustrated breath.

Caroline looked up from her call. "I got a hold of my friends. They're on their way to the warehouse. Hopefully, they will stop them before they get inside."

"I don't know why her phone's going to voicemail." Erik paced the floor staring at his phone.

"Come on, let's go. I have people who will try to beat them, but we need to go, in case they need our help." Caroline grabbed her purse and stopped next to Erik. "Ready?"

"Yeah, we need to save them." Erik shook slightly as he followed Caroline out the door.

Caroline started the car and threw it in drive. She flew down the side streets and got on the highway.

"Um, Caroline, what about the kid we left at your house?" Erik looked over.

"I'm having someone take care of him. We have more important things to do."

"Okay." Erik picked up his phone and dialed Mike again. "One of them has to pick up, eventually." He tapped his thumb against his pants as he listened to the phone ring. He brushed his hair back with his hand. "Shit, voicemail. I hope the others get to them in time."

Chapter 13

S loane blinked her eyes open once, then shut again. Her arms ached, her head was pounding. She tried to reach her hands up to her head but pulled on the zip ties that bound her wrists. Shit, where the hell am I? She thought. Sloane blinked her eyes open again. Looking around, her eyes met a silver crossbar. She kicked her feet out and connected with the wall. The sound of a humming motor filled her ears, and she was jostled when the car hit a bump. *Shit, I'm in a trunk. How in the hell did I get in the trunk? I was on the phone with Mike; then everything went black.*

Sloane rolled onto her back to see what she could grab as a weapon. She yanked and wiggled her wrists, but the zip ties bit into her skin. She could feel the hot blood drip down her hands. She bent her knees, trying to pull her arms around to the front. The zip ties cut further into her flesh, but she managed to get her hands to the front. Her shoulders burned, and she bit her lip to stop a moan from escaping. She didn't want them to know she was awake. She kicked out the back taillight with her boot. She scooted until she could peek out at her surroundings. All she could see was the passing trees on the highway. There was a burgundy Buick behind her. Maybe they saw her kick out the tail light. She moved to kick out the second. She was grateful that she was in an older car. This wasn't always possible in newer models. If she were in a newer model, she could pull the trunk release cord and jump out. This old boat didn't have one. It was quite a spacious trunk though.

As she watched, they took an exit, and after a few blocks pulled into a parking lot. Sloane figured they were in Denver but didn't recognize anything around her. She reached down into her boot. She breathed a sigh of relief when she found her blade still there. These dumbasses didn't even search me for weapons. She chuckled. She gripped the knife in both hands, listening for the crunch of their footsteps. She glanced out of the hole. She could hear two men talking.

"Mr. Hall said to take her in the back. He'll be here soon," the husky voice said.

"Good, we have the other one here, too. Are we ready when the others come to find them? We want the one with the power to freeze time. She'll be an asset to our team." A deep, smooth voice spoke with authority.

"We have thirteen, here. Two guys are loading up the materials for the others. We've printed the spells and information we've gathered from the others. We also have many of the athames and amulets to help ward against the hunters' power. We are ready to start distribution. Is there anything else we'll need?" The husky voice asked.

"We may need a few of those crystals posted around the building. We don't want the blonde one to be able to freeze us once she gets here. We need to get them both possessed for our plan to move forward. Have you contacted the others in Kansas City? Are they ready for us?" the deep voice asked.

"I am doing that next. Anything else, sir?"

"No, go get the room ready. This one may put up a fight. I'll get her in there." He turned and walked toward the trunk. Sloane could see his indigo jeans through the hole. She gripped the knife ready. She needed to get out of here. They were going after the leaders in Kansas City. She needed to warn them. She needed to warn Jessie. She couldn't let them get her. They'd all be fucked if they got her. She wasn't sure how they were managing to possess Shikari, but they had figured out a way.

She heard the key in the lock and held her breath. She was ready to fight with everything she had. The trunk lid lifted, and she kicked out at the man standing in front of her. She landed her kick in his stomach, and he doubled over. She jumped up and swiped her knife in the air, slicing his bicep. She dropped down from the trunk and kicked out again. This time her kick landed against the man's jaw. He flew backward, hitting the pavement with a crunch. She took a moment to try to flip the knife to slice off the zip ties. Suddenly she felt a sharp pain on the back of her head, and everything went black.

The pounding in her ears was getting louder. A constant, sharp pain filled her head. She swallowed hard before opening her eyes. Pain shot into her eyeballs when the light hit them, and she closed her eyes again. The metallic taste in her mouth let her know she probably had a concussion. She realized the pounding she could hear in her ears as her heart beat. She tried to swallow again, but her mouth felt like sandpaper and metal. She took a deep, steadying breath before braving the fluorescents again. She had to see where she was. She remembered attacking the guy with a husky voice in dark indigo jeans. He was handsome, and in another life, Sloane would have hit on him, instead of hitting him. She squinted through the pain. The walls were tinged yellow. She could smell the tobacco in the air. Across the room was a card table with ashtrays and Mountain Dew cans. She could see a sink to the right of her. This must've been a break room. The whir of a refrigerator came from behind her.

The large steel door was closed. The scent of old tobacco permeated the air, so she knew someone had been here smoking recently. Thinking back on what had happened before she got knocked out again, she remembered there were fifteen of them, including the two guys talking. A knot formed in her stomach. They were trying to get Jessie. This was a trap. She needed to get out of here and warn them. Jessie couldn't come here. They were expecting it. She yanked on her restraints, and a biting pain shot up her arm. She felt fresh blood dripping down her fingers. She didn't care; she needed to get free. She moved her hands against the metal chair. She tried to move her hands up and down against the edge. It was no use, it was rounded and would never cut through. She yanked her hands apart as hard as she could, but nothing happened. She could feel more blood dripping down her hands.

She tried to kick out her legs, but they were against the metal legs of the chair. She looked over to the ashtrays. Maybe she could hop over to try to burn the zip ties enough to get free. She took a few hops, and the chair moved slightly over. She did it a few more times. She pushed herself despite the pain coming from her wrists. She needed to get the hell out of here. She knew if she stayed, they were going to possess her or torture her for information. She'd rather die than tell these fucking demons anything. She got in a few more hops before she could hear voices outside. The husky voice was back.

"Give me five minutes with the bitch. I owe her a good ass kicking," he said.

"Tom, you know I can't let you do that. I will be handling her from now on. Please make sure they are getting everything loaded. I will talk to the woman. Remember, we need to be ready when the others come for her. We want the tracker to come here, but we also don't want her to be here. I want that girl who can freeze time. She is vital to our plans in Kansas City. Now go, I want my time with her."

"Good fucking luck," he said. She could hear his loud footfalls down the hall.

"Imbecile," she heard the other man say. He had a smooth drawl almost like he came from the south. Sloane made a mental note of that.

The door opened, and a tall dark-haired man stood before her. He had days' worth of stubble on his chin. He wore a long black peacoat with the bill flipped up behind his neck. His dark gray suit beneath with a midnight blue tie felt out of place in this room. She studied him, looking for weakness. The stubble let her know he was stressed. Anyone who wore that designer suit, wouldn't have gone a day without shaving. She could tell he'd gone a few. She noted that for later. She hoped that meant things were not going as he'd planned. She planned to make a few more things not go according to plan.

"Hello, Sloane," he said, her name rolling off his tongue in a caress. She didn't like it.

"Hello, asshole," she spat back.

"Is that any way to talk to a superior? You may call me Mr. Hall. I believe we will be good friends very soon, my dear." He smiled, and she could see all the way back to his molars. It made her want to puke.

"I'm not your fucking, dear. We're not going to be friends. I'm going to kill you as soon as I'm free." She glared at him, fire in her eyes.

"Oh?" He pulled a chair over from the table and straightened his coat before he sat in the chair. He looked her dead in the eyes. "I believe I have the upper hand here, my dear, Sloane." He said the words as a caress again, and it bothered Sloane. She felt a shiver as he spoke. She wondered what the headmaster's power had been. He was having an effect on her, but she wasn't sure what it was. It reminded her of what Bryant could do. She was fighting it like she did with her father, but it was still affecting her. She didn't like it.

"So, it does seem you do have the upper hand, for now. I can't imagine you want to defeat me in such a weak manner. I'd think you'd want to fight me on an equal footing, like a real man." She smiled one of her dazzling smiles at him.

"Oh dear," he lifted his hand and ran the tip of his finger along her cheek. "I don't care how I defeat you, as long as I do. Before the night is over, I will break you. I will do whatever is necessary to break you, Sloane. I promise." He stopped a finger below her chin and raised her head so that her eyes met his. "You are such a beautiful woman. I'd hate to waste this opportunity with you." His sardonic smile made her stomach turn. Sloane spat in his face.

He moved back and took the handkerchief out of his pocket to wipe his face. "Now, was that necessary? I was admiring your beauty. Don't worry; I'll take my time with you, as soon as you're possessed. I know you'll feel every moment of it, just as the man inside me feel everything. I can feel him squirm inside me. You'll be squirming, soon." His mouth turned up into a sly smile.

"The fuck you will. I'll die before I let you possess me. Keep dreaming, asshole," she spat. She knew she shouldn't show him a weakness, but she wasn't kidding.

"Oh? How do you propose to stop me from doing whatever I want to you? Currently, I have you tied to a chair. I'd love to hear how you'd manage to stop me in your current state." He moved to gaze into her eyes. She felt a chill run down her spine again, but this time it was one meant to make her feel fear. She shook her shoulders in response, and Mr. Hall's smile widened.

Sloane began rubbing her wrists against the restraints causing her wrists to bleed. She smiled wickedly, "I have my ways." She knew that if she could continue cutting her wrists, she'd bleed enough to die if he didn't notice.

"You may think you do, but I'll bandage your wrists before you can cause enough blood loss. You are wasting your energy, dear. You could accept the demon, and I'll let you free." There was a fire in his eyes as he stared at her. It was a combination of power and desire. He was getting off on having her bound and helpless. She knew she needed to show no fear.

"Fuck you," she glared back at him, fire in her eyes.

He sat back, an amusing smile on his face. "Maybe, I'll let you sit in here and think awhile before I bring in your demon. Don't worry, I chose a very special demon for you, dear. She's a little spitfire, and I think she's perfect for you." He stood and placed the chair back at the table. "Although, the anticipation to have my way with you may win out. I can't resist seeing you squirm. We'll have to see. I do believe you'll be a good time." His eyes raked over her body, and Sloane's stomach turned again. "Yes, a very, very good time." He licked his lips and strode out of the room.

Sloane began frantically rubbing and pulling at her wrists. She needed to get the hell out of here. There was no way in hell she was being possessed or used by that fucker. She knew she would still be in her mind, but she'd have no control over her body. What that bastard was considering. She shook her head; she couldn't think about that, now. She had to get the hell out of here. She kept pulling, ignoring the pain. She'd be in a lot more pain if she were possessed. The kind of pain, you didn't recover from easily. She felt bile rise in her throat. She needed to get free. She hoped that the others knew where she was. She hated to admit it, but she hoped that Mike was on his way with reinforcements. She wasn't the type of girl to want to be rescued, but right now, she would give anything to see his beautiful face come through that door. She could feel blood dripping down her hands. She knew it wouldn't be long before she passed out. She was already feeling light headed. She closed her eyes and tried to call forth a vision. Maybe she would see what was going to happen next. Anything would be a comfort as long as she wasn't possessed.

Chapter 14

"Do you think we'll make it before they possess her?" Jessie asked, shifting nervously in her seat.

"I can't even think about that, right now. I need to get to her. We need to stop them. I can't imagine her letting them do much to her. She'll fight to the death before she'd let them possess her. That's why we need to get to her. She won't think about her own life. Only stopping them." Mike gripped the wheel tighter and pushed the gas pedal down further. He was determined to get to Sloane before she had to fight them. Because she would, and it wouldn't be pretty.

"Oh yeah, you're right. I didn't even think about that. She'd fight them with everything she had. Shit, yeah we need to get there, now." Jessie glanced to her phone. The screen was black. She hit the button to illuminate the screen, and nothing happened. "Shit, my phone is dead. I was going to check with Erik to see what they learned." She looked around the car for a charger.

Mike fished his phone out of the center counsel. He held it out to Jess. "Here, use mine."

"Thanks." She pushed the button. "Ah, you have five missed calls."

"Oh yeah, who called?" He looked over at the phone.

"Erik and Caroline. A few times. I should call them back. It seems like it might be important."

"They probably got info from the demon you grabbed." Mike focused back on the road.

"Yeah," Jessie hit the send button on the phone. The screen went black. "What the hell?" Jess hit the power button on the phone. "Mike your phone died, too. Do you have a charger in here?"

"Shit, I grabbed a different car from Magnus. I don't think there's one in here."

"Seriously, so we have no way of getting in touch with the others. What the hell are we going to do?" She set the phone in the counsel.

"We're going to go get Sloane. We can find out what they learned after we have her with us."

"Okay," she tucked her hair behind her ear and sat up. She was nervous. She had a bad feeling in the pit of her stomach, but she wasn't sure why. She laid her hand against her stomach. Something wasn't right. She wanted to be able to talk to Erik. She wanted to know what they found out from the demon. She hadn't even thought about how she was using her phone when they were at the school in the car. Now, she could kick herself for not thinking ahead. She didn't even grab any weapons before she left. She felt largely under prepared for the challenge they were charging toward. "Are you sure we should be rushing in like this?" She looked over at Mike.

"What? Yes, we need to get Sloane away from the demons. Why?"

"I don't know. I just have a bad feeling that's all." She gripped her hands together in her lap.

"It'll be fine. We'll get Sloane, and everything will be fine." Mike said it like he needed to convince himself as much as her.

"Are you sure? You sound like you need convincing as much as I do." She studied Mike.

"Yes, I know we have to get Sloane. She can see the future. If they can access her power, we'll all be fucked. They will use her to tell them when we're coming, and how many will be there. Not only that, but she can see every detail of any future battles. If they can see the future, we'll never be able to fight them without them knowing. We have to get to her. We have to." Mike gripped the wheel; his voice shook as he spoke.

"We will." She placed her hand on her stomach, worried. She knew something wasn't right. She wanted to talk to Erik but had no way to. She took a deep breath. "How far behind them are we?" she asked.

"Not far, but there's no way we're stopping them before Denver. They're too fast. They have a destination. We won't be able to stop them before they get there. We'll have to confront them wherever they're going. Are you ready for that?" Mike asked.

"I'll have to be. We don't have much of choice, do we? They can't possess Sloane, which is what they intend to do. We have to get her back before they have a chance. You know they'll try right away. I wish I had a power boost, but between the two of us, we'll have to make it work.

"Good, cause we're getting close to wherever they took her. The pull to her is getting stronger. We're going in blind, so we have no idea how many will be there. You freeze and we'll both fight. We don't have time to dispossess them. I'm hoping there are only a few taking her hostage. If we make it there while they're still transporting her to the building, we'll have a better shot at getting to her before we have to fight. But again, we have no idea what we're walking in to."

"That's what has me nervous. We can't even call for back-up. We have no way to communicate with anyone where we are. What if we get into trouble? Mike, they can't get all three of us. What do you know about their plan? Aren't they trying to get Shikari members with powers they can use? Could you imagine the advantage they'd have with all of us? Mike, I think we need to think this through before we charge in blind. At least with Erik or another mind-reader, we'd know what we were walking into." She bit her lip and peeked over at Mike. She hoped he would listen to her. What if this whole thing was a trap?

"I can still sense them. I'll be able to identify how many are in there. If it's too much for us, we'll get help. I want to know where she is and try to get to her before they possess her. We need to at least try, Jess, for Sloane. You know she'd charge in there for us, no matter how many demons she had to fight." Mike glanced over to Jess. She could see the fear in his gaze.

"I know, but I think that's because she has some crazy death wish. She's been careless with her own life since she lost her mother. We need to be smarter than that if we want to get out with her. Otherwise, the demons win, we lose. We can't let that happen, either."

"Okay, okay, we'll make the decision when we get there. If we get in over our heads in there, you run and get help. I will stay with Sloane until you bring reinforcements." Mike nodded his head.

"If you think I'm leaving you with the demons, you're crazier than Sloane is. I'm not going to leave you behind."

"Well, if you won't leave me, why would you leave, Sloane?" He questioned.

"They already have her. We need you to get her back. Come on Mike be rational. If there's too many, we get help, agreed?" She studied his face. The muscle in his jaw twitched, and he gripped the wheel until his knuckles turned white.

"Fine, if there's too many, we'll get help. But I don't like abandoning her to them. We need to get her out of there as soon as possible. She's reckless with her life, and she'll get herself killed to stop from being possessed."

"Well, let's just hope this works out for us, then."

Mike exited the highway and turned down a side street. "We're getting close. I can feel her."

"Okay, what do you have in here for weapons? I didn't grab anything before I left the house."

"Look through the duffle in the backseat. I don't have much, but it's better than nothing. They must be in one of these factories." He drove by a brick warehouse. He slowed and took a left at the next street. She's in the brick warehouse back there. He took another left at the end of the street followed by another to bring them back to the factory. He slowed a few buildings down and parked on the side of the street. "She's in the one right up there." He pointed to the brick building with a few windows that were covered.

Jessie glance around. There were four other cars on the street, but there was a small parking lot on the other side of the building. "Is there a good way to get into the building without being noticed? The windows on this side are covered, but we can probably get around that. We need to get eyes on how many are in there. Should we scope out around the building to find the best way in?" She tucked a gun in the back of her waist band and continued to lean forward in the seat observing the building.

"Yeah, we can go around the back of the building to try to get a view of the inside. We'll start on this side and move to the back-parking lot. If we can get inside without being noticed, we do it. Once inside, we find Sloane. Hopefully, you can freeze any demons we spot." Jessie observed Mike as he spoke. Jessie could see the worry lines around his eyes. She could tell he hadn't gotten much sleep over the last few weeks. He had dark circles under her eyes, and they were bloodshot. She figured she probably didn't look much better. They both could use a good night's sleep.

"Sounds like a plan. What if they have the building warded against my power as they did in Minneapolis?" She took a deep breath.

"If they don't freeze, we fight. If we get in over our heads, we fight our way out and run. Our priority is to get Sloane without being noticed. If we don't have our powers, we leave and get back-up. I'll know right away because I won't feel the pull toward Sloane I'm feeling now. If you give me a minute, I'll gauge how many are in there before we go in. I should be able to get a pretty accurate number for us." He closed his eyes and lowered his head concentrating his power on the building. "Shit, there's around fifteen of them in the building, and two in the parking lot. Sloane is in the back room, which we may be able to enter closer to the back to get her. I can't tell if it's warded from out here. There's another Shikari in the back next to Sloane. They haven't been possessed, yet. We may be able to get them both out." His eyes met Jessie's, and she nodded.

"Okay, let's go around back and see if we can get to them, trouble free." She raised a brow.

"Love, you know that's not going to happen. We've never been that lucky," he accentuated the last word.

"Maybe you haven't." She cracked a playful smile and wiggled her brows. She was still worried, but she also loved the rush a battle brought her. She was scared for Sloane, but at the same time, she was relieved she hadn't been possessed. If the other Shikari hadn't, maybe they were waiting for someone. They still had time to get to her.

"Ready?" Mike studied Jessie.

"As I'll ever be," she responded.

"Alright then, let's do this thing." His smile was playful. She knew he was trying to lighten the mood for what they were about to do.

"Mike, I love you." She smiled as she eased out of the car.

"Ah love, now you tell me. We could have been together years ago. I guess I have something to live for." He bit his bottom lip and quirked up the side of his mouth trying to hold in his laugh.

She stepped beside him and elbowed him in the side. "You are so, not funny. Come on we need to focus and get the real love of your life out of here before she does something monumentally stupid like take on all the demons in there at once. You know she'd try to lose." She shook her head as they made their way to the back of the building.

"I know no such thing. I mean, she could win. She's certainly got the fire within her to put up one hell of a fight. I know that fire all too well." He winked. Jessie moved her finger to her lips to quiet him, so they could try to see into one of the windows. She stopped next to a window that didn't look like it had been covered entirely. She peeked through the tear in the plastic and could see three guys sitting around a card table. There were cards in front of them. Jessie suppressed her urge to laugh. Demons were in there playing cards. She could see through the doorway into the hall. She saw one dark-haired man walk to the back of the building. She took a deep breath. There wasn't much to see here.

She turned to look at Mike. "There's not much to see, here. Three guys are in there playing cards, and one dark-haired guy just walked toward the back." She shrugged.

"Okay, let's head further back. See if anyone is guarding, Sloane." He walked in front of her, ducking under the next window and stopping on the other side. Jessie stopped to see what she could. Being a head shorter than Mike, she had to stand on tiptoe to see through the small hole in the bottom of the window. She observed two men standing near a cork board with pictures and lines drawn between the pictures. There were maps of different buildings; one looked like the school they'd been scouting. She glanced to Mike, who was looking through on the other side of her.

"After we get Sloane, we need to torch this place. Get rid of their plans," he said in a low voice.

"Absolutely. We should try to dispossess a few, too."

"If there's time." He cocked a smile.

Jess shook her head at him and focused back on the building and what was happening inside. "We should keep going. See if we can see where they've got Sloane."

"We're getting closer. I can feel her." He carefully made his way to the back of the building. He closed his eyes a moment, and Jessie glanced around making sure no one noticed them standing at the back of an old warehouse.

"She's on the other side of this wall." He took a few steps. There are no windows here, so we need to find another way in." He glanced over. "Shall we?" he indicated the door about ten-twenty feet away from where they stood.

"You open, I'll freeze." She responded and followed behind as he made his way to the door. He looked her in the eyes and nodded once. He reached his hand out to take the door handle.

He met her eyes again. He mouthed, "one, two, three," and pulled the door open. Her hands were up ready to freeze anyone on the other side, but the hallway was empty. She took a tentative step through the door, and Mike followed behind. He took his gun out of his waistband and held his finger ready on the trigger as he pointed it in the direction they walked. Looking behind her every few steps, she continued down the hall. He stopped in front of the solid green door on the left. He jerked his head to the side. They had been lucky so far, but neither of them wanted to attract any attention by talking.

He reached for the handle and pushed. The door didn't budge. "Shit," he whispered.

Jessie slipped two pins from the back of her hair and inserted them into the keyhole. She twisted just enough to hear a slight click and turned the handle. She opened it slowly, and Mike held the gun in front of him with his back to the door. He was watching her back as she stepped into the room. Sloane was slumped in a chair in the middle of the room. Droplets of blood ran down her wrists behind the chair. Her wrists were twisted at her back and held together with zip ties that were biting into her skin. Jessie could tell that she had tried to pull her hands free but to no avail. Her ankles were secured to the legs with more zip ties. Her face was ashen and pale. Mike dropped down in front of her and cupped her cheek in his hand.

"Sloane, love. Sloane, can you hear me?" he pleaded in a soft voice. She didn't move.

"I'm going to need to carry her out." Mike reached in his pocket and took out his pocket knife. He cut loose her legs then her wrists. He kissed her palm when he was finished and lifted her into his arms. "Are you ready?"

"What about the other guy? I thought you said there was someone else." Jessie studied Mike.

"There is but can we get her out of here first. As soon as we have her tucked away in the car, we can come back. Come on Jess; we don't have time for this. What if he's passed out, too? I can't carry them both, and you need your hands free to freeze if we have any hope of surviving a run-in with any demons. Be reasonable, please." His eyes pleaded with her, and she knew he was making sense. It felt wrong to leave someone behind when they were so close. Mike did make some awfully good points, but every part of her knew it was wrong to leave a fellow man behind. She huffed out a breath, "Fine, but we're coming back for him."

"Yes, now let's go. We've been extremely lucky thus far. Let's not take any more chances."

"Fine, but I don't like it." She moved to open the door. Her hand reached for the handle, and it flew open, nearly clocking her in the face. She jumped back startled but regained her composure quickly. She raised her hands to freeze him. He didn't stop. "Shit," she kicked forward, connecting with his balls. He slumped forward grabbing his crotch.

"Fucking bitch, you're going to pay for that." He raised, hands in fists. She kicked forward again, hitting him a second time. He coughed forward, and she kicked him in the head. He held his hands to his crotch, guarding it against another attack. She kicked him again in the face, and his eyes rolled back and closed.

She took a deep breath. "You just had to say it, didn't you?"

"What?" Mike asked.

"Now, we have to go. You just jinxed our assess. Come on." She ran through the hall. She had her gun in her hand, now that she knew the place was warded. She didn't care if they were possessed, people. She'd kill the next one she saw. She heard running steps behind her. She got to the door and flung it open. Mike ran through it. She turned and saw two tall, burley men following. She pointed the gun and fired. The bullet struck one on the right side of his chest. He slowed on impact but didn't stop.

"Fuck," she slammed the door closed and ran toward the car. Mike was a few steps in front of her. She heard shots coming from the building behind her. "Come on; we need to get to the car." She called, moving to run next to Mike. A bullet lodged in the grass next to her last footfall. "Holy shit, they don't even care that they are shooting outside, in the middle of the day."

"Hate to state the obvious love, but they're demons," Mike spoke, out of breath as he ran.

Jessie ran around to the driver's side and opened the backseat for Mike. Mike flung Sloane and himself into the seat and slammed the door behind him. Jessie jumped in the driver's seat and yelled, "Keys."

Mike tossed the keys from his pocket to her lap. She started the car and put it in the drive. She peeled out of the space and headed toward the highway. She glanced into the rearview mirror. "Shit, we've got company." She stepped harder on the gas as two black sedans pulled behind her.

She looked behind her, and Mike was shifting Sloane over next to him in the seat. "I'm going to shoot at them. Hopefully, I can slow them down or get them off our assess." He rolled down the window and shifted to look out the back.

"Hold on." Jessie took a turn, and Mike dropped the gun to the floor when he hit the side of the door.

"You think you could give me a little more warning. I dropped the damn gun."

"No, I'm going to lose these fuckers." She took another corner.

"Can I get in at least one shot, Jess?" Mike pleaded.

"Fine, fucking do it already."

"I would love to, quit taking the damn corners so hard."

"Do you even know how a car chase works? I have to take the corners hard. Would you rather I slow down, so they can shoot us?"

"No, but I'd sure like the chance to shoot them," Mike said.

"Fine, whatever, shoot them then. I'll go straight for a minute, maybe two."

"Your sarcasm doesn't help."

"It helps me." She uttered under her breath. She glanced in the rearview mirror, and Mike was lining up in the window to take a shot. She shook her head; it was taking him forever. "Will you take a shot already?"

"Jess, I'd like to hit them. No use wasting a bullet." He fired and hit the front right tire. The sedan began swerving recklessly, finally slamming into the other car. The other car slowed, then slammed them back. Jessie let out a laugh.

Sparks flew from the right side of the car, and they slowed. "Do you think you can do that again?"

"I plan on it." Mike held the gun steady to fire a second shot. Jessie hit a bump, and Mike cursed behind her. "Jess, please. Do you think you could try to help me, here?"

"No, I like to watch you struggle." She stressed high-pitched giggle.

"Seriously Jess, what the hell? I'm trying to save us here."

"Okay, fine. I'll try to be good." She smirked and took another turn.

"Jessie!" Mike shouted from the backseat.

"What? I'm still trying to lose them."

"You are going to pay for that, so help me," he muttered. He fired again. The bullet went wide to the right. "Fuck!" Mike said. He steadied again and fired. This time the bullet went through the windshield. The car jerked to the side and slammed into a car parked on the side of the road. Jessie breathed a sigh of relief.

"Well, we lost them. You ready to go back and get the other guy now?"

"No, are you fucking kidding Jessie? They know we took, Sloane. They'll be waiting for us. We can't go back there."

"We have to get the other guy, Mike."

"Ah, no we don't. We have to get help. Then, maybe when we have fifteen other people with us, we go back and get him."

"How many were in there? You said fifteen. How many do you think followed us in those cars? We have to be down to at least ten maybe less. I think we can go back and get him."

"Jessie be reasonable. You can't freeze them in the building. We barely fought off the one guy when we were in there, and we almost got shot. We absolutely can't go back. It's a suicide mission. I thought you were smarter than that." Mike blew out an exasperated breath.

"I know that if it were any of us in there, you'd go in. Come on, Mike. We just went in blind to get Sloane, and we made it out. We can't just leave him there." Jess pleaded.

"No, Jessie. We need to get Sloane some medical attention. Then we need to call Erik and find out what they learned. We can't go back, right now. We will save him, but we can't do it without help. Go to Magnus' house. He'll get us help. We can go save the guy but only if we have some more people, okay." Mike's voice was soft, and she knew he was probably right. Jessie didn't like the idea of leaving the other guy there. She wanted to turn around and get him. For now, she would head to Magnus' to get help. Then she would go back and get the other guy. She wanted to call Erik. He would come to help her if she asked. He'd go back with her right now if she were with him. She blew out a breath she hadn't realized she was holding.

"Fine, I'll go to Magnus' house, but I'm going back as soon as I can. I don't care, Mike. We need to save that guy. He's Shikari, and we don't leave one of our behind, ever." She took a sharp turn and exited onto the highway. She wanted to get to Magnus' as fast as possible. She also wanted to get her hands on a phone.

She pulled into the driveway and parked. Mike opened the door and lifted Sloane out. Jessie knocked on the door, and Jolene answered. "Oh my, what happened?" she asked.

"Sloane was kidnapped. We got her out, but she's lost some blood from the cuts on her wrists. I think she got hit in the head pretty bad, too. There's blood in her hair. Can we get a medic here, immediately?" Mike asked.

"No need, I'm a nurse. I can get her all patched up in a jiffy. Bring her on into the house. I'll get my supplies." Mike walked into the living room and laid her gently on the sofa. Jolene hurried in with a black leather medical bag in her hand.

"Do you mind if I use your phone? Ours are both dead, and I'd like to let Erik know what's going on." Jessie asked as she watched Jolene open the bag for supplies.

"Of course, dear, go on into the kitchen. My phone is sitting on the counter. We have chargers in there as well if you'd like to plug yours in." She continued to kneel in front of Sloane. "Mike would you mind going and fetching Penelope for me. Ask her to bring some wet cloths. We need to clean up all this blood on her before I patch her up."

"Sure, no problem." Mike headed for the kitchen.

Jessie turned and walked back out to the car to get their phones. She wanted to call, Erik, but she'd rather call from her phone. He was probably worried about her, and she wasn't sure if he'd answer an unfamiliar number. She retrieved the phones and plugged hers into the charger in the kitchen. She tapped her foot as she waited for it to turn on. She was dying to talk to Erik. The adrenaline from the chase had left her system, and she needed reassurance.

When the screen was finally on the startup page, she hit the phone icon. She scrolled to find Erik and hit the send button. She breathed a sigh of relief when she heard his voice on the other end.

"Jessie? Hello, Jess are you okay?" Erik's voice was frantic.

"Yes, babe. I'm okay. We got Sloane out," she said.

"Oh, thank god you're okay. It was a trap. They knew you were coming. They were trying to get you, Jess. I was so worried they would." Erik's voice was full of concern, and her heart swelled. She wanted to feel him in her arms.

She dropped her voice low, "Erik, we have to go back. There's another guy in there. We had to leave him because we were being chased, but we have to go back and get him. We just have to." She pleaded.

"Jess, it was a trap. They wanted to get you. You can't go back there. Do you know how bad it would've been if they got you?" He sighed into the phone.

"I know, Erik. But we can't just leave him there. He's one of us. We have to save him."

"Jess, you don't even know this guy."

"It doesn't matter if I know him. We have an oath or have you forgotten? I'd think you of all people would support me, Erik." She spat his name. She couldn't believe after everything; he wasn't supporting her in this. He left her because of his damn sense of duty. Why wouldn't he agree with her? Jessie slumped against the counter. She'd never felt so lonely, at this moment. She took a deep breath.

"I know the oath, Jess. But I love you, and I don't want anything to happen to you."

Her heart skipped a beat. "What did you say?" She was surprised. She wasn't expecting him to say I love you.

"Jess, I said I love you. Now, will you please wait until I get there? Caroline and I are on our way. We're only about ten minutes from Denver. Please, just stay put until I get there." He pleaded.

"Fine, I'll stay. But this conversation isn't over. We are going to save that guy."

"Okay, okay, just stay there. I'll be there soon."

"Okay, bye." She hung up the phone before she could hear him say anything else. She would wait, but she didn't like it. The longer they waited, the more demons could show up at the warehouse. She knew if they'd gone back right away, they wouldn't be expecting it. They would have had a better chance against ten; now they would have to go against however many they would call in for reinforcement. Which meant it would be even harder to get Erik to let her go. She wasn't sure there was even enough Shikari in Denver to scale a full-on attack. Demons had possessed many of them. Jessie cursed and walked back into the living room to find Mike and check on Sloane. Sloane would be willing to go back. She was sure of it.

Chapter 15

"Have you woken her up, yet?" Jessie asked as she walked up to the sofa.

"Not yet, why?" Mike asked.

"Just asking." Jessie studied Sloane's still form.

"You're never just asking, Jessie. What's up?" Mike held Sloane's hand in his as he studied Jessie. She felt his eyes bore into her as she crossed her arms over her chest.

"Fine, I want to go back and get the guy we left behind. I know Sloane will side with me on this one. She'll want payback for those assholes taking her. She can't side with me while she's passed out." Jessie bit her lip and studied Sloane. Her face was ashen and pale. Jessie could see the blood around her wrists from the restraints. Jessie looked to the ground. She knew she was selfish. Sloane shouldn't be going to battle in her current state. She just wanted one person to agree with her.

"Jessie, you think Sloane is going to be ready to fight? She lost a lot of blood and had a pretty bad concussion. I'm not even sure she's going to wake up easily. She's got a bad head injury from when they knocked her out at the school. I think they may have knocked her out twice based on the size of the bump. She's in no shape to fight." Mike traced a finger along her cheekbone, admiring.

"I know, but it'd be nice to have at least one person on my side." She stood rigid.

The door opened, and Erik strode through, "I'm always on your side, babe." He reached his hand out and laced his fingers with hers. "Unless it's going to put you in extreme danger." He gazed down at Jessie knowing why she was asking.

"We can't just leave one of our own. It's not right." Jessie dropped her head. She let go of Erik's hand, crossed her arms, and walked back to the kitchen.

A moment later, Erik walked through the door behind her. "Jess, we will go back for him, but we need help. It was a trap. They were trying to get you. Did your powers even work when you got in there?" He placed his hand on Jessie's shoulder and squeezed lightly.

She turned around, head still down. "No, my powers didn't work at the warehouse." Her voice was small.

"I know. We found out from the kid; it was a trap meant for you. You're damn lucky they didn't get you. Jess, I was so scared when I couldn't get a hold of you." Erik stepped forward and wrapped his arms around her. She dropped her hands to her sides and let him hug her.

"I don't like it. We need to get back there. The longer we wait, the more time they have to plan for us. Then we could have an even harder time. They could also speed up having him possessed because we were there. We need to save him." She pleaded, gripping Erik's shirt in her hand and looking up into his eyes.

"I know, babe. We need to save him, but we also need to be smart about it. We can't go charging in there without a plan. They want you, and I absolutely will not let them have you. Jessie, I love you. I can't let anything happen to you." He placed a hand under her chin and raised her head to meet his eyes. He bent and kissed her. His kiss was filled with worry and relief. She responded instantly, wrapping her arms around him, and pulling him closer. She needed him, his comfort. She always felt safe with Erik. She kissed him for several minutes before breaking away.

"Okay, so let's make a plan. The sooner we get on with it the better." She grabbed his hand and pulled him back into the living room. "Okay, Mike we need to make a plan to go get the guy. We're going to need help — any idea where Magnus is?" she asked.

"No, I only saw Jolene since we got here. Speaking of Jolene, I haven't seen her in a while. She bandaged up Sloane and disappeared." Mike ran a hand down Sloane's face before standing. "We should find her. See where Magnus is, and if we can get some help from the Shikari here in Denver." Mike strode down the hallway. He opened doors along the way looking for Jolene.

"Jolene?" Jessie called down the stairway. "Isn't Magnus' study down here? We should check for him here." She turned toward Erik.

"Yes, we'll check downstairs. Mike, you want to head upstairs."

"Yeah." He turned around and left.

"Magnus, Jolene? Anyone down here?" Erik called as they walked down the hallway.

"Well, where the hell did, they go. I know Jolene and Penelope were here when we got here. Jolene took care of Sloane. Where did she go?"

"I don't know. Maybe they're upstairs. Hopefully, Mike had more luck than we did."

"Oh yeah, didn't you come with Caroline? Where is she? You didn't come in with her."

"She was checking in on her daughter. She attends school here. I'm not sure what's taking her so long. She said she was just going to make a quick call." They reached the kitchen and went back into the living room. Caroline was standing over Sloane. She looked up when they walked in. "Hey, did you get ahold of your daughter?" Erik asked.

"No, I haven't been able to reach Nick or Nicole. Neither of them is answering their cell phones, which isn't like them at all. I'm going to try again in a few minutes. If I have to, I'll drive over to the house, then the school." She clenched and unclenched her fists.

Mike and Jolene walked down the stairs. "So, we need to make a plan to go back and get the guy at the warehouse. Jolene, do you know where Magnus, is and can we get any help to go back?" Jessie asked.

"I can certainly call him, dear. I didn't realize there were pressing matters such as these. I will call Magnus straight away and see what he can spare to help. If you'll excuse me." She walked into the kitchen.

"Caroline, do you think you could help, too? You and Erik have the power to hear thoughts, so we would know where everyone is before we go in. Last time it was just Mike and I, and we didn't have an advantage." She studied Caroline.

"I don't see why not. I do agree with you that we need to get him out of there. Did you find out anything about the man while you were there?" Caroline asked.

"I know he has power over the elements, but that's about it," Mike explained.

"What? That's a unique power to have. I only know of one person to have that particular gift." She pulled her phone out again.

"Who do you know who has that power?" Erik asked.

Caroline dialed a number into her phone. She met Erik's eyes and said "Nick." She turned away from the group and began pacing, the phone pressed to her ear.

"Oh shit," Erik said. "Okay, time to wake up Sloane." Erik looked to Mike. He nodded and knelt next to Sloane. Mike reached his hand to shake Sloane's shoulder lightly. "Sloane, love, Sloane wake-up. Sloane?" he called, leaning over her. He had one arm on her shoulder, the other he ran down her bare arm.

Sloane bolted upright in an instant colliding with Mike. "What the hell? Where am I?"

THE SHIKARI 2: THE EVIL HEADMASTER

Mike lifted his hand to his head where Sloane had just connected with it. "Love, you're at Magnus' with us. You're safe." He took her hand in his and lifted it to his lips.

"Oh shit, sorry babe. Are you okay?" She scooted closer to him, placing her hand on his cheek, and examining his head.

"I'm fine. I should've expected it. At least you didn't wake up swinging this time." He curved up the side of his mouth, and she blinked. "You okay?" he asked.

"I think so. My head hurts like hell. How did you guys get me out of there? It was a trap. Mr. Hall wanted Jessie, bad. He was going to get a demon to possess me." Sloane lifted her wrists to examine them. "When he threatened to have a demon possess me, I tried to get free. I would rather die than be possessed." She looked into Mike's eyes. "Thank you for coming for me."

"Of course, love." He lifted her wrist to his lips placing a gentle kiss on the bandage. "My life would be boring without you in it," he whispered.

Sloane blushed and captured his lips with hers in a fiery kiss. She curled her fingers in his hair pulling him to her. She kissed him wildly for several seconds before Erik said, "Ahem, do you two mind? We have some pressing matters to attend to."

"Oh, of course." Mike moved to sit next to Sloane on the couch, taking her hand in his as he went. Jessie smiled at the closeness of the two. She was genuinely happy for her friends. She glanced over to Erik, and the look of pain on his face surprised her.

"Sorry Sloane, we have to go back to the warehouse. There was another Shikari member there. We think it may be Caroline's ex-husband Nick. He has power over the elements, so we need to save him. Are you up for that?" Jessie asked.

"Yes, I want a piece of the asshole who got me. I'm going to have a bruise on my head for weeks. I'm in; I'm always in for a fight. Do you have to ask?" She huffed and touched her head.

"Love, you were just unconscious. Are you sure you're up for it? No one would fault you if you sat this one out." Mike reached his hand to cup her cheek and looked into her eyes.

"Hell no, I'm not staying here. I'm going. I want to get my hands-on Mr. Hall. That bastard deserves a good beating. I wanted a chance at him back at the warehouse. Now, I get one." She rubbed her hands together, eyes alight with glee.

"Sloane, you scare me sometimes." Jessie shook her head.

"Sloane, you always want to charge in. We need to think this through. You guys already charged in without thinking about what could happen." Erik eyed Jessie. "We need to have a plan."

"I don't feel right leaving that guy in there. He's one of us. We need to try to get him out of there if we can." Jessie glanced to Erik and held his eye. "You'd do it for one of us." She whispered.

"You're right; I would." Erik took Jessie's hand.

"Okay, so we're going. Hopefully, Magnus will come through with some help for us." She looked over to the kitchen door. She was wondering what was taking Jolene so long. "I'm going to check on Jolene." Jessie strode into the kitchen. Jolene was dropping the phone from her ear. She turned and jumped.

"Oh dear, Jessie you startled me." She raised her hand to her chest.

"I'm sorry. I was just checking on you. What did Magnus say?" she asked.

"He said he would have a car of four head over to the warehouse to meet you there. He was hoping with you four it would be enough. He has another matter going on of some urgency, and that's all the men he can spare. Bryant will be with them, I believe." Jolene set the phone back on the counter. "If you'll excuse me, I need to fetch something for Magnus. Will that be all?"

"Okay, is he sending them now?" Jessie asked.

"Yes, he said they would be on their way, but they're coming from the other side of town, so it might be about fifteen minutes before they arrive." Jolene turned and walked down the stairs.

"Okay," Jessie went back to the living room. "Magnus is sending four guys to the warehouse to help us. Bryant will be with them. They'll be there in fifteen minutes. Is everyone ready to go?" Jessie looked to each of them. Caroline was still pacing with her phone in her hand. She took a step toward Erik and lowered her voice. "Has she gotten ahold of either of them, yet?"

"No, not yet. We need to go to the warehouse. If it is her ex, we need to get him." Erik laced his fingers with Jessie's.

Sloane stood with Mike. "We're ready." She turned to Mike. "Do you have weapons in the car or should we load up here?"

"I have everything you need, love." He wrapped his arm around her and pulled her into a kiss. She pulled back and laughed.

"So, we're ready." She looked to Jessie and Erik. "Let's do this." Her eyes were alighted with anticipation. Jessie knew Sloane loved the fight. Jessie knew they were necessary but didn't get nearly as excited as Sloane did. She was like a little kid every time a battle presented itself. Maybe it's because she hasn't been doing any fighting for years like Jessie had. She'd been heading into battle since she was a teen. As soon as the order knew what her power was, they would use her to defeat demons whenever they could. Jessie just wanted a break from all the fighting. Maybe when all this was over, she'd convince Erik to take a vacation to a secluded cabin where they could be alone together without any thoughts about demons. She smiled at the thought. She looked up and met Erik's curious gaze.

"What's going on in that pretty head of yours?" Erik asked.

"Nothing, just thinking about what it'd be like to have a break from demons."

"Oh, that's all? Hopefully, we'll get to find out soon." He placed a kiss on her hand, keeping their fingers intertwined.

Jessie and Erik followed the other two to the car. Caroline came up a minute later. "I'm going to follow you in a separate car. I may need to take off if I can get a hold of Nicole. I don't know what's going on, but I don't like it."

"Okay, do you want us to ride with you?" Jessie asked.

"No, it's fine I want to be able to run if I need to. You understand?"

"Of course, your daughter is the most important thing. If you have to go to her, we understand completely." Jessie reached out and took her hand.

"Thank you, Jessie. You always have such a kind heart. I will meet you at the warehouse." She turned and walked to her car. Jessie and Erik got in the backseat behind Sloane and Mike.

"Ready?" Sloane turned and asked.

"Yeah, Caroline took a car in case she has to dart off for her daughter. She's meeting us there." Jessie explained. She reached to take Erik's hand. He squeezed her hand when she took his hand, and she could see the worry lines around his eyes. She still had a bad feeling in the pit of her stomach, but she also knew they couldn't leave one of their behind. She hoped she was right to push everyone into going back to the warehouse.

"Okay, and you said Bryant would be with the others?" Sloane asked.

"Yes, Jolene said he would be one of the four Magnus was sending. They are meeting us there but were driving from the other side of Denver." She looked down at her phone. It was between rush hours, so hopefully, they would get there around the same time.

"So, what's our plan once we get there?" Erik asked.

"We planned to go around back. We know that's where they are holding him. Mike could sense both Sloane and him in the back. It should be the third door down on the left." Jessie said.

"Okay, so our best bet would be to split up. Half going through the back to locate the guy. The other half was going through the front and dispossessing as we go. We need to find whatever they have affected our powers. We do much better in a fight when we're at full capacity." Erik explained.

"We also know that at least a few of the guys who've been possessed are Shikari. I could still sense them even though Jessie's power didn't work, so whatever they are using is ineffective against my tracking ability." Mike explained.

"So, it may not affect my ability, either. That could be an advantage if I can still hear their thoughts. I know I was able to hear the couple in Minneapolis even though they had the amulets. We need to talk with a leader of the order. Someone who knows the extent of these amulets and how in the hell they could've gotten this information." Erik shook his head. Jessie reached a hand to cup his cheek. She could tell he was worried about everything going on. The worry lines on his forehead softened when he looked at her.

"Let's focus on one thing at a time. Once we get this guy out of there, we can focus on what's next." Jessie rubbed his cheek. She dropped her hand to take his.

"Okay, I agree we need to split up. Let's send the others through the front, and we focus on getting to the guy. He's our priority. Caroline can join the other group, so we have someone who can listen to thoughts at both entrances." Erik put his finger on his mouth, thinking.

"We'll need to fill in the other group before we go in. We have a layout of the building. We've seen some of it when we rescued Sloane. We need to let them know how many are in there." Mike glanced back in the window and met Jessie's eyes. She nodded.

"Okay, can you call Bryant? He's with the other group. It'd be good if we were all set to go when we got there." Jessie asked.

Erik looked down at his phone. "Ah, he's calling me," he said in surprise. He hit the button and raised it to his ear. "What's going on?" Erik listened. He raised his hand and ran it through his hair. "Shit, okay," he nodded. "Okay, I'll tell them. Yeah, we'll figure it out." He dropped the phone to his lap. His voice dropped in surprise. "Bryant and the others aren't coming." He stared forward for a few moments.

"Wait, what? Are they not coming? How can they not be coming?" Jessie blurted.

"Something's going on. It must be big. Bryant didn't give much of an explanation, just said that they couldn't come. He said there was an emergency, and they had to go."

"Okay," Jess spoke slowly as she processed what that meant for them. "So, we have to go in there with the five of us." She nodded, wrapping her mind around the idea.

"I'm not sure we should go in there with only us. We needed back-up, and now we have none. If something happens, we've got no one else coming to help. It must be pretty damn bad for them not to be coming to help." Mike said shaking his head in disbelief.

"Well, there are only ten of them since our last visit. Does that help?" Jessie shrugged. She was grasping at straws, and she knew it. They needed to save the guy.

"You're counting on them not bringing in anyone else. If they called in help, we're screwed. They will get us with our collection of powers, and the rest of the Shikari would be fucked. I don't think this is a good idea." Erik ran his hand through his hair again.

"Erik, we have to save him. We can still pull off the same plan as before, but we split up. Our focus is on getting the guy in the back. Maybe, we don't dispossess them. Maybe we just focus on getting him out of there. We worry about the rest later." Jessie knew she was rambling, but she needed to convince them to still go through with the plan.

"Okay, okay, maybe we all go in a back way. I think splitting up would be a bad idea. We need to stick together. We're better as a group. Sloane could you focus on getting some vision of what we're walking in to. I know you're weak, but anything could help us." Erik looked to Sloane.

"I can try." Sloane settled into the front seat and closed her eyes.

"Mike since your power still worked, you need to tell us what we're walking into. When we get there, focus on how many are in there, and what powers we might be facing. I will do the same. I'm going to try to pick up any thoughts about the amulets. Maybe we can deactivate them, so Jessie can freeze again as we go." Erik reached for Jessie's hand. "We could use you, so we need to see if there's any way for you to be able to use your power." Jessie nodded.

"I overheard they were loading up amulets for other areas in the warehouse. I forgot about that part. If we can locate those, we can stop this from happening to others. That would put a huge dent in their plan." Sloane said, darting up in her seat.

"Yeah, it would. Okay, so we need to locate the amulets while we're there. Our priority is to get to the guy. If he's conscious, we could use his help. Then, we move on to the amulets," Erik said.

"Well, we're about there, time to start praying to whatever God you believe in." Sloane slapped Mike playfully on the arm.

"What? It's a good idea. We're about to go into a warehouse full of demons that outnumber us. I'll take all the help we can get." Mike shrugged.

'We don't need help. I'm all the help we need. Now, let me focus will you." Sloane relaxed back.

"Ever the humble one, huh sis." Erik shook his head.

"Shut it, I'm amazing, you know this." She crossed her arms over her chest.

"I know no such thing. Although, if you get a vision before we go in, I might change my mind."

"No pressure or anything," Sloane said and held her hand up for silence.

Mike parked a half a block down from the building. Jessie took Erik's hand as he focused on the thoughts in the building. It felt as though everyone in the car was holding their breath while concentrating. The tension was so thick you could cut it with a knife. Jessie waited but began drumming her fingers against the door.

Erik's eyes snapped open, and he placed his hand over hers on the door. "Jess please."

"What? You guys ready, yet?" Her tone was biting, and she bit her lip after she'd said it. "Sorry, I just hate waiting in here when we need to be in there." She clasped her hands together.

"We need to know what we're getting into before we go charging in, Jess." Erik placed his hands over hers, and she unclasped her hands to take his.

"Okay, I know. I'll be patient." She blew out a breath.

"That hard, huh?" Mike joked. "I'm ready; there are still only about twelve in there. They didn't call in reinforcements which are good for us. I can't sense any special powers beyond the guy who's still being held in the back. How about you, Erik? What do you get?"

"I agree with you. There are twelve in there. They didn't call for back-up. They didn't think they needed it since Sloane was gone. I guess you guys are taking her spoiled their plans." He looked to Sloane. "I have bad news for you, Sloane. Mr. Hall isn't here. He left before they even got to you. Something else is going on, but I don't know what for sure. It has to do with a school here. That's all I know. I think if we go in through the back like we planned, we should be fine. There's no one back there right now, so we'd be smart to go now."

"Alright, let's do this." Sloane clapped her hands together, smiling.

"Sounds good to me." Erik turned to look out the back window. "Where's Caroline? She said she would be joining us. It's been a while. She should have a say in this plan." He tried to peer out of the window to see if he could see the car.

Jess turned to look. "Yeah, she should've been right behind us."

Erik closed his eyes a moment. "I don't hear her thoughts. She's pretty good at blocking me out, though." He reached for the door handle and stepped out of the car looking around for her car. Jessie got out with him. "Shit, her car's not here."

"I know she said she'd leave if she had to, but you'd think she'd at least let us know."

"It must've been important for her not to come," Jessie said.

Erik shook his head in disbelief, "Yeah, it better have been damn important."

Chapter 16

"Where's Caroline?" Mike asked as Erik got back into the car.

"I don't know. The car's gone." Erik's voice was concerned. "You think she'd have sent me a message before just taking off like that."

"It must've been an emergency, Erik. There's no way she would have left us, otherwise. You know she was taking her car, in case she had to leave because of her daughter. She must've heard something and had to run. Come on, let's get on with this." Jessie said.

"Okay, well we better get on with it. We may need to help with the emergency when we're done here. It must be big considering both Bryant and Caroline left." Erik shook his head.

Jessie looked to the front. "You two ready to go?"

"Yeah, let's do this." Sloane rubbed her hands together in anticipation. She looked over to Mike. "You ready?"

"Always ready, love." He lifted a brow at her answering smirk. She bit her bottom lip thinking about the last time they'd been together.

"Let's do this." She raised a brow at Mike, running her hand up his thigh before turning to get out of the car. Mike slid out, and Sloane met him on the other side. He hooked a finger in her belt loop and pulled her against him. "You know you're paying for that when we're alone." He whispered in her ear.

She leaned against him and turned to whisper next to his ear. "Looking forward to it." She reached one hand back to run up his thigh, stopping to cup him through his jeans. She looked over to Erik and Jessie, thankful that for the moment, they seemed to be occupied.

Erik looked over to Mike and nodded. Mike grabbed Sloane's hand and brought it back around to her stomach. "Babe, we have work to do." He whispered in her ear. She pulled on her bottom lip with her teeth slowly releasing it.

She turned around. "So, you got any guns in this car?"

He shook his head and laughed. "Love, I told you I have everything you need."

"Good, because I want a big one." She smirked.

"Of course, you do. I would expect nothing less." He shook his head again and walked to the trunk to get the weapons he'd stored when he'd gotten back to the car. "You can have all the big guns you want." He dropped his hand and slapped her ass. She jumped in surprise and then cast him a devilish grin.

Erik walked over. "You two done? Cause we have work to do."

"Yeah, we're ready," Sloane said, as she tucked a 9mm in her waistband.

Jessie walked over to join them. "Okay, we make our way to the back. I'm going to check the windows as we did before as we go." She looked to Mike, and he nodded.

"You know I can just tell you where they are, right?" Erik moved to stand next to Jessie.

"I still want to check. I like being able to see them." She rolled her eyes at him. She headed toward the building. The others followed. She stopped when she reached the first window. She peeked through the same hole as before. Erik leaned next to her against the building and gave her a playful look.

"There are two guys in there." He leaned next to her ear. "One's thinking about the sex he had with his girlfriend last night. He's trying to conceal his erection by staying seated at the table. The other guy is thinking about the last hand they'd played. He had cowboys and thought he could have pushed harder to get more of their money, but he played it safe. They're taking a break cause the third guy is in the bathroom. I won't tell you what's taking him so long. Anything else you want to know?" He smirked at her annoyed look.

"Okay, I get it. I'll follow your lead." She glared defiantly into his eyes, and his smile grew wider.

"Now, was that so hard?"

"Whatever, let's just go." She huffed out a breath and walked along the side of the building. Erik took a few hurried strides to catch up to her. He reached out to grab her wrist.

"Jess you need to let me lead. Your power isn't going to work in here." His look was stern.

"Fine," She swept her hand in front of her, palm up. "Go ahead."

He shook his head, "Always so stubborn." He glided past her to the back door. He stopped and waited. "You ready?" He looked into Jessie's eyes.

"Yes," she said.

He placed his hand on the door and opened it, knowing no one was on the other side. He took a step in, and the others followed. Jess stood at the ready next to him. He took a few steps toward the first door. He listened. No one was in the room. He took another few steps to the next door. He stopped., There were two men on the other side. He nodded to Jess, then Mike and Sloane. He mouthed, one, two, three, then he swung the door open. Mike went for the one on the right. He had his back to the door and was pouring himself coffee. He set the carafe down as Mike hit him in the back of the head with his gun.

The second guy whipped toward the door with stunning speed. He reached for the gun in his belt. Sloane pulled the trigger, hitting the arm reaching for his gun. She took a step toward him and rounded a kick to his face. He stumbled a moment but got his grip on the gun.

"For peat's sake." She rounded again kicking him square in the jaw. He stumbled sideways but raised his gun level with Sloane.

"Fucking bitch." He spat. Mike moved silently behind him and hit him in the back of the head with his gun. This time he fell unconscious, making a loud thud when his head ricocheted off the table as he fell.

"Thanks, babe," Sloane said. She stepped over the guy to take Mike's hand.

"Two down, ten to go." Erik turned, and another guy stopped dead in the hallway looking from the group to the two guys on the floor.

"Holy Shit, Hunters!" He yelled. He reached for his waistband, his focus on Erik. Jessie came from the side and landed a jab to his jaw. He shook his head, and Erik stepped forward, pointing his gun at the man.

"Move your hand up, slowly." The guy stopped mid-motion.

"Or what?" The guy glared at Erik's gun.

"Or I'll shoot you in the head," Erik said.

"Oh? You don't care that I'm in one of your own. You would shoot your own man?"

"Absolutely." Erik didn't flinch. Jessie moved around him and ripped the chain from his neck. Once he was free, she raised her hands to freeze him.

"Ah, much better. I like it when they don't talk." Jessie rubbed her hands together. "I noticed that they are all wearing the amulets Sloane mentioned. That means it's not the building that's protected, it's the individuals. So, if we can get the amulets off their neck. I can freeze them, and we can dispossess them. If they're Shikari, they can help us." Jessie cracked her knuckles looking at the frozen man.

"Okay, well we got a girl and three men sprinting down the hall. Back in the room, we've got a better advantage if they don't know where we are. Jess, Sloane you go one room down, across the hall. Jessie be ready to freeze when we get the stones off their neck." He stepped back into the room with the two unconscious men. He could hear them running. He stood on the side of the door frame, and Mike took a position on the other. They had weapons and planned to shoot them. One had the gun aimed down the hall, but Erik knew from his thoughts that he'd never actually shot a gun before. "Ready?" he whispered. Mike nodded.

They reached the doorway and stopped, looking at the two men on the ground. The woman hurried into the room not noticing them in the doorway. The woman dropped down next to one of the men. "Scott, baby are you okay?" She shook him.

The men looked around the room, guns up. Neither turned toward the door. They turned back, looking down the hallway. Mike and Erik moved quickly, grabbing the men from behind. They yanked the chains off. "Now!" Erik called. Jessie stepped out and froze them.

The woman turned, "Wha…" Sloane stepped in the room and hit the woman in the back of her head. She slumped over the man who she'd been shaking. Sloane ripped the chain from her neck, tucking the amulets in her pocket.

"Did anyone else hear him?" Jessie asked.

"I don't hear anyone else coming, but if they stay in the hall, someone will see. We have to move them."

Mike took a step forward. "How about we drag them into the room with the other two, so they're out of the way and this time? When we dispossess them, we close the door." Mike raised his voice at the end. His sarcasm was thick.

"Oh, now you got all the bright ideas. Where was that genius two minutes ago?" Erik shook his head. Mike raised a brow at him and moved to cup his arms under the largest of the three, dragging him back toward the room. The back of the man's heels left a black mark along the floor as he went. Erik grabbed the other while making sure to stay alert for anyone coming. He didn't want to screw it up again. If the other guy hadn't been so surprised, he could have easily got a shot off. Erik couldn't let any of them get hurt.

They got the three in the room, and Mike and Sloane went to dispossessing them. When they were finished, Erik went for the door again. The men who had been playing poker were still in the room. They hadn't made it to the Shikari man, yet. They had taken care of five of them. There were still seven of them in the building. Erik listened for a moment to take a mental inventory of where each of them was. He had the three in the room playing poker. Two were at the front of the building packing boxes to load into their pickup. They needed to get a few things to the school here in Denver. It sounded like these demons were also taking on some of the life events of the people they possessed, just as the couple had in Minneapolis. He concentrated. He could hear two other men discussing some plan that had to do with the school. One man was arguing about which door they should enter through, and whether the girl would be there as they planned.

Erik blew out a breath. He looked wide-eyed to Jessie, then Mike and Sloane. Jessie's eyes narrowed. She looked in the direction of the hall. "Erik, what is it? Is someone coming?"

"No, no one is coming here. I think I know where Caroline went though, and it's not good."

He clenched his hands into fists at his sides. "We need to make this quick. Caroline is going to need our help." Suddenly a dark flash of fabric caught his attention. He forgot he had already opened the door while he was listening. Jessie stood next to him, staring up at him in concern.

As he listened in shock at the thoughts of the two men, he heard a subtle click and looked up just in time to see a guy standing with a revolver pointed at Jessie. He reached his arm out and pulled her towards him as the bullet left the barrel. Erik wasn't fast enough, and the bullet went through Jessie's arm and lodged in the wall behind her. Erik heard the click again as he went for a second shot. Before he could fire, Jessie raised her hands to freeze the guy, but nothing happened.

Mike and Sloane both moved behind the wall. Erik saw red in an instant. He flew forward, knocking the gun out of the guy's hand and shoving him against the wall. His fingers wrapped around his throat. He pressed so hard his hand turned red.

"You will pay for that." Erik spat through clenched teeth. He tightened his grip and pulled him back to slam his head into the wall. He felt the shock reverberate down his arm. His eyes shut, and a stream of blood ran down his nose. Erik dropped him to the floor and whirled. Jessie was holding her hand pressed against her upper arm.

"Are you okay?" Erik asked, fear shaking his voice.

"Yes, I'll be fine." Her eyes were wide as she looked down at the blood soaking through her clothes to her fingers.

Sloane took a step forward and yanked a stone from around his neck. "These fucking amulets. We need to stop the guys from loading these up to bring to the others. They put us at a serious disadvantage."

"Agreed." Erik huffed as he looked down to the guy limp on the floor.

Mike walked up and grabbed the guy and dragged him back into the room with the rest. "You think next time you don't almost kill him. I thought we were only supposed to dispossess them."

"You're just mad because it wasn't you, who kicked his ass," Erik said.

"True, true. Okay, how about a compromise? You let me kick the next guy's ass."

"Deal," Erik took a deep breath to try to steady his nerves. He clenched his hands into fists.

"Ah, guys can we move this along. I'm kinda bleeding over here." Jessie held her hand to her arm, but blood was dripping through her fingers and down her arm.

Mike walked over to one of the guys on the floor and ripped a large chunk of the bottom of one of their t-shirts off. He walked to Jessie and wrapped it tightly around her wound, tying it. "There, love. That should help the bleeding until we can get you stitched up."

"Thanks," she breathed. "Okay, let's get this over with. There's somewhere else we need to be." She looked meaningfully toward Erik. He nodded.

"Yes, let's go get the idiots playing poker. They won't even know what hit them. Plus, no one will find them. They've been playing together for hours. I want to save the two in the last room on the left for last. They are in on a big plan happening at the school, and I'd like to know more about it."

"Okay, so poker room it is," Sloane said. "Lead the way, bro."

"On it." He started walking down the hall, muscles tense. He didn't want any more surprises. Erik kept a hand on Jessie as they walked. He needed the reassurance that she was okay. When he heard the click and knew on instinct it was a gun, he had pulled Jessie out of the way, but far not enough. He would make it up to her later. His heart was racing as he stopped in front of the door. He leaned down to her ear. "You ready?" He gazed into her beautiful steel-blue eyes. Her muscles were tight, and she unfurled her fist to be ready to freeze. He could tell she was in pain, but he knew she would continue on no matter what. It was her fighting spirit he loved. He knew, no matter what if she could, she would keep going. It killed him now that she was in pain, but they'd done this many times before. He needed to stay focused.

He reached a handout and slowly opened the door. Jessie raised her hands, and the men at the table froze. "Hey, it's about time my power works."

Sloane and Mike walked into the room. Sloane leaned over the guy furthest from the door.

"Ooh, he had aces. Maybe we should let them finish this hand." She smirked.

"Sloane just do it already. We have work to do." Erik shook his head.

"Fine, you are so not fun." She plucked the cards out of his hand and threw them on the table. She said the incantation for the men, then flipped the river card. It was an ace. She smiled,

"See, it would had been a great hand: full house, Aces over eights. He could have gotten a nice pot since he sucks. I'll just have to take his pot for him." She smiled and picked up the bills in the middle of the table and shoved them into her pocket.

"We're not here to steal from the demons." Erik cocked his head at her.

"Why not? It's not like they're going to miss it. These idiots probably didn't even have the money, to begin with. Besides, we should get something for our troubles. I saw a new Glock the other day that I would kill for."

"Careful, sis. Some might think you would kill for it." He lifted his mouth in a sly smile.

"Whatever, I like riding the world of demons. If I can steal a little of their loot in the process to buy new, pretty guns all the better." His eyes were bright, and she tapped her pocket for emphasis.

"You're incorrigible," Erik said but went back out of the room. He looked to Jessie. "We have two more packing boxes up front. Then maybe we can capture the other two making the plan and get some information out of them."

Sloane bounced up behind them. "Oh, this may be a promising mission, yet. Can I do the torture? I do enjoy getting information out of demons. Besides, I haven't found the asshole who hit me, yet. Maybe, I'll get lucky, and it will be one of them. Then, I can have some fun." She raised her eyebrows and bit her lip, looking at Mike. He shook his head at her.

"Ever raising hell, my love," Mike said.

"Oh, what? You know you love that about me." She walked over, stopping next to his ear. "Especially in the bedroom." She winked before following Jessie and Erik. Erik made a gagging sound as he walked. She slapped his shoulder. "Knock it off."

Erik stopped next to an open steel door. He looked to Jess and jerked his head toward the opening. There were two guys in there loading boxes into a truck. Jessie glanced around the door to see that the men's backs were to them. They looked like strong carpenters with their muscled backs covered in flannel. She raised her hands and froze them in place.

"Seriously, they're loading the amulets but aren't wearing any?" Jessie questioned.

One man had the box outstretched toward the tailgate of the truck. She giggled. Erik raised a brow but then became concerned. Her face was growing pale. They continued into the room, and Mike and Sloane had already moved to dispossess the two. Sloane bent to the ground and picked up a silver chain with a sapphire stone at the end.

"Looks like it fell off him." She held the stone next to the blue flannel. "At least he put to match." She slid the necklace into her pocket with the others. "I have to say; I'm getting quite a collection of precious stones." Sloane clapped her hand together. "Now for the fun part." She bounced as she walked back toward the entrance. "Where are they? I want to get my hands on them. One of them has to be the guy who knocked me out. He wasn't any of the others." She bounced on the balls of her feet as she waited.

"Okay, they are in the room on the left. They are still talking about the plan. I'll fill you in when we are sure there's no one else.

Jessie, you freeze them, and we'll secure them. Then you need to sit down. You're getting pale." Erik reached his hand to brush her cheek, his concern evident in the lines of his face.

He took Jessie's hand and led her to the other side of the door. He squeezed her hand and reached for the handle. He nodded toward her, and when her eyes met his, he opened the door. She raised her hands to freeze them. One man froze at the board, hand outstretched pointing at a picture there. The other man whipped around toward the door, realizing his friend had stopped mid-sentence. He reached for his belt, but Mike was faster. He lunged toward the man, hitting the end of his gun against his temple. The man's knees gave, and he slumped to the floor.

"Hey, I wanted to do that." Sloane protested.

Mike's eyes shined as he looked to her. "You don't get to have all the fun."

"Hmph," she crossed her arms over her chest. She walked over and bent before the slumped man. His face was soft. She ripped the necklace from around his neck. "How many of these guys have these damn things? Someone in the order has to be giving them to the demons. We need to find out who the hell that is and make them pay for it. I'm sick of these assholes having an advantage over us."

"They've always had an advantage; they're demons." Erik pointed out.

"Whatever, you know what I mean." She scrunched her nose up at him.

Mike grabbed the man at the board. Jessie pulled over a chair, and Mike pushed him into it.

"I'll go grab the zip ties they used on me." Sloane strode out of the room. She was back a moment later with a handful of heavy-duty zip ties. She handed them to Mike. "Erik, you and Jess want to go wake up the guy being held in the back?"

Erik looked to Mike, "Actually, I should probably stay to listen to this guy's thoughts when he comes to. Mike, you want to get the guy out to the car?"

"Yeah, no problem." He walked out the door.

Erik glanced over to Jessie. She was as white as a sheet. She was leaning with one hand clutching her arm. He could tell she was in pain and had lost a lot of blood. He took a few steps toward her and cupped her cheek with his hand. "Jess, you need to go to the car, too. I know you're trying to be strong, but you've lost a lot of blood. You look like you're about ready to fall flat on the floor. Sloane and I can take care of this." He gazed into her eyes, and she nodded. She followed Mike out of the room.

Sloane looked over to Erik. "You ready? Cause he'll wake up as soon as Jessie makes it to the back room."

"Yeah, you?"

She licked her lips, "Always." Her eyes were alighted with anticipation. She looked over to the man strapped to the chair. He wasn't the guy who'd knocked her out, but he was the one who was with him. She waited for him to unfreeze so that she could ask him questions. She took her butterfly knife out of her pocket and began flipping it open and closed. She looked to Erik, and he was shaking his head. She tapped her foot and when the guy unfroze a smile spread across her face.

"Well, hello there." She said moving to stand in front of the man.

"What? What the fuck is going on here?" he shouted.

"You're tied up like a good little demon, and you're about to tell us all about the plan you and your buddy were discussing." She looked up to Erik, and he nodded.

"I'm not telling you anything, bitch." He spat.

"Oh, you're not?" She feigned innocence and batted her lashes at him; then her eyes turned dark as she looked into his. "Good, I don't like it when you're too easy to break. I'd like to have some fun, first." She trailed the side of the knife up his arm. Not cutting yet, just to get her point across. The demon's eyes were wide as he watched the knife move up one arm and down the other. "I do enjoy drawing blood from demons." She pushed the knife down on his forearm and watched as the blood pooled, then spilled over the side of his arm.

"I'm not telling you, shit. By the time you're done with me, it'll be too late, anyway. You can't stop it. We'll destroy you, worthless hunters."

"Oh, you think so? Well now, I know it's happening soon. See, you're so cooperative. Too bad I may have to cut up this pretty face of yours to get what I want." She ran a finger down the boy's cheek as she leaned forward, her cleavage in the demon's face. His eyes watched the hand with the knife but when she leaned with her face only inches from his. "I think you're going to tell me exactly what I want to know."

He raised a brow, "Oh yeah?"

She moved the knife to his leg and stopped with the tip pointing down toward his thigh. "Yeah." She plunged the knife in, and the man screamed out. She was sure to stab just off to the side as to not hit an artery. She didn't want him to bleed out before they got their information. She glanced up to Erik, and he nodded, letting her know he'd gotten the information.

"Now, tell me what the hell is going on, or I'm going to give you matching scars." She pulled the knife out of his leg and poised it on the other side pointing down in the same spot. She began adding pressure until she knew he could feel the tip entering his leg.

"Bitch don't fucking stab me. Are you fucking crazy?" he yelled.

Sloane smiled wide. "Yes, I do believe crazy is a word used to describe me often. Now are you going to tell me what I want to know, or am I going to keep putting holes in you with my knife?" She inched the tip down further.

"It's at the school," He cried out as Sloane slowly pushed the knife further into his leg.

"Which school? There are hundreds of schools in Denver?" She inched the knife down infinitesimally.

"Mullen, they're at Mullen. We know Shikari have the local kids go to high school there, so we went after your kids. There's nothing you can do about it. We've already possessed most of them. It's fucking perfect. You won't kill your kids to dispel us." The demon threw his head back and laughed.

Sloane looked to Erik. "We good?"

"Yes," he said through gritted teeth. Sloane read the incantation, and the man's eyes went wide, but he slumped when the demon exited in a mass of black smoke. "You want to take care of the other one. I'm going to go let Jess and Mike know what's going on."

"Sure," she knelt next to the other as Erik strode out of the room. She said the incantation and grabbed a towel that had been sitting next to the sink in the back. She walked over and tied it tight around the guy's leg to help slow the bleeding. She hadn't hit an artery, but he was still bleeding. She would need to get him to a hospital soon. She should feel bad that the young man had to suffer the injuries of the demon, but she didn't. He would recover and not remember anything about what happened. When she was finished, she went to find the rest of them. She knew they were needed to help with the other issues happening in Denver. The demons had been pretty slick to go after the Shikari members kids. It would be harder for them to take out any demons they needed to when they wore the skin of those they loved, especially children. Sloane took a deep breath. She saw Erik and Jessie in the back room.

"I thought you were supposed to be resting in the car, Jessie?" Sloane stepped next to her in the room.

"My sentiments exactly," Erik said.

"Whatever, I came back to see what you found out. Besides, I'm fine." She shrugged, but the color of her face indicated she was not fine, not by a long shot.

"Let's get you back to the car, and we can talk there. Then we can plan our next move." Erik took a step and slipped his arm around Jessie's waist. He guided her out of the room and toward the back entrance. Mike had pulled the car around to the back-parking lot and idled while the three got in. Erik guided Jessie to the back where the other man was passed out against the window.

"Why didn't you wake him up?" Erik asked. "We could ask him where he'd been taken. What he knows about what's going on."

"I figured I'd wait for you before I woke him. Maybe once we get him to a safe place or something. I called Magnus. He said we could go back to his place since we're in Denver. He's with Bryant, now." Mike explained.

Sloane turned around to look at Erik. "We need to call the cleaners in to get that guy to the hospital. I tied off his wound, but he's already passed out. They need to deal with the clean-up. We don't have time. We need to get to Mullen."

"On it." Erik pulled out his phone and dialed.

"Mullen? What's going on at Mullen?" Mike asked.

"The demon said that's where they are, right now. The demons possessed all the Shikari kids knowing we would have a hard time hurting children, especially since they are our children. It's ingenious really. I think that's where everyone rushed off to. We need to get there, pronto. It helps that we stopped them from bringing the amulets, but they're still going to need help." Sloane looked meaningfully at Mike. He nodded and put the car in reverse to back out of the space.

Sloane looked back to Jessie. "You up for another round, or do we need to get you to Magnus' before we go to the school?" She looked at Jessie's ashen face and knew the answer. She needed to get treated, but she'd never admitted to it. She couldn't blame her. Sloane would do the same thing.

"I'll be fine, just get to the school."

Erik's eyes blazed as he hung up his call. "Like hell, you need to get her back to the house. She can't fight anymore today." He took Jessie's hand. "Jess, you need to go take care of yourself. We can take care of the demons." His voice was soft as he spoke.

"No, you need me to freeze them. No one should have to fight their child, Erik." Her voice shook with intensity.

He reached his hand to cup her cheek. "Jess, you need to rest." He gazed into her determined eyes. "Fine, I'll do what I can before we get there. Sloane, you want to grab what we have for first aid in the center counsel. I can at least try to bandage this before you go in again." He sighed in defeat.

Sloane opened the center counsel to find a box. "Damn, there's a first aid kit in here." She pulled it out and handed it back to Erik.

"Thanks." He opened it and found gauze, alcohol pads and tape. He took the cloth that had been tied around her arm and Jessie winced. "Sorry, babe." He kissed her lips softly.

"It's okay, just do what you gotta do." Jessie looked into his eyes and nodded once.

Mike took a corner, and they both slid into the guy next to them. "Mike, do you think you could not take the corners quite so fast? I'm trying to bandage Jess, back here."

"Ten-four." He said and eased off the gas pedal.

Erik cleaned the blood off Jessie's arm with the alcohol wipes. She winced when he went over the bullet hole. He took out the gauze roll and held the end against her arm. "Can you put your finger here to hold this a moment?" She placed her finger to hold the gauze, and he wrapped it around her arm. She moved her finger when he reached the spot and continued wrapping it tightly around her arm until it was a few rows thick. He took out his pocket knife and cut it. He held it and placed two pieces of tape on end. He admired his work a minute then met Jessie's eyes. She smiled warmly at him.

"Thanks," she said.

He leaned in and touched his lips to hers in a gentle kiss. She nipped his lip and reached her hand up to grip his head closer to hers. She opened her mouth and slipped her tongue hungrily into his mouth. He kissed her back as though he were starving for her. She gripped his hair between her fingers and enjoyed the taste of him. The vanilla mint combination was intoxicating. He rubbed his hand on her thigh. She gripped her fingers tighter before pulling away and closing her eyes. She dropped her hand to his chest, and she could feel his heart race through her fingertips. She steadied her own heart and breathing as she stared into his eyes.

He smiled, "There, that put a little color back in your cheeks." He winked.

She took a deep breath and met his eyes. His were on fire with desire. She moved her hand up to his shoulder to massage his shoulder a second then dropped her hand. "I promise we are finishing this discussion later." She whispered.

He dropped his head next to her ear. "You can count on it." He breathed. She could feel his hot breath on her neck before he withdrew. A shiver ran down her back.

"If you're done, ahem, bandaging Jessie, could you wake up the guy next to you? It'd be nice to have some perspective on how he ended up in the building with the demons but not possessed." Sloane turned slightly to roll her eyes at Erik before facing forward again.

"Sure," Jessie turned to place her hand on the guy's shoulder. "Hey, wake-up." She pushed him a little harder.

Sloane reached inside of her bag and handed Jessie a capsule. "If he didn't wake to you two back there, I don't think he'll wake up to a few shoves. Try this."

Jessie took the capsule and snapped it under his nose. He blinked and sprang forward. "What the hell?" he said. "Where am I?" He looked to Jessie then Erik.

"You're in a car. Don't worry we're Shikari. We got you away from the demons who took you." She rolled her voice to be soothing.

"Oh shit, where's my daughter?" he asked, eyes darting around the car. "Did you get her?" His voice became panicked. He reached his hand out and gripped Jessie's arm. "Tell me you got to my daughter?" he pleaded his eyes sad.

"Ouch, can you let go? I just got shot." He dropped his hand. "Thank you. She wasn't in the building with you. We're on our way to the Muller school because demons have possessed students there. Could your daughter be one of them?" Jessie asked. He focused on her as she spoke.

"Yes, she goes to school there. They grabbed her first. I tried to fight them, but one of them knocked me out before I could do any real damage. Her mom lives in Colorado Springs. I need to call her. Do any of you have a phone?" He asked.

Erik handed him his. "Who's her mother?"

"Caroline, she'll freak out when I tell her I lost our daughter. She's at the very least going to kill me." He began dialing, and Jessie placed her hand over his on the phone.

"She already knows," she said, her voice low.

"What? How could she already know?" he asked.

"She was with us when we arrived. She must have heard something. She took off, and my bet is she's at the school, now with the others." Jessie explained.

"Oh, others? What others?" he asked.

"My father is Bryant. I talked to him before we went in to get you. He said there was an emergency, and they were all headed there. We didn't know what it was until we got it out of the demon here. Now we're going there to help them." Erik said.

"Why didn't you go right away? I'm only one; they have many," he said.

"Because they had me, too," Sloane said. She waved a hand up but didn't turn around. She was slumped in her seat as Mike focused on driving.

"Oh, I see," he said.

Mike took the next turn, and they could see the school in the distance. "You guys ready? Because there's going to be quite the battle inside here." Mike looked to Sloane and reached his hand out to take hers.

"Always," she squeezed his hand tight.

Chapter 17

"Okay, do we have a plan or are we just charging in?" Erik asked from the backseat.

"Erik, why do you always need a fucking plan?" Sloane asked, throwing her arms up.

Mike placed his hand over Sloane's and shook his head. "We don't know what's going on in there, so for now, we're charging in. We don't have much of choice."

"Well, I'll go first. That way I can freeze any demons as I go. As long as they don't have the amulets, I should be able to freeze them," Jessie said.

"I also know the school. I can lead you through it. I'm Nick, by the way. I don't know if Caroline told you anything about me." He shrugged. "She isn't a forthcoming person, so I doubt it."

"No, she hasn't told us anything about you. We know a little about your daughter and that she lived with you. That's about it." Jessie said.

"Yeah, as I said she isn't forthcoming. I think she likes to keep the world from knowing about us. Our powers might have something to do with it. She keeps us protected, even from our people." He looked from Jessie to Erik.

"I completely get that." Sloane huffed up front. "So, this whole getting to know you stuff is fun and all, but we kinda need to get in there right now."

"Yes, of course. My daughter may be in there." He moved his hand to the door and jumped out. Erik grabbed Jessie's hand, and they both exited the car. Sloane and Mike got out at the same time.

"Does anyone need weapons? I have a duffle in my trunk." Mike asked.

"I could use something. Although, I'm not sure I need it." Nick followed Mike to the trunk. He tucked an XDS-9 into his waistband and patted Mike on the back. "Thanks, man."

"Anytime." Mike closed the trunk. Jessie, Erik, and Nick took the lead. Mike and Sloane followed close behind.

Erik stopped momentarily at the door to gaze into Jessie's eyes for just a moment, then opened the door for them to stroll through. He shook his head as Sloane bounded on the balls of her feet ready for anything. The entryway was empty. Erik stopped to listen. He figured he could find where they needed to be quickly. Most of the thoughts were coming from the chapel.

He glanced toward Nick. "There's fighting in the chapel."

He narrowed his eyes at Erik. "Can you hear thoughts, too?" He asked.

"Yes," he hustled toward the chapel. He wanted to reach out to Caroline, but he wasn't sure he could. He'd never tried.

Caroline made it seem easy, but her power may be different from his. He reached out as if he were trying to talk to her. He pictured her sitting across the table from him and sent out his thought. *Caroline, Caroline, are you there? Are we heading to the chapel?* He stopped and listened. He blew out a breath when nothing happened. Then he felt a small flicker in his mind. *Get your damn walls down, idiot!* Caroline screamed in his head. *Get your ass in here, now. We need you.* She projected. He reached the door of the chapel and threw it open.

He saw Bryant first, punching a young man in the nose. The boy doubled over and held his hand to his face as blood streamed over his lips and chin. He saw Caroline was fighting hand to hand with another female girl. He looked to Jessie, "Freeze them, quick. They're all possessed students and Shikari. Please, Jess, we have to save them." His gaze looked desperate as he scanned the room.

She raised her hands and froze the students nearest to them. She began running to the back of the room, and Erik followed. She froze as she ran. Some students didn't freeze as she went, but she didn't stop until she'd made it around the room. The students who hadn't frozen were being knocked to the floor by other Shikari members in the room.

Caroline walked toward Erik and Jessie. "It's about time you got here. It took you that long to get through the damn building?" She scolded.

"Well," Nick stepped forward. "They were saving me."

Caroline's mouth dropped, she recovered and closed it quickly. "Oh, it's good to see you, Nick."

"Is it?" he asked, narrowing one eye at her.

"Of course, when I heard about students being possessed at the school I rushed over here." She looked to Erik and Jessie. "You understand why."

"Yes, is your daughter okay?" Jessie asked.

"I don't know. I got here and started helping. I haven't been able to find her in the crowd of students." Caroline looked around frantically. "I need to find her." Caroline rushed around the room checking each of the students as she went.

Sloane walked up to Jessie and Erik. "Looks like we missed all the fun." She crossed her arms over her chest. Mike walked up behind her and rubbed her shoulders.

"We've got bigger problems. They've possessed more students at the school in Colorado Springs along with adults there. If they can accomplish that, they will go after the order. I don't know how they've been able to possess Shikari, but they are. We need to figure out how before this goes any further." Erik said.

Bryant walked up to the group. "I couldn't agree more. We need to contact the order. Let them know what's going on here. They need to be aware that they may be next."

"Isn't that what you normally do, being the head of the Minneapolis area and all?" Sloane said a little too cocky, and Mike squeezed one of her shoulders a little harder. Bryant glared at Sloane, and she felt a wave of calm spread over her. "Oh, no, you don't. You can't use your power on me. I know better."

"This isn't the kind of thing you discuss over the phone, dear. We wouldn't know who was possessed over the phone. If they've already gotten to them, we will tip our hand. The demons cannot become aware of our knowing. We're going to need to go there in person." Bryant explained.

"Well, we need to take care of the school here, first." Sloane shot back.

"I do believe we need to split up. Some of us will need to travel to the order to warn them. Sloane, Mike, Jessie and Erik, I trust you can stay and take care of the school." Bryant looked to Erik then Sloane.

Mike wrapped an arm around Sloane's waist, and she leaned into him.

"We should be getting to the other school. We believe the headmaster there may be a leader of the demons. He seems to be masterminding the operation here in Denver. We need to find out who's behind all of this if we have any chance of stopping these demons." Erik explained.

"Agreed," Bryant said. "Erik, Mike, Jessie, and Sloane should go back to Colorado Springs. You can handle the situation there. You'll need Shikari hunters from Denver to help. There very well may be quite a few possessed at the school. Coordinate with Magnus. He'll get you the help you need." Bryant stroked his beard as he directed everyone.

"Okay, so we regroup after everything is cleaned up here?" Jessie asked.

"I think we need to wait until tomorrow to go after the other demons in Colorado Springs. We'll need to keep this quiet until then, so the other demons don't know we've stopped them." He stopped and gave Jessie a meaningful look. "Jessie, you need to rest. You're supposed to be recovering from a bullet wound. We need to recuperate before we go into another battle." Erik said.

"We should go back to Caroline's house." Jessie looked around the room. Various students were being dispossessed and helped. There was a young girl being held by a woman in an iron embrace. Many were being attended to and bandaged. "Speaking of Caroline, where is she?" Jessie asked.

"I don't know. She went to look for her daughter. Do you think she found her in another room?" Sloane glanced around, but there was no sign of her.

"We should go find her. Make sure her daughter is alright." Jessie strode to the door of the chapel.

"I'm going to find Magnus and discuss who should be going to Colorado Springs and Kansas City. I will meet up with you shortly." Bryant turned and headed toward the pew.

"I'll try to reach out to Caroline." He concentrated and tried to send his thoughts out to her.

Caroline, where are you? Erik projected.

He got a quick reply. *Erik, I can't find her. She's not here. What happened to her?* Her thoughts were jumbled and panicked.

"We need to find her. Caroline's daughter is still missing. She's freaking out." Erik hurried down the hall in the direction of Caroline's frantic thoughts.

They found her in the band room. Jessie stepped in front of her. Caroline whipped her head around. "Her stuff's here, but she's not. Why isn't she here? I found her backpack in the practice room. I thought maybe she hid in here, but I can't find her anywhere. Come on we have to keep looking." Caroline raced out of the room.

"Okay, everyone split up. We have to find Caroline's daughter, Nicole." Jessie followed behind Caroline.

"Do they just forget I'm a tracker?" He glanced to Sloane and jerked his head back toward the band room. She followed him to the girl's backpack. He picked it up and closed his eyes. He took a deep breath. "She's not here." He opened his eyes slowly and spoke low. "Go let them know. We are wasting time here. She's not in the building." Erik nodded and raced to find Jessie and Caroline.

Sloane took Mike's hand. "Any idea where she is?"

"I think they are on the way to Colorado Springs. I think she's possessed; her essence isn't as strong as another Shikari. I can't explain it exactly, but it's faint. I'm not sure how long I will be able to feel her if they get too far away. We need to head toward her now." Mike carried the backpack and headed in the same direction as Erik.

Erik was stopped at the end of the hall. His hand was on Caroline's shoulder. She was hunched over, gripping her stomach. Mike called, "Come on we need to go after her."

Caroline snapped up and went running in his direction. Her eyes wide, "You know where she is?"

"I can sense her, but it's faint. We need to go before I lose her altogether."

"Okay, lead the way." The determination in her voice was strong.

"Alright, let's get to the car. Caroline, give your keys to Erik. He and Jessie can follow us in your car." They raced to the exit and into the cars. Mike raced onto the highway and sped toward Colorado Springs.

"Could she be going home after her school was attacked? Maybe she was coming to see me." Caroline said as she realized they were heading out of the city.

Mike exchanged a glance with Sloane. "Yeah, maybe," he said focusing back on the road.

"That's got to be it. She got away from the fighting and ran. I taught her well and with her gift. I'm sure she got away." Caroline was speaking more to herself than anyone in the car.

Sloane looked over to Mike, and her lips thinned into a hard line. "Are you going to tell her, or am I?" She asked Mike.

"I think we should wait." Mike cautioned.

"She deserves to know."

"Fine, Caroline, your daughter's essence is faint because I think she's possessed by a demon," Mike spoke smoothly.

"What? That can't be she's too powerful. She'd never let herself get possessed by a demon."

"What do you mean, she's too powerful?" Sloane asked.

"She has a special gift. Unlike any, I've heard of in the Shikari. It's why I try to keep her away from other Shikari members. She went to school here, but she knew not to talk about her abilities. Just like she's not supposed to discuss Nick's ability." Caroline took a deep breath. "I guess it's important for you to know. So,

Nick's power is to manipulate the elements, and I can read minds as well as send thoughts. My daughter, well, she can influence your thoughts. It's like she can plant a thought in your mind and compel you to act on it. That's why I try to keep her protected. She lives with Nick because he can protect her. They both have very special powers. It's also why we chose to live in Colorado Springs rather than Denver. Nick chose to move to Denver after the, ah, the divorce." She sat back in her seat, chewing her lip anxiously.

"Wow, that's one hell of an ability." Sloane blew out a breath.

"We need to save her. That's my baby." Caroline gripped her hands into fists.

"Of course, Caroline we'll get her back," Mike said giving Sloane a look. She rolled her eyes back at him.

"Did anyone tell Nick?" she asked. "He should know."

"He's in the car with Erik and Jessie. They're following us. He said Nicole was with him when they took him. When he woke in the car on the way to the school, he asked where she was. I'm sorry, we didn't know at the time the demons had her. We'll get her, Caroline. We won't stop until we do." Mike reassured.

Chapter 18

The shrill of the phone broke the silence in the car. "Who is it?" Jessie asked.

"Bryant," Erik swiped his finger over the phone to answer. "Hey, what's up?"

"Magnus is sending help your way. They will be there in the morning after everything is cleared up here. We're still discussing going to Kansas City to alert the order in person. We'll work out the details, and I'll inform you of our decision."

"We may need help sooner than that. Demons have taken Caroline's daughter. We're in route to Colorado Springs. We're following Mike, who is tracking her. Any chance we can get some help sooner than tomorrow?" Erik asked.

"I'll confer with Magnus and let you know as soon as I can," Bryant said.

"Okay, call me back. We need to know. If we track her to the school, we're going to need help. Is there anyone in Colorado Springs you can call to help?" Erik asked.

"I'm not sure. I'll get back to you." He hung up.

"Ah, okay." Erik set the phone down in the center counsel.

"Bryant said they're sending help but not until tomorrow. I let him know we needed them sooner. He's getting back to me, I guess. He hung up kind of abruptly." Erik shrugged and focused on keeping up with Mike who was racing down the highway.

"Caroline is the head of Colorado Springs. She could call in help sooner than Magnus. I'll call a few friends and let them know what's going on. I'll see what assistance I can round up." Nick sat back in the seat and began scrolling through his phone.

"If the battle is at the school, I'm not even sure we have enough people in the area to go against them. The school had so many possessed teachers and students. They've been working on this plan for months. I can't believe no one was noticing." Erik shook his head. They weren't supposed to be able to possess hunters.

Erik's phone began ringing again. "It's Mike. Hey, man, we're right behind you."

"I know, I lost Nicole. I could sense her one minute and the next she was gone. We're going to drive by the school, but I don't think it's a good idea to go in." Mike's voice was somber.

"No, there are way too many possessed to go in. Bryant and Magnus are sending help, but they won't be here until tomorrow. Bryant was going to check with Magnus to see if they can get here sooner. Nick is making a few calls to friends in this area, but we can't just charge in." Erik explained.

"I agree, Sloane is trying to get that exact point across. I think we should rendezvous at Caroline's before we go to school.

Figure out who can aid us and how to strategically go in, so we don't all end up possessed or dead." Mike huffed into the phone.

"Sounds like a plan. I'll follow you there," Erik said.

"Ten-four," Mike said.

Erik hung up the phone and looked to Jessie. "We're heading to Caroline's. Caroline's daughter suddenly went off Mike's radar. We don't want to go to the school without a plan." Erik brushed his hand through his hair.

"Yeah, I heard most of what you said. I think it's a good idea to go back and figure out what we are going to do. Now, how in the hell are they going to get Caroline to go along with us when it's her daughter?" Jessie shook her head and reached over to take Erik's hand.

"No idea, let's just hope they can." He looked back in the mirror to Nick who was talking on the phone to someone behind him, not paying attention to their conversation. Erik knew that if it were his child, he wouldn't be going to make a plan. He'd be charging in guns blazing. He also knew he'd probably get himself dead. He glanced back in the mirror again. He was pretty sure Nick was a reasonable guy. He'd probably listen to them and go with them to the house. Erik wanted to listen in on his thoughts but refrained. He looked over to Jessie. She had her hair pulled up into a high ponytail. He wanted to pull it out and watch her hair fall past her shoulders. He hated when she wore her hair up. He shook his head and focused on the road, following Mike.

They pulled into Caroline's driveway. Erik put it in park and watched as Caroline bolted out of the car, slamming the door.

"Oh shit, I gotta go. I'll call you back soon or better yet, just come to Caroline's house. We need all the help we can get." Nick hung up the phone and rushed out of the car after Caroline.

Erik looked to Jessie. "Well, this should be fun."

"Come on, Erik. It's her daughter we're talking about. We just brought her home instead of to the school where her daughter is. Wouldn't you be pissed off?" Jessie slid out of the car, closing the door before Erik could respond. She hurried after Nick and Caroline into the house.

Erik got out and walked up to Mike and Sloane. "So, I take it she didn't want to come here."

"No, she's pissed off that we didn't drive straight to the school. I didn't want even to chance driving by, for fear she might jump out of the car. She's not all that pleased with us, right now. I'm hoping Nick can calm her down." Mike wrapped his arm around Sloane's waist.

"I tried talking sense into her, but she didn't hear it. We can't go in there without more people. Even I can see that. Usually, I wouldn't care, but there's no way we'd even have a chance at the school without help. They already know Caroline and me. We'd be spotted and taken before we could even locate Nicole." Sloane rested her arm over Mike's on her waist. She leaned back into him and closed her eyes a moment. Erik was happy to see his sister with Mike. He hoped this meant she might stick around. Although, they were close when they were young, and that didn't stop her from leaving. Erik shook his head, trying to dislodge the thought. The fear she would leave was always there. He wasn't sure he'd ever been free of it. Everyone around him left eventually. The only constant he had was his father.

"Well, we better get in there." Sloane huffed and walked toward the house. Mike shrugged, took a step, patted Erik on the shoulder and followed Sloane inside.

"This could get interesting," Erik said before following them inside. When he walked through the door, Caroline was pacing frantically around the room. Jessie threw her hands up, "Caroline, can you stay here until we have some plan and more help? We need you. You're the head of this area. Call others, get help before you race in and get killed. You know, it's in the best interest of Nicole to wait." Jessie took a step toward Caroline and put her hand on her shoulder. "Please, Caroline. We need you."

She stopped and looked into Jessie's eyes. "Okay, Jessie. I'll try."

"Alright, Nick, who have you already called?" Jessie looked to Nick.

"I called the Steele's and Carrie and Jon. They'll be on their way here shortly. I didn't call Brett. I figured I'd leave that call up to you, Caroline." He stormed into the kitchen, hitting the door open on his way.

"Ah, okay. Caroline, who else should we be calling?" Jessie looked to Caroline.

"I'll take care of it." She picked up her purse and strode into the kitchen behind Nick.

"What was that about?" Sloane asked.

"Probably, why they're divorced. Let's give them a few minutes. Erik, when was Bryant getting back to you?" Jessie asked.

"I'm not sure. He said he would call as soon as he talked to Magnus."

"Okay, can we start making a plan for how we'll enter the building. How many people would be ideal for that? Erik, any idea how many possessed we're talking about. You were listening to their thoughts. I figure you've got about as good an idea as any of us for how many we're up against." Jessie studied him.

"Jess, we're looking at about forty, maybe more. I'm not sure exactly, but there were quite a few. We have no way of knowing how many they've added since we were there last." Erik bent his head looking grim.

"I'll go grab the blueprints of the school. I had Magnus get these for me before I left Denver. They're in the car. I'll be back." He strode out to the car.

"Sloane, any chance you can try to get a vision? I know they can suck, but we could use a bit of supernatural help right now." Jessie looked to Sloane.

"I can try. I'll need to focus all of my energy on it. I'll be up in my room. If you need me, come find me." She flew up the steps.

Mike walked through the door. "Where'd Sloane go?"

"She's upstairs working on getting a vision," Erik said.

Jessie bent to move the crystal bowl from the coffee table. "Here lay those out here." She stood up and wobbled a little on her feet. Erik was next to her in a second, placing his hands on either side of her waist.

"Jessie, I know you think you're superwoman, but you were shot a few hours ago. You're not ready to go running into another fight. We're not going to be able to go to the school today, anyway. Maybe you should go rest." Erik cupped her cheek with his hand. He gazed into her eyes. She closed her eyes and nodded.

"Okay, maybe you're right. How about I sit here for a little while and help you guys plan? Then, I promise, I'll go get some rest." She placed her hand over Erik's on her face.

"Okay, here sit." Erik sat next to her on the sofa.

Mike spread the plans onto the table. "Okay, there are four different buildings. There's a courtyard between them. There's a parking lot for each building and a road that wraps around each building. The headmaster's office is the first building you see when you drive up the hill. That's where I suspect many of the possessed adults congregate, so we'll want a team going in there first." Mike pointed to the first building. "Okay, so there's six entrances, two each on the North and South ends and one each on the West and East ends. We won't be able to cover all the entrances, but I believe if we want to go in unnoticed, we should take the West entrance, it's near the janitorial and loading dock. It might even be a good idea to go in disguised as one of the delivery drivers. We could manage it with a little help from Magnus. That guy has connections like no one I've ever met. I think it might have something to do with his side weed business, but it's to our advantage, so hey." Mike shrugged.

"I think that could work." Erik leaned forward studying the plans before them. Jessie had lounged back against the couch. Her eyes drooped, but she nodded her head as Mike spoke. Erik turned toward her. "Jess, babe, please go up and get some rest. I'll come and get you the minute I know anything new. I can fill you in on anything when I get up there." He lifted her hand to his lips and kissed it gently. "Come on; I'll walk you up." Erik stood and pulled her up with him.

"Ouch," Jessie said.

"Oh, sorry babe," Erik blanched, his eyes were wide as he dropped her arm.

"It's just my bad arm. I'll be fine." She wobbled. Erik reached his hands out to steady her.

"Yes, you will after some rest. Come on." He wrapped his arms around her and guided her up the stairs. She flopped down onto the bed. Erik bent and slipped off each of her shoes. He reached his hands to unbutton her jeans. Her eyes flitted open, "Oh, I thought I was supposed to rest?"

"You are going to rest, babe. You'll be more comfortable resting if you're not wearing jeans. Besides, it's not like you're going to come back downstairs without pants on." He winked at her. He unbuttoned her pants and started sliding them down her hips. He bent to kiss her thighs, her calves; then he nibbled her toes after he pulled her jeans off. He crawled up next to her and captured her lips with his. He pulled the elastic band from her hair, letting her blonde hair fall back onto the pillow. He sighed, "Much better." He kissed her again, lingering gently massaging her tongue with his own. "Okay babe, get some rest." She reached her hand and twined her fingers in his hair. She pulled his lips back to hers.

She whispered, "Stay a minute longer." She kissed him, sucking his bottom lip before dropping back down to the pillow.

"Get some rest. I'll be back as soon as I can." He bent to kiss her forehead before he glided out of the room, closing the door quietly behind him.

Chapter 19

Sloane relaxed back against the pillows she propped against the headboard. She closed her eyes and tried to concentrate. She heard the door open and was enveloped in the familiar Sandalwood smell she loved. Her lips curved into a smile. She felt his weight on the bed, and his lips met hers. She moaned at the softness of his lips. She brushed her hands through his curls and clutched the back of his head in her fingers as her passion grew. She gripped his shirt with her hand and pulled him to her. He swung a leg over her and cupped her breast in his hand, rubbing his thumb over her nipple. It peaked through the thin fabric of her shirt. She pushed him away a moment to catch her breath.

"You know I'm supposed to be up here getting a vision. How am I supposed to concentrate with you here?" She opened her eyes to gaze into his. She still gripped his shirt in her hands. He leaned back straddling her on the bed. He looked so hot, his tight jeans. Sloane bit her lip as she assessed him. "Oh, fuck it." She pulled him back to her mouth and ravaged his tongue with hers. She reached her hand to unbutton his shirt. When she reached the last one, she slipped the shirt off him, feeling the contours of his shoulders. Relishing in his hard pecs. She pinched his nipple, and he smiled against her mouth. He backed away, and her mouth followed, hungry for more.

"Love, I'm not sure we have time for what you have in mind." Mike slid his shirt back onto his shoulders.

Sloane stuck her lip out in a pout. "We always have time for us. Besides, I need to relax. I can think of nothing better than you to help me with some relaxation." She rubbed her hand over his pecs, sliding them down to his abdomen, stopping at his waistband. She gazed into his eyes, biting her bottom lip as she pulled the button of his jeans free. She looked up through her lashed before slowly sliding the zipper down. She licked her lips and watched his gaze alight with a hungry desire.

"Dammit, Sloane." He captured her mouth with his. His kiss was hungry, and she knew he wouldn't stop her. She slipped her hand beneath his waistband. She wrapped her fingers around him and his breath caught against her mouth. His hands moved to grab the headboard on each side of her head.

"Sloane, I'm yours," he breathed against her mouth in desperation and desire.

"Always," she breathed.

"Always," he repeated against her lips.

After they were satiated, Sloane rolled back onto the pillows, "Oh Mike, you always know just how to help me relax." She placed her hand on her chest and felt her heart race beneath her palm. She placed her hand over Mike's chest, to feel his racing heart. Mike placed his hand over hers.

"Always, happy to oblige, love." He gazed down into her eyes. He brushed his fingers down her cheek. She gazed up into his eyes, brushing her fingers through his curls. She loved his black spirals that fell in different angles around his face. They were never the same. His dark eyes were locked on hers. She leaned up to kiss him tenderly. She wasn't sure when she fell in love with Mike, but at that moment she knew she loved him. She was happy. She turned her back on her old life to embrace what she'd always known she would return to. She had thought she loved Mike when they were young, but that was nothing compared to what she felt for him now. Her lips moved so easily against his. She sucked on his soft lips, slid her tongue along his, relishing in his gentle caresses as they kissed.

Suddenly, she was someplace else entirely. *What the hell,* she thought. *Looking around, she could tell she was outside of the school. The same girl from before was leaning against the building. She looked right at Sloane.*

"Well it's about time you got here," she said, eyeing Sloane.

"What do you mean, I'm not late?" She looked down at her phone.

"I'm not talking to you. I'm talking to Sloane." She studied her.

"What are you talking about?" the voice asked.

"Sorry Katie, I used you to bring Sloane here. She needs to be warned before they come to the school."

"Ah okay," the girl said.

"Sloane, you guys can't come to the school, yet. They know about Mullen. They're planning for you. There are too many of

them, and they've possessed too many students who have powers. There has to be another way. We need to separate the students who are possessed from the ones who aren't. I can help you. I go to school here, and many of us know what's happening. I'm going to meet with everyone tonight. We're going to plan to divide and conquer. We don't want to see our friends hurt. Meet me at the Cariboo off Woodman road; eight am sharp. We need to discuss our next move. You have to stop everyone from coming. It will be bad, really bad." The look she gave Sloane was grave.

"Ah okay, Chloe are you done now, cause I'm starting to get a headache," Katie said.

"Yes, remember, eight am. Sloane." Then she was gone.

Mike stared back at her, eyes full of concern. "There you are, love. Where did you go?"

"I think I got pulled into someone else's head by another Shikari. The girl's name is Chloe, and she goes to school here. She warned me not to let anyone go in until we meet. The demons know about Mullen, and they are preparing for us to go there next. She said the students have a plan to divide and conquer. She wants me to meet her tomorrow morning at Cariboo." Sloane yawned. "I wish my visions weren't so exhausting."

"It's okay, love. You got us what we need. I'll go down and tell everyone. Stay here, rest. I'll be back shortly." Sloane yawned again. Mike's mouth turned up at the corner as he looked at her.

"Okay, babe. Don't be gone too long." She sighed.

Mike bent to kiss her after he'd gotten dressed. "I wouldn't dream of making you wait too long." He swiped a few stray hairs from her forehead. Sloane sighed, happily. She heard the door close softly, and she drifted off to sleep.

"Hey, it's about time. Sloane get a vision or something?" Erik asked.

"Yeah, actually, she did. A girl from the school sent it to her. She wants Sloane to meet her at Cariboo tomorrow morning. The girl said they know we're coming, and she needs to meet with us before we go in. She has a plan to divide and conquer, I guess." Mike shrugged.

"A girl sent her a vision? That's new. Do you think we can trust her? How do we know she's not possessed?" Erik asked.

"I don't know. I guess we go with her tomorrow to check her out. If she's legit, we trust her, and they help us dispossess the demons at the school. It's a win, win from our standpoint." Mike sat on the couch next to Erik. "You come up with any ideas, yet?"

"Not really, I keep staring at this map. I heard Caroline and Nick argue for a bit. Now, it's crickets. I don't know where they went, but I didn't hear a car leave. They're still in the house somewhere. I was hoping to hear from them about how many people would be able to help. I still haven't heard from Bryant. I texted him a few minutes ago with no response." Erik brushed a hand through his hair.

"Stalemate, then. Maybe, we call it a night. Wake up early and be ready to fight. It's already been a long day. We could use the rest." Mike stood.

"Whatever, you just want to get back to whatever you and Sloane were doing." Erik narrowed his gaze.

"Oh yeah, like you don't want to go join Jessie." Mike side-eyed Erik. "Yeah, that's what I thought. Have a good night, brother." Mike patted Erik on the back and hurried up the stairs.

Erik shook his head. He wanted to at least check on Caroline before he disappeared. He didn't think she was going to just go to bed when demons possessed her daughter. He wasn't sure what they were doing, but he doubted they were sleeping. He walked into the kitchen, but it was empty. A glass of water was on the counter next to the sink. It was the only sign anybody had been in here. Walking down the hall toward the study, he stopped at the closed door. He wanted to walk in but thought better of it. When he turned to walk back to the kitchen, the door opened.

Nick was coming out of the room. "Oh hey, what are you doing out here?"

"I was coming to see how it was going. Jessie is resting since she was injured today. Sloane had a vision about a student at the school and is meeting her tomorrow at a coffee shop. I guess the students have a plan about dispossessing the students. I'm not sure what else we can do tonight until we know who all is going to help us. I haven't heard back from Bryant, either." Erik slouched realizing he wasn't sure what he should do.

"Caroline is in there calling friends in the area. We have friends coming from all over. We'll have at least fifteen to twenty people coming, but most won't be here until tomorrow. You might as well catch a few hours of sleep. It's going to be a big day tomorrow." Nick patted Erik on the back.

"I guess. I just don't feel like sleeping."

"How about a drink, then? I know I certainly could use one." Nick walked toward the kitchen. He pulled out two glasses and a bottle of Highland Park. He poured two finger's width into both glasses and slid one across the counter to Erik.

"Thanks," Erik took a drink from the glass. It was smooth going down. "So, how did you convince Caroline not to go to the school tonight?"

Nick scoffs, "That's what you want to talk about? Okay, Caroline is a reasonable woman. She knows if we go tonight, we'll lose. She just had to see reason and have actionable steps to take. She's making calls to everyone and arranging travel. She has something that will keep her busy and dull her thoughts about Nicole for the time being." Nick shrugged.

"Good, I wasn't sure she'd be persuaded. We might have to tie her down or something."

Nick laughed, "Yeah, good luck with that."

"Would you like to take a look at the blueprints we have for the school? I can go over what we discussed on the best way to go into the school. I'm not sure if it will still work considering Sloane will be meeting with one of the students tomorrow, but it's something to do. I'm too wired to sleep, yet."

"Yeah, I'd like to take a look. Caroline and I were going to send Nicole there at one point. If we were still together, she'd probably be going to school there." Nick looked down and shook his head.

Erik could hear the pain in his words but didn't ask about them. When they got to the plans, Erik sat and pointed to the West Entrance. "We think it'd be best to go in here undetected. We thought we'd talk to Magnus about getting a delivery truck, so we'd be able to blend in when we arrived. Mike said he thought Magnus would be able to help us get the truck. We could load everyone in the back. The delivery entrance has the fewest people. We also thought it would be unlikely any of them would be possessed like the people in the office." Erik explained.

"That's not a bad idea. You think Magnus can get the truck by tomorrow? I'm not sure I'll be able to hold Caroline off much longer. We should have enough people joining us by tomorrow afternoon. If we can get a truck by then, we'd be all set to go by late tomorrow afternoon. Does anyone know the delivery schedule or anything?" Nick asked.

"I'm not sure. Sloane could ask the girl tomorrow, or we see who we can find on the inside who might know. I can do some scouting in the morning. If I can listen to their thoughts about who they're expecting, we can match the truck or stop the truck before it goes to the school. That could be an option, too." Erik pulled out his phone. "I'm going to send a quick message to Magnus. I think it's weird my father hasn't called me back, yet." Erik typed a message about getting a truck to Magnus and asked if he had any people, he could spare to help them tomorrow. He included the details about Sloane meeting with one of the students to elicit help from them.

"I'm going to go inform Caroline of what's going on and see what she may know about the school and deliveries. I think we have a good start for tomorrow and she'll be appeased by this information. You should try to get some rest. I think it's a good idea for you to a scout who they may be expecting tomorrow, which means you may need to be at the school around six am. You might want to catch at least a few hours of sleep before then." Nick placed a hand on Erik's shoulder and looked at him, before standing to go back to Caroline. Erik sighed. He wanted to be with Jessie, but at the same time, he wasn't sure he'd want to let her go once he had her in his arms. Today scared him more than he was willing to admit. He let out a heavy breath and trudged up the stairs. He longed to wrap Jessie in his arms and hold her close to him. He also feared how close he came to losing her today. If that bullet had been a few inches over, she'd be dead. He couldn't think about that. He needed to hold her. Forget about today and relax, knowing she was safe.

He quietly opened the door. He took off his shoes, jeans, and t-shirt and slipped into the bed next to her. She moaned softly when he wrapped an arm around her and pulled her tightly against himself. He'd missed being this close to her after he'd broken it off. Today was a reminder of his reasoning, but he could never bring himself to do it again. He'd just have to get better at protecting her. He couldn't stand the thought of being away from her again. He rested his head on the pillow and blew a heavy breath over her neck. She placed her hand over his arm and rubbed.

"Erik, it's okay. I'm here." She snuggled closer to him. The friction of her hips against his boxers elicited an immediate response. He couldn't help it. He always had the same response to her closeness. He wanted to be insider her even now, sharing this tender moment. Every nerve in his body was excited by her closeness. He felt her like an electric current through his body.

She turned and placed her hand on his cheek. "I'm glad you finally came to bed. I missed you." She kissed him gently at first but then with growing need. She wrapped her arms around him and pulled him flush to her, she wrapped her leg around his waist, and he lowered his hand to skim her bare thigh. Their mouths moved with frenzied passion. She splayed her hands over his bare chest and rubbed her fingers over the light hairs on his sternum, scratching lightly. He laughed against her lips.

"Playful, are we?" He looked into her eyes lit with fire.

"Well, it took you so long to get back here." She smirked and scratched his chest again.

"I slept a while. Now, I want to enjoy being alive, with you." She captured his lips and clutched at his back with one hand while the other gripped his hair. She was fierce and hungry in her embrace. He was more than happy to give all of himself to her. He needed to feel her vitality as much as she needed to give it. He nipped her lip and went to memorizing her skin with his lips. Tonight, he wanted to cherish every inch of the woman he loved.

Chapter 20

"Oh coffee, how I love thee." Sloane gripped her mug in both hands and took a sip. Mike rolled his eyes at her but took a drink from his mug.

"Maybe, if you slept more, you wouldn't need coffee so much," Erik said as he stood in front of the stove, stirring the scrambled eggs in the pan before him.

"Shut up and finish breakfast. I'm starving." She smirked.

"Hey, don't talk to him like that. He's making us all breakfast. You should be nicer to him." Jessie walked behind Erik, pinching his butt. She leaned in to kiss his cheek. "I appreciate you making us breakfast."

"Thanks, babe. Sloane can make her damn breakfast." He scrunched his nose in her direction.

"Whatever, Erik you know you love me and would miss me if I were gone. Besides, who else here is going to give you shit? I'm just trying to keep you humble, little brother." She squared her shoulders.

"Humble my ass," Erik muttered under his breath.

"Okay, so let's get our morning straight. Sloane and Mike are going to Cariboo to meet Chloe. Erik and I are headed to the school to see what deliveries they'll be expecting. Then, we're meeting Scott at nine to get a truck. We will all rendezvous back here at say, ten to plan how we're going to the school. Caroline is meeting her friends and making sure everyone gets here. Anything I'm missing?" Jessie asked.

"What about Nick?" Mike asked.

"He'll be helping Caroline and meeting with the people Magnus is sending from Denver. He's been on the phone all morning according to Erik." She leaned against the counter and met Erik's eyes.

"I still can't believe you woke us up before the sun to do this. Just because you have to be at the school by six, doesn't mean I had to get up at the butt-crack of dawn. I don't have to be to the coffee shop until eight." Sloane huffed and took another drink from her mug wrapping both hands around it.

"We all needed to be on the same page. The best way to do that was to be in the same room. Besides, Erik offered breakfast. I know you'd roll your ass out of bed for breakfast." Jessie chided.

"True, I do love breakfast and coffee." Sloane took another drink. "Mmm, coffee."

"I think we can find something to do for a few hours, love." Mike winked at Sloane.

"Could you two not do that while I'm here? That's my sister. I'd rather not think about that, like ever." Erik dished the eggs onto six plates. Jessie opened the oven and took out a pan of steaming cinnamon rolls. She set it on the counter and began icing them. "Babe, you should wait a minute for them to cool first." He bent to kiss her on the cheek, and she set the knife down on the lid and turned.

"Whatever, I could hear Jessie all the way down the hall last night. What time did you two finally decide to sleep, or did you sleep?" Sloane narrowed her eyes at Erik.

"Sloane, do you mind?" Jessie said, placing her hand on her hip.

"Not at all, you sounded like you were having a good time." She winked at Jessie.

"Ugh, Sloane!" She turned and went back to icing the cinnamon rolls. Erik pinched her butt, and she jumped, then relaxed when she met his eyes. He bent and kissed her lips gently then moved to stand behind her, resting his neck on her shoulder, wrapping his hands around her waist as she finished.

He whispered next to her ear, "I had a good time." He nibbled her earlobe and backed away to put bacon on each of the plates. Jessie set a frosted cinnamon roll on each plate and walked two over to the table, setting them in front of Sloane and Mike. Erik took the other two and set them in the open spots. "I'm going to run two plates to Caroline and Nick. I know they haven't slept and could probably use some food." He walked down the hall to Caroline's study and was back, sitting to eat his food.

"Damn Erik, who knew you could cook?" Mike said as he shoveled eggs into his mouth quickly.

"I'll take that as a compliment since you barely came up for air to say it." Erik bent to eat his eggs.

"Yeah, bro this is delicious," Sloane said, finishing off her bacon and going for the roll.

When they were finished, Erik grabbed his leather coat and looked to Jessie. "You ready, babe?"

"Yeah, I just want to grab a few things upstairs. I'll be back in a sec." She bolted up the stairs.

"Mike, you'll call if anything changes." He looked to Mike expectedly.

He nodded. "Yeah, I'll call you after the meeting."

"Sounds good," He looked as Jessie came back into the room. "All set?"

"Yep, see you guys later." She walked out the door and to the car.

"So, you feel up to this today?" Erik asked Jessie when they were alone in the car.

"Of course, why?" She narrowed her eyes at him.

"Just checking, I know you put up a front to everyone else, but you can be honest with me Jess. If you're not up to this, you can take it easy. No one would fault you for it." Erik reached to take Jessie's hand, but she pulled her hand away. He turned quickly.

Her eyes narrowed, glaring at him. "Thanks, for caring or whatever, Erik, but I'm fine. I can handle myself, okay?" She said and crossed her arms over her chest.

"I know you can handle it, babe. You can handle anything. It's just that sometimes I worry you push yourself too hard for others.

I want to make sure someone is taking care of you." He placed his hand on her thigh and squeezed.

Jessie dropped her hands and gazed into Erik's eyes. "Thank you," she breathed. "I'm fine though, Erik. I promise. I need to be able to help later today. I'm the only one who can freeze the students. I don't want anyone to have to fight our kids. What the demons are doing isn't right. I want to make sure that no one has to fight their kid." She dropped her head and balled her hands into fists. Erik reached to take one of her hands. He understood. He couldn't imagine being in Nick or Caroline's shoes right now, and to think about them possibly having to fight their daughter. It was unimaginable. He squeezed Jessie's hand and drove the rest of the way to the school in silence. He pulled up and parked in the lot nearest the loading docks. He wanted to keep an eye on who was coming and going. He would bring back notes to the others about how many demons were in the building.

Jessie lounged back putting her foot up on the dash. Erik looked over at her foot and took a deep breath. He always hated it when girls did that. No guy would ever put his foot up on the dash. He had too much respect for his car. He looked back toward the building and began sifting through thoughts for something useful.

He heard the kitchen manager was expecting a delivery from the food wholesaler and Pepsi to fill the vending machines. He took a mental note and continued to listen. They were both supposed to be there in the afternoon which he wasn't too happy about. They usually received their food order early in the morning, so he could have it all put away before they had to serve. Now, the truck would be coming in the middle of the day. He would have to pull a few people off prepping for dinner to put the food away. He picked up the phone to see if Carlos could come in early to help. Erik knew he might have just found someone to help them.

He looked to Jessie. "Text Magnus and let him know the food truck is delivering late today. Sometime late afternoon. Also, text Nick and ask him if he can find out who Carlos is. He works at the school. He's coming in early to help put away the food. If we come in that truck, maybe we can get Carlos to help us so that we won't be noticed. If he's already expecting the truck and coming in just for that, it'll be perfect. I don't know how we got so lucky, but we did." He squeezed Jessie's hand.

Jessie reached for her phone and typed messages to the two. Erik continued to listen for how many demons were in the building. It was harder to tell since many of the people here were still sleeping. He slipped between dreams to see whose thoughts may be off. The demons wouldn't influence sleep, so they'd be dormant. He wouldn't have a good number until everyone was awake. No one had even come into the office, yet. The only people who were awake in the building were the kitchen staff and the cleaners.

"Jessie, I know this may sound crazy, but what if we went in and planted some bugs around the offices? Especially, say, Mr. Hall's office, so we could hear what was going on even away from here." He looked over to her, and she furrowed her brow in confusion.

"How would we do that? Aren't there people in the building, right now?"

"The only people in there are the kitchen staff and cleaners, and just as we thought, they're not possessed. We could slip in undetected before anyone else wakes up." His eyes were lit with excitement.

"I guess we could. Do you even have any bugs in here? We didn't exactly plan for this." She shrugged. "I don't think we'd have time if we had to go back for them."

"I have a few in my duffel in the back. It's the same one I always take when doing any recon. I keep bugs in there just in case. Today that will come in handy. It has come in handy a lot. It's why I always keep a stash of them in there. They are connected to my laptop so that I can listen in as far as ten miles away without interference. You up for it?" He looked over at Jessie. He was worried about her, but her face wasn't ashen and pale like it was yesterday. She had gotten rest and seemed to be doing good. He didn't want to put her in any unnecessary harm, but he could use her skills if he wanted to make this a quick run into the building.

She could easily freeze anyone as they went. It would be easy with her help. "Yeah, I'm up for it. We could easily slip in and out as long as all the people are out of the offices. You're sure that no one is in there? We won't have any surprises?" She focused her attention on Erik.

"I don't hear anyone. They could be wearing amulets, but it's not even seven yet. My bet is they're all still sleeping. We could sneak in easily, plant the bugs and be back in the car before anyone notices. It'll take ten, fifteen minutes, tops." He studied Jessie.

She nodded her head. "Alright, let's do it."

He took the key from the car and slipped out toward the trunk. He grabbed the bugs and tucked a 9mm into his waistband. He never went into a building without a weapon. He had another tucked into this boot. Jessie did the same, pulling her jacket down over her back. He looked her in the eyes.

"Ready?" he asked.

"Yep," she responded, nodding her head once.

"Alright, let's slip through the employee entrance. Mike was right; it's the easiest way to get into the building without being noticed. It's also the only door unlocked at this hour. If you see anyone, freeze them. It'd be nice not to have to answer any questions as we go." He took her hand in his.

"Got it." She squeezed his hand and walked alongside him to the door. He dropped her hand to open the door for her. No one was on the other side, so they walked down the hall. When they were approaching the break room, Erik reached his hand out to take Jessie's. He jerked his head to the side, and she nodded. She froze the few that were in the room and unfroze them after they'd strode by. She did the same when they walked by the doors to the kitchen. They made it to the stairs, and they both hustled up, Erik taking two at a time.

They reached the door to Mr. Hall's office. Erik reached for the handle, but it was locked. He swept his hand out giving Jessie space to work. She took two pins out of her ponytail and put them in the lock, twisting until it clicked. She opened the door, and they both slipped inside. Erik closed the door and let out the breath he'd been holding.

"Well, that was easy," he said.

"Dammit Erik, you're not supposed to say that. You'll jinx us."
Jessie shook her head.

"What? We'll be fine. As long as I have you, nothing will go wrong." He bent to kiss her.

"What the fuck? Seriously, you are trying to get us killed? You did it twice. Plant the damn bugs before the cavalry comes rushing through the door after your stupidity." Jessie stepped away from him.

Erik followed and grabbed her belt loops and kissed the crook of her neck. "How about we have a little fun while we're here." He whispered in her ear. He nibbled her earlobe and wrapped his arms around her waist.

"Are you crazy? First, you jinx us. Now, you want to spend more time here than we need to." She took a step forward, but Erik went with her. He cupped her breasts in his hands, massaging each nipple through her shirt. She moaned and leaned into him when his tongue dipped into her ear, and his fingers pinched each nipple. "Dammit, Erik. We don't have time for this." Her breathing became ragged.

"Come on, Jess. I will hear if anyone is coming. Haven't you always dreamt of doing it in the headmaster's office?" He continued to work his way down her neck, toying with her nipple in the process.

She turned and captured his lips. Raising both hands to his face. She wrapped her arms around his neck and pulled him into her. She kissed him passionately, winding her fingers in his hair. He responded instantly, his jeans tightening.

He moved his hands to cup her butt and lifted her. She wrapped her legs around his waist, and he carried her to the desk, depositing her on top of it. His lips still locked with hers. He lowered his hands to lift her shirt, cupping her bare breast beneath. "Mmm," she moaned against his mouth as he toyed with her peaked nipples. "Erik," she breathed. He raised her shirt above her head. She reached her hand behind her to take the gun out of her waistband and set it on the desk. He moved his mouth to suck and nibble her breast. She clutched his hair in her hand, moaning. Her head fell back as he continued to make her writhe beneath his mouth. He reached his hands to the button of her jeans.

He moved back to her mouth to capture her lips. One hand continued to pinch and rub her nipple; he lowered her down to the desk. He moved back to unzip her jeans. He slid the denim over her waist and froze. "Shit," he whispered and bolted upright. He leaned forward holding his hand out to Jess. "There's someone up here." He took her hand and pulled her down behind the desk.

"Erik, what are we doing?" She reached her hand up to pull her gun down off the desk. Erik popped up to straighten the few things they'd disturbed in their passion. He bent back behind the desk.

"It's not a demon, but if they open the door, it's better if they don't think anyone is here," Erik whispered.

"I told you that you jinxed us. What the hell were we thinking?" Jessie's eyes widened.

"We were thinking about having a little fun." He moved and nipped her lip quickly. "Now, shush, before he hears you." He put his finger to his mouth. Jessie bit her lip and looked toward the door.

Erik moved his hand to her face and cupped her cheek. He didn't like that they'd been interrupted. He looked down at Jessie's taut nipples. *Shit, where's her shirt?* He thought. He turned and peeked around the desk. Her shirt was on the floor next to the desk. He reached his hand out and grabbed it. He held it out to her. "Not that I don't mind your current attire, but here." He winked at her.

She slipped her shirt over her head. "Thanks," she mouthed.

"Have I told you, yet how happy I am you chose not to wear a bra today? Because I am, really, really, happy." He looked down at the two beads which were sticking out through her thin cotton shirt. He raised his eyebrows at her. She shook her head, hitting his arm playfully and rolled her eyes at him.

"I think the coast is clear. So, where were we." He moved to kiss Jessie. She put her finger up on his lips before he could reach her mouth.

"Oh no, you don't. We are planting those bugs and getting back to the car. There's no way we're getting caught in here when the demons show up." She tucked the gun back in her waistband and pulled her shirt down. Erik looked down to his too tight pants and back up to meet Jessie's eyes.

"Not even a quickie under the desk?" he smiled and stuck his lip out in a pout.

"No, it's your fault we're even here. Now, let's get this done and go back to the car. We have work to do." Jessie stood up and walked away from the desk.

Erik stood, trying to think of anything other than Jessie sprawled over the desk a few minutes ago. If he hadn't heard the guy outside, he'd be enjoying himself. He cursed his power and planted a bug under the desk. He'd already put one under the lamp when they'd come in.

"Last chance to finish what we started." Erik raised his eyebrows toward Jessie.

"No, let's go before we have any more trouble. They should be coming into the office soon."

"Ugh, fine." He crossed his arms over his chest. Jessie laughed her sweet laugh, and he couldn't help but smile.

"You're cute when your pouting. Don't worry we're not done, just done for right now." She winked and opened the door. No one was in the hall, and they took the same route back to the car. They had made it in and out without being noticed, and they had ears in Mr. Hall's office. They would be able to hear what was going on back at Caroline's house. Erik was happy with what they'd gotten done that morning.

Sloane leaned back in the cozy loveseat at Cariboo. The fire was lit in front of them, and both she and Mike clutched cups of coffee in their hands.

"I thought she was supposed to meet you at eight?" Mike asked. He moved his arm behind Sloane and rested it around her shoulders.

"She said eight, sharp. It's only five after. I'm sure she'll be here any minute. I should've asked her what she drinks. I could've gotten her a drink while we're waiting." Sloane snuggled closer into Mike, taking another drink from her cup.

The chime on the door rang, and Sloane looked up expectantly. Chloe strode in with another girl behind her. She saw Sloane, and they both sat in the chairs next to them.

"Hello, Chloe, nice to finally meet you," Sloane said, taking a sip from her coffee. "Can we get you something?" she asked.

"Uh, sure," she looked to Katie. "You want something?"

"Yeah, I'll get it." She stood.

"Cool, you want to get me the light roast, black." Katie nodded. She walked to the counter.

Sloane elbowed Mike, "Go with her."

"Fine," he stood and followed Katie to the counter. After she ordered, Mike extended his card to the cashier. "I got it," he said. Katie smiled and went to fill their mugs with coffee.

"Okay, Chloe, what did you have in mind for the school?" Sloane sat forward, setting her mug on the table in front of her and rested her elbows on her knees.

"Okay, so there are over thirty students that know about the possessions. We know at this rate it won't be long until they have all of us possessed. We have been watching helplessly because the teachers aren't teaching what they should be. All the books with the dispossession information have been removed from the school. We've been searching for ways to dispossess our friends but haven't had much luck. I had a vision of you coming to help, so I reached out to you. If we have a way to dispossess our friends we can start when we have them separated." Chloe took her cup from Katie and took a careful sip of coffee.

"Okay, we need to move a little faster. We are going in today. How fast can you spread the incantation to the students who aren't possessed?" Sloane asked.

"Ah," she looked over to Katie. "We can send out a mass text. We have to make sure it doesn't go out to any of the possessed students, but we can get it to them in minutes. As soon as we all have it, we can start dispossessing them. As long as we do it quickly, we should be able to start without anyone catching on. When are you guys going into the school? You know they know you're coming, right?" she asked.

"Yeah, we think we have a way to get in without anyone knowing we're there until it's too late. I don't want to give you all the details, just yet," she said.

"You don't trust me?" Chloe questioned. "Of course, you don't. You just met me. Okay, well what's the incantation. I'll send out a text. Maybe that will sway you into trusting us. If we can dispossess the students, you'll have a better shot at winning the fight. You guys don't want to go up against the students at the school. Some of us have some serious juice." She looked over to Katie, and she was nodding.

"Okay, hand me your phone," Sloane said. Sloane typed in what she needed and handed it back. "I put in my cell phone. You'll find it's an easier way to contact me." She smirked.

Chloe took the phone and messaged Sloane. "Now you have my number. Will you call me with a plan? I'll go back to the school now and see what we can do before you get there. The more students we can change the better. Then you'll only have the teachers left to deal with. Oh yeah, and Mr. Hall. That guy such a phony. He acts all nice like he's saving the school, but in reality, he's the one getting all the students possessed." She shook her head.

"Alright, we need to go meet up with our friends to continue planning before we go into the school. Oh yeah, Chloe, can you find a girl named Nicole and try to dispossess her? She's the daughter of my friend, and we'd like not to have to go against her. Could you try to find her for me?" Sloane asked.

"Yeah, I'll see what I can do." Chloe got up and nodded toward Sloane.

"Thanks, until we meet again." Sloane waved her hand in the air. They left and walked to the car.

Mike got into the car, "Well, that was a quick meeting. Do you think they'll be able to dispossess students without being caught in the process?"

"I don't know. I hope they can. Chloe seems smart, but I don't know anything about her. She jumped right in, so I hope she knows what she's doing. If not, we'll end up fighting the students. I'd like to avoid that if at all possible." Sloane took Mike's hand.

"I couldn't agree more, love." Mike looked into Sloane's eyes. Sloane noticed his mouth was tight with worry. She couldn't blame him. She was worried, too. They were only kids, fighting against demons.

"Okay, now we've handled the meeting. Are we going back to Caroline's? Erik and Jessie will be there shortly." Sloane tried to calm her nerves. Felling Mike's hand in hers helped.

"Yeah, we need to go back and talk with the others. Let them know about Chloe and see what they found out." Mike took the last turn and pulled into Caroline's driveway. "Shouldn't there be other people here by now?" Mike asked.

"I thought so. Maybe they just aren't here, yet. Our meeting was pretty quick." Sloane shrugged and got out of the car.

'Yeah, maybe." Mike said and followed Sloane into the house.

Chapter 21

Caroline was sitting in the kitchen, clutching a cup of coffee. "Hey, I thought there'd be more people here by now. It's almost ten." Sloane said as she moved to sit next to Caroline.

"They're coming. Some are just further away than others." Caroline shrugged.

"Did you get any sleep?" Sloane asked.

"No, I can't sleep with my daughter out there, possessed. I'll sleep when she's home safe." Caroline looked hollow. Dark circles rimmed her lower lashes.

"Aren't you worried you won't be able to fight if you're too tired?" She asked.

"No, I'm not." She lowered her head and took another drink of her coffee. "You'll understand when you're a mother." She muttered.

"O...kay, so, did you get the text from Erik?" she asked.

"Yes, Nick is finding out about Carlos. Magnus already got a truck for us to use. Jessie and Erik are picking it up now. They'll be parking it at a nearby dock. I called a friend. When we're ready, we can load up in the back at the dock. I wanted to make sure it was ready to go nearby." Caroline glanced at her watch. "They should be back here any minute. If you'll excuse me, I'm going to check on Nick. Hopefully, he found this Carlos to help us." She rose and trudged back to her office.

Sloane was concerned about her. She figured she'd be the same in her situation. She looked up, and Mike strode into the kitchen. "Hey, I think I just saw Erik and Jessie pull up. I thought they were bringing the truck?" Mike asked.

"They parked it at a loading dock nearby per Caroline. They couldn't exactly drive a semi down a residential street. Especially one so close to the mountains." Mike stood behind Sloane and began rubbing her shoulders. "You're too tense, love." He continued rubbing. Sloane closed her eyes as he worked to relax her.

Jessie and Erik came into the room. "Hey, so we parked the truck." Erik said, "How was the meeting?"

"Good, Chloe has the incantation to dispossess the students. She sent a mass text. They said they'd try to dispossess as many students as they could before we got there. I told her I would let her know when we were going in. I also sent her to try to find Nicole. She mentioned some of the students there have some serious powers that we don't want to go against. I'm hoping she focuses on dispossessing them, first. I can't imagine having to go against our own. Especially students." Sloane shook her head.

"Yeah, can you imagine being Caroline, right now." Erik sat across from Sloane.

"Ah, no and I'm worried about her. She doesn't look so good."

"She's not going to rest until we have Nicole. Can you blame her?" Jessie sat at the table next to Erik and reached for his hand. He gave it to her and squeezed.

"No, I just needed to say that. When she was in here, she looked worn. She hasn't slept any. I hope she makes it through the battle. It can be even worse when you're sleep deprived to make quick, accurate decisions. I'm just worried about her." Sloane clasped her hands together.

"Sloane, you live your life sleep deprived." Erik cocked his head to the side, giving her a knowing look. She narrowed her eyes at him.

"I know, I know." She shook her head.

"Okay, so what's next? We have the truck. Nick is working on Carlos. What should we be doing? I'm surprised no one is here, yet." Jessie looked around the kitchen.

"I said the same thing when I came in here to talk to Caroline. She said some were coming from further away, and they would be here soon. I thought they started calling last night? I'm surprised no one has arrived." Sloane shrugged. "I guess, I can try to get a vision while we're waiting." She slouched further. She didn't like the idea because her visions were often draining, but she needed to try.

"Okay, we have bugs planted in Mr. Hall's office. We'll listen in on what's going on to find the best time to go in. Magnus is working on stalling the actual food delivery truck until later. I think our timing is going to be around two to three this afternoon, but I'll let you know if anything changes." Erik stood.

"I'm going to make a few calls. See if I can get any more people here. I'll be up to join you shortly." Mike bent to kiss Sloane before walking out of the room.

Sloane walked to the fridge, to make herself and Mike a sandwich. She went up to her room to focus. Sitting at the desk, she looked at her phone. It'd been a long time since she'd checked on anything from her other life. Even the thought of opening Facebook gave her a knot in her stomach, but she wanted to know. She needed to at least see that everyone was okay. She was trying to distance herself from the life she couldn't go back to, but there was still a twinge of guilt for disappearing so abruptly. Amy knew what was going on, but she'd been calling. Sloane hadn't answered a single call. She wasn't ready to explain anything to her. She sighed and turned her phone upside down on the desk and took a bite of her sandwich. She needed to keep her head in the game.

She took a few steps over to the bed and slid to the middle. She cleared her mind of all thoughts. She focused on herself, her power. She focused on the future. After a few moments, Sloane huffed. She was sick of how temperamental her power was. She needed to be able to get visions when she needed them. Not whenever the universe felt like it. Mike opened the door and popped his head in.

"Mind if I join you?" he asked.

"Of course not. I made you a sandwich." Sloane pointed to the sandwich on the desk.

"Oh, thanks." He walked over to the desk and took a bite of the sandwich. "So, any luck?"

"No, I never get a vision when I want one." She clasped her hands in front of her. Mike set down his sandwich and slid in front of her on the bed. He took her hands in his.

"Love, you need to stop putting so much pressure on yourself. You'll get a vision when you need one. You know your power doesn't work on command. You've gotten lucky so far. Have you messaged Chloe about when we'll be there?" he asked.

"Oh, no. I probably should." She went to the desk to grab her phone. She grabbed their sandwiches and handed Mike his plate. She sent Chloe a message saying they'd be arriving at three. She didn't want to give her the details as to how they planned to arrive. She figured giving her the time would be good enough.

Her phone lit up a moment later. Okay, we've dispossessed about fifteen students. No Nicole yet though. I don't know where she is or what she looks like. Can you send a pic?

"I need to find a picture of Nicole." Sloane looked to Mike.

"There's a few in picture frames when you walk up the steps. I think they're her school pictures. The closest to the bottom is her most recent, I think." Mike explained.

"Okay, I'll be right back." She hurried to take the picture and sent it off to Chloe.

She came back, and Mike was brushing crumbs off the bed and setting his empty plate on the desk. He walked back to the bed and slid against the headboard. He patted the space in front of him. "Come here, love. I'll try to help you relax."

She slid in front of him. "Okay." He massaged her shoulders. She moaned as he dug his fingers into the muscles in her shoulders and back.

"Oh God, Mike. That feels so good," she moaned.

He bent to whisper in her ear, "I love you, Sloane."

She tensed, "What?" She turned to face him, eyes wide.

"I said, I love you." He blinked.

"Why would you say that?" She tensed. He couldn't love her. They were just having fun. She shook her head and looked down to her hands. She began picking at the cuticles on her nails. So much for relaxing.

"I said it because it's true, love. What's wrong? I would think you would love to hear me tell you; I love you." She felt his eyes studying her. She continued to pick at her cuticles. She had thought the same thing the other day, but she wasn't ready to tell anyone, especially him.

"We haven't even been together that long. How can you know you love me? Why would you say it, now? We were just having fun together." She got up from the bed and walked out of the room.

Mike sat, mouth open. Then he scrambled to follow her. "Sloane, Sloane, where are you going?" Mike called. She turned toward him in the hall.

"Downstairs," she stared at the floor. Mike placed his hand under her chin, lifting it so she would meet his eyes. Sloane could see the calmness in his eyes. She only felt fear.

"Love, we're about to go into battle, again. I didn't want you going into it without knowing how I felt. You don't have to say anything. I just wanted you to know." His eyes glistened in the light. She could see the gold flecks in his eyes as he watched her. She nodded slightly.

"Okay," she muttered softly.

"Come on, let's go back to the room." He held out his hand to hers. She looked down at it wearily, then back up to his eyes.

"I want to go check on, what Erik and Jessie have learned from listening to Mr. Hall. Maybe they know where Nicole is since Chloe hasn't been able to find her." She turned and hurried down the steps leaving Mike to stare after her.

Jessie and Erik were sitting on the couch with Erik's laptop on the coffee table in front of them. "Hey, hear anything interesting?" Sloane asked when she reached the landing.

"Yeah, but none of it is good. They have Nicole. They're using her to get others to do what they want. It's not looking good for us." Jessie looked back at Sloane. She walked over to take a seat in one of the chairs.

"That's why Chloe hasn't been able to find her." A moment later, Mike reached the living room. He met her eyes momentarily and sat in a chair across the room from her.

"Did you let her know we're going in at three?" Erik asked.

"Yeah, they've dispossessed fifteen students so far. Do you have any idea how many are possessed in there?" She asked.

"No, we didn't stay long enough to get an accurate number, but there are plenty. I'm hoping they put a good dent in it before we get there. I'm not sure we'll have enough of us to go up against an entire school of possessed Shikari. That would be a suicide mission if I ever heard one." Erik shook his head.

"I'm sure they have. I'll message Chloe in an hour for an update. How many of us will there be?" She asked.

"About twenty-five, I think. Caroline and Nick keep changing the number and Magnus is on his way here. Bryant is with him. They're putting off going to Kansas City until everything here is wrapped up. Magnus said he didn't feel right leaving when his city is in turmoil. He's bringing as many with him as he can spare. There are still demons in Denver he needs to deal with." Erik shook his head.

"I called in a few people I know from the area. You can add four more. They weren't happy to be pulled out of hiding, but they're coming for me." Mike looked to Erik. He nodded.

"Thanks, that will help," Jessie said.

"Why are they in hiding?" Sloane couldn't help herself.

"Some don't trust the order. Especially, if they have a particularly useful power." He studied Sloane. "You should understand that." His tone was biting as he spoke.

"I do understand." She shot back.

"Oh shit," Erik said. "What's going on with you two?"

"Nothing." They both said in tandem.

"Ah, okay, I don't believe either of you." Erik looked from Sloane to Mike. "You need to get your shit together because we need to fight in a few hours. The truck is already. We're just waiting on more people."

"We'll be ready," Mike said.

"Do we have a plan for how we're going into the building? Who is focusing on what? Anything like that?" Sloane asked. She knew Erik was the king of planning, and if she asked, he would forget all about their issues.

"Yes, Nick got Carlos to help us. He's Shikari, which was surprising. He's meeting the truck as expected. Jessie will freeze the other workers when he opens the door for them. We're going for the leaders in the offices first. Then we'll spread to the different buildings. Jessie will help as much as she can to freeze. The rest of us will spread out and try to dispossess without too much of a fight if possible. I'm hoping the students are taken care of by your friend. Do you think the students will help when we get there? Do any of them have similar powers to Jessie?" Erik looked expectantly toward Sloane.

"I'll check." She reached for her phone but remembered it was still up in the bedroom. "Oh, I left my phone upstairs. I'll go text her." She stood.

Mike stood. "I'm going with you."

Sloane's eyes widened. "Why? I'm just going to get my phone."

"We should talk," he said.

Erik looked between the two, "Yes, you should."

Sloane glared at him. "You promised you wouldn't read our thoughts, Erik." She spat out his name.

"It's obvious you two are having issues. It'd be good if you resolved them before we left."

"Ugh, fine." Sloane stomped up the stairs. Mike shook his head and followed her.

Sloane went right for her phone and messaged Chloe. Mike watched her. Then she put the phone down on the desk and met his eyes. He strode toward her, his eyes never leaving hers. He captured her lips with his. She gasped in surprise, and he slipped his tongue in her mouth. She savored his soft lips on hers. The hunger in his kiss. His hands tightened around her, she felt safe, and dare she say it, loved. He pushed her against the desk. He dropped his hands, skimming her thighs before gripping them and lifting her onto the desk. His lips moved from her mouth to her neck. She ran her hand through his dark curls. He drew in a quick breath.

He stopped and rose to look her in the eyes. "Sloane, love is it such a bad thing to be loved by me?" he asked. His eyes searched hers. She took a deep breath.

"No," she breathed.

"So, what are you so worried about?" he brushed his hands along the lines forming on the side of her eyes. He caressed her cheek with his fingers.

"I'm not ready. I can't say it back to you." She looked down and gripped her pointer finger with her other hand.

"Sloane love, you don't have to say it back. I still love you regardless." His eyes were soft, patient as they looked at her. He took her hands in his. "Love, I just wanted you to know. I don't want to lose you again. Please, just talk to me. Don't close up on me." He kissed her hands, then her lips. He was so gentle in his kisses. His lips caressing hers with feather-light pecks. He kissed her lips, her jawline, savoring every touch. He brushed his fingertips from the back of her neck down her spine. Sloane felt tingles go down her entire body as he savored her.

She ran her hands through his curls again. "You're amazing, Mike."

He smiled and met her lips with his. "Glad to hear it, love." He breathed the words against her mouth. She wasn't sure if she was ready to tell him, yet. She knew she didn't want to lose him, either. She wanted to stay with him. To keep him with her like this. Was that enough? His thumb flicked over her nipple, and her breath caught. For now, it would have to be. He wasn't asking for her to tell him, right now. He tugged at her shirt. She raised her arms as he pulled it over her head. He took her nipple in his mouth, and she'd forgotten her train of thought.

She wasn't sure how long they'd been in the bedroom, but no one had come looking for them. Mike gazed at her. His head propped on his hand as he lay on his side on the bed. He ran his hand down her face, and she stared back at him. She could stay in this bed with him forever. "This is enough," he said.

She closed her eyes. She wanted to say she loved him, she did. She tried to pull the words out. She took a deep breath. Instead, she said, "Are you sure?"

His laugh rang out, "Yes, love. I'm sure." He caressed the lines on the side of her eyes again. "If you're not careful, these worry line will stick." He kissed the side of each eye. "Stop worrying, love. I'm a very patient man. I know you. When you're ready, you'll say what you mean. You always do." He kissed her. "Now, come on. There's a fight happening, and I know you're not skipping it." He held his hand out to her. She took it, and he pulled her into his arms for a kiss. She giggled at his eagerness. "Oh, how I love the sound of your laugh." He kissed her again. He let her go, and she felt his absence immediately. She grabbed up her phone. She had messages from Chloe.

I don't know anyone with the power to freeze, but I'll ask around. Brb.

Nope, no one can freeze time. Super cool power. We'll be ready to help when you get here. We're spreading around campus, so we're not suspicious. We can dispossess while you guys go after Mr. Hall. lmk when you're here.

"Chloe says there's no one there that can freeze time. What powers do your friends have that are so secret?" She pulled her shirt back over her head. Mike had his jeans back on and was pulling his belt tight. She licked her lips at the sight. She wanted to jump him all over again. The muscles in his arms tightened. She wanted to run her fingers over his abdomen. Feel each curve of muscle under her fingertips. She bit her lip and walked over to him. She splayed her hands over his chest, rubbing. He smiled down at her.

"Couldn't resist me, aye?" He placed a hand over hers on his chest.

"You're so beautiful." She breathed and bent to lick his chest. She couldn't help herself she wanted to taste him. He lifted her hand to his mouth and kissed her palm.

"So are you, love." He smiled as she met his eyes. "We have some pressing matters to attend." His smirk was playful. She could tell he enjoyed her preoccupation with his body.

She juts out her lip in a pout, "Fine." She turned and went back to the desk and plopped down in the chair. He shook his head and laughed at her. He reached down and picked up his shirt. He pulled it over his head.

"You ready to go battle some demons?" he asked.

"I guess." She pouted.

"You love battling demons." He walked over and brushed his hand down her cheek.

"I love being with you, more." She looked up at him through his lashes.

"Good to know." He held his hand out to her. She slipped her hand in his and followed him out of the room.

Erik and Jessie had moved into the Kitchen. Caroline and Nick were there, along with about seven other people. Sloane looked around at each of them. Her eyes stopped at one guy, leaning against the counter, popping a grape into his mouth. His dark hair was swept back out of his face. One piece rebelled and hung down the side, next to his eye. He had the beginning scruff of a dark beard around his mouth. Sloane could tell he'd trimmed it all but around his mouth in a sexy goatee. Mike walked up to him.

"Hey Ely, it's good to see you, brother." Mike took his hand and pulled him into a quick hug with a single pat on the back.

"Yeah, you called, I came." He glanced over at Sloane. He raked his apprehensive gaze over Sloane. "This your girl?" He asked.

Mike looked over to Sloane. "Yeah, Sloane meet Ely." He held out a hand. She placed her hand in his. He turned it and placed a kiss on her knuckles, looking deep into her eyes.

"It's nice to meet you, Sloane." Her name sounded like velvet coming from his mouth.

Mike wrapped his arm around Sloane. Ely smiled up to Mike. "She's a beauty, Mike." He looked Sloane up and down again. Mike tightened his hand around her shoulders. Sloane looked to him, was he jealous? She narrowed her eyes on the tightness of his face. She'd never seen him jealous; her heart swelled at the thought.

"She is." Mike gazed into Sloane's eyes. She caressed his cheek with her hand. When he smiled, she could see the brightness of it in his eyes. They were about to go into a huge battle, and Mike's smile meant everything.

"Ahem," Erik stood next to the two. "Nice of you to finally join us. You know we have to leave in ten minutes, and you don't know what's going on." He looked at them with annoyance.

"Okay Erik, what's going on?" Sloane turned on her brother.

Mike wrapped his arm around her waist and pulled her into him. "Erik can you fill us in. We're all getting in the truck, right? Anything else we need to know." Sloane placed her arm over Mike's.

Erik looked down at Sloane, then up to Mike. "Yes, we're all going in the truck. Then we'll go through the offices as we discussed. A few groups are breaking off to go after the teachers in other buildings. Caroline is staying in the offices since her daughter is with Mr. Hall. Jessie will be going with her. I'm going to another team to the West. I can hear the thoughts of everyone, so I'm going to help distinguish between demons and Shikari." He paused to look at Sloane. "What's the status on Chloe?"

"There will be students spread around campus to assist. They know we're coming and can help identify those who are demons. She said they were still working on dispossessing as many students as possible. I need to text her when we're on campus." She explained.

"Good, they'll be a big help." Erik looked over to Caroline, and she nodded. "Looks like it's time to head to the truck." He walked over and took Jessie's hand.

Sloane looked to Mike, "You ready?"

"Always," He bent and kissed her lips quickly before following everyone outside.

Chapter 22

Erik bent to Jessie's ear. "I thought there would be more people here. What did Caroline say to you?"

Jessie clutched Erik's hand. "Nothing, just that more people were coming, but they were driving. I thought there would be more, too. She said we'd have twenty-five at least. I only count thirteen of us total. I'm not sure it's a good idea to go in with only thirteen of us." Jessie's eyes were creased in worry.

"Magnus and Bryant are meeting us at the truck. He has people with him. We should be up to twenty with them. I'm still worried. I don't like the idea of being away from you in the fight." He slid into the driver's seat of the car. Sloane and Mike slid in the seats behind them.

"What do you guys think? Do we have enough people?" Erik looked back at Mike. He was the more reasonable of the two.

"I was wondering about that, myself. I thought you said we'd have twenty-five. I only counted thirteen people including us. Caroline wouldn't send us in without enough people, would she?" Mike grasped Sloane's hand in his.

"Yes, when it comes to her daughter, she'd do anything. We have to save the school. Besides, Chloe and the other students will be helping us. There's no way they outnumber us if we have most of the students dispossessed." Sloane squared her shoulders in confidence.

"I'm just worried. We'll see how many people show up at the truck. I think one group of us needs to arrive in a separate car, in case anything goes wrong. I hate the idea of us all sitting in one truck." Erik drove to the warehouse. He parked next to the procession of cars. "It looks like Magnus brought a few people. I just wish we had someone with the power to freeze time besides Jessie." He gave Jessie a concerned look.

"Erik, I'll be fine. We can do this." She gripped his hand tighter.

"Let's get a count on how many people we have and their abilities, so we are sending everyone to the place best suited to them," Mike suggested.

"Sounds good. Hey, what does your friend Ely do?" Erik asked.

"Astral projection." He answered. "That's why he hides out. I only came across him when I was looking for someone else in Southern Colorado. He keeps himself pretty hidden away. When I sensed his ability, I was curious, so I found him. We've been friends ever since. He's from New York City originally, but he came out here to hide in the mountains."

"Wow, that's a pretty cool ability." Sloane peeked out the window to see Ely, lounged against his black Chevy Impala. Mike rubbed his thumb across her knuckles.

"Okay Mike, can sense them? What are we working with here? It'd be nice to know who we have on our side. We need to be quick though. They'll be expecting us to join them soon." Erik darted a glance out the window. Magnus was talking with Caroline. They were probably talking logistics before loading up.

"Okay," Mike closed his eyes to concentrate. "So, Caroline can read minds like you can, Erik. Nick can manipulate the element of water. He can freeze people, but in a very different way." He chuckled. "Magnus is copying Jessie's power, right now. That should come in handy." He continued.

"I'll listen to what I can while you do your thing." Erik began scanning the surrounding minds. Usually, he wouldn't do this to people he knew, but he needed to know who was here.

"Whoa, one girl here can overload another's mind with voices. That could come in handy to distract others while we dispossess them." Mike looked from Sloane to Jessie. "She could go with one group while Jessie goes with another. You freeze, and she distracts. Another guy has the power of augmentation, his being here boosts all our powers. He's probably the reason I'm getting such a clear picture of what everyone can do. I have to say; Caroline and Magnus have a powerful group of friends." Mike felt pleased with the prospective fight, knowing they would have some serious help to go into it.

"Um, Rachel can do fear projection. It's freaky. She just blasted me with it when I tried to listen in on her thoughts. She let me know what she thought of the intrusion. I think I'll stop. We have a pretty good idea of how we should split up. Magnus and Caroline are going to be the ones making the decisions, anyway." He shook his head to clear it. The image Rachel sent him sent shivers down his spine. He drew in a few deep breaths. Jessie cupped his cheek in her hand.

"Are you okay?" she asked.

"Yeah, just remind me not to piss her off. She's got some serious talent. She sent me an image of my worst fear. It looked so real. It felt real. It was only there for a split second, but it was long enough." Erik shook again. He didn't want to see that ever again. He'd seen Jessie lying dead, blood soaking the floor. He didn't want to think about her being hurt, especially after the last fight. He gripped her hand in his. "Promise me; you'll be careful." He whispered to Jessie, half-frantic.

"Of course, I'll be careful." She narrowed his eyes at him. "Who is she? I'll gut her if she hurt you." She said the words with such force, Erik believed that she would. His mouth turned up in a slight smile. He forgot she was just as protective of him. He brushed a strand of hair from her face.

"It's fine. It was just a warning. Trust me; I won't do it again. Come on, let's join the others. I'm ready to get this party started." He reached for the handle of the door. Jessie pulled his arm toward her, and he turned to look at her. She leaned over and kissed him fiercely. He gasped when her mouth touched his. He met her fierceness with a desire all his own, and when she backed away from his mouth, they were breathless.

Erik and Jessie walked up to Magnus and Caroline, hands clasped. "Is everything set?" Erik asked.

"Yes, here are your coms. We will be communicating with each other through earpieces. Jessie, you will be with team red. We're going into the offices, first. Our target is Mr. Hall and

Nicole. Erik, you're with Team Blue. You will focus on the West building. You are acting as the guide. You will listen to thoughts and direct the team to the existing demons in the building. You'll have Rachel, Ely, Peyton, and Mya. Rachel can distract any demons as you go. She's very effective. She'll be your number two. You okay with that?" Caroline asked, almost as an afterthought.

"Sounds good. You'll be with Jessie?" Erik asked.

"Yes, we'll all be on the same frequency, so you'll be able to hear what's happening with our team," Caroline explained. He knew she was trying to reassure him since they would be separated in the fight.

He nodded, "Okay."

Caroline turned to Jessie. "You'll be with me, Sloane, Nick, and Mike. We're focusing on the offices. You'll be my second. I will listen for the demons, and you freeze. Our priority will be to get to Mr. Hall and my daughter."

"Sounds good, what about the other two buildings?" Jessie nodded.

Magnus stepped forward. "I'll be leading team green. I have copied your ability to freeze, so I'll be following Bella with my team. Kim will be leading the fourth team into the North building. They will be driving in separate cars. We wanted a few groups to be outside the truck to guard our entry. Carlos is on point to meet us there. I believe we're all set." Magnus looked around the group who began to gather around the small group. "Is everyone set? Do you all know your teams and locations?" Magnus called out.

Many heads nodded or called out in agreement. "Alright, ear pieces in and let's go." Magnus walked to a Black Escalade. Erik watched in puzzlement.

"I thought he was heading up the green team? Are they taking separate vehicles?" Erik narrowed his eyes.

"I guess, Magnus said there were groups going separately." She shrugged and walked to the loading dock with the others. Erik followed. He felt uncomfortable getting in the back of the trailer. He appreciated that benches had been lined up along the walls for them to sit for the drive to the school. There was something off-putting about not being in control. He sat next to Jessie and took her hand. He knew they could handle anything as long as they were together. Sloane and Mike sat in the seats across from them and had been oddly quiet during Magnus and Caroline's explanation.

"Have you texted Chloe, yet?" He asked Sloane.

"No, I figured I'd wait until we were ready to go. I didn't want to screw up any plans by informing them. I'm still weary of letting her know exactly what's going on, but at the same time, I know we need her." Sloane pulled her phone out from her pocket.

"Someday, you need to get over your trust issues." Erik shook his head.

"What? I doubt I will ever get over my trust issues. By the way, did you see Bryant with Magnus? I thought they were coming together?" Sloane asked. She had begun typing a message into her phone. Mike was reading it next to her and smiling.

"No, come to think of it, I didn't. Where would he have gone? He knows this is a big deal. We're talking about kids and demons being able to possess Shikari. You'd think he'd be here." Erik looked down the rows of people. Bryant was nowhere in sight.

Jessie squeezed Erik's hand. "I'm sure he has a good reason for not being here."

"Whatever, he'll show up after all the fighting is over and declare a miraculous victory. He'll make some grand gesture like it was all his doing, I'm sure." Sloane rolled her eyes as she tucked her phone back in her pocket.

"When have you ever known our father to do that?" Erik asked.

"I don't know, like every battle we've faced since I've come back." She waved her hand in the air as she spoke.

Erik shook his head. "So, the one time, then. Besides, that's not true he was with us in Minneapolis."

"Ah, no, he was sneaking out the back door when all the fighting began. Then, he was there at the end of it all. I'm sure we'll see him when everything is over." She rolled her eyes again.

"There's no reasoning with you," Erik said.

"We're here; game faces people, game faces," Mike smirked at Erik. Erik watched as he reached for Sloane's hand. Erik looked down to reach for Jessie's hand, but she already moved closer to the door. He sighed. He wasn't ready to go in without her, but he didn't have much of choice.

Sloane met Mike's eyes for a split second. He gripped her hand tighter before turning to the door. They waited patiently for

Carlos, who was supposed to meet them to open the door. The truck had backed into the dock two minutes ago. Sloane looked over, Caroline and Jessie were standing by the door, huddled in a quiet conversation. Nick stood a little ways behind them, his thumbs through the loops of his jeans. He was poised like he was relaxed, but Sloane could see in the tightness of his features, he was ready for anything.

Mike pulled her toward him and bent next to her ear. "You think it's strange the door hasn't opened, yet?" he asked.

She bent closer to him. "I don't know. We have coms so that we can communicate to the world outside. I don't like this." She scanned the room and noticed the same unease spreading. Erik stood clenching his hands in fists at his sides. Suddenly, there was a click near the door, and it slid open. A tall, dark-skinned young man stood at the door; his hand raised over his head.

"Sorry, my manager was asking a lot of questions about why I needed to open the door alone. It took me a bit to convince him." He spoke with a tinge of a Spanish accent. Sloane released her breath slowly. This was it. They filed out of the truck and broke into teams. She noticed her brother split off with two other girls and Ely. She didn't like being separated from him. She took comfort that he could contact them if he needed to through their coms. She met Mike's eyes and wondered if he was thinking the same thing. She sighed, probably not.

Caroline made a motion for them to move forward. She drew her dagger out. She chose to bring knives for this fight instead of a gun. They were fighting against their warriors. She didn't want to kill anyone in this battle. She would only do enough damage to give them time to dispossess them. The thought of killing Shikari members made her cringe. She relished killing demons, not hunters.

Caroline led them through the first floor, past the kitchens, and to a back staircase. They crept up the stairs. Caroline reached a hand out to stay Jessie a moment, then turned and nodded toward her. Sloane strained to hear what was going on beyond the stairwell. Caroline touched her hand to her ear.

"There are six in the first set of offices. There is a workroom around the corner to the right. Three are in there. We need to move swiftly." She nodded toward Jessie. They both whipped around the corner. Jessie reached her hands up and froze the one man walking down the hall. Nick stood next to him, whispering the incantation. Jessie followed Caroline to the right. She swung the door and held her hands up again. The people in the room froze. She walked in and said the incantation next to the lady standing in front of the copier. She glanced over; Mike had moved next to a man in a gray pinstripe suit.

Caroline and Jessie were waiting next to the open doorway. Caroline's forehead was furrowed in concentration, and Jessie was watching her. Sloane stole a glance around the room. She was feeling pretty useless. Jessie looked back, and the others had moved behind her and Caroline. Caroline moved to whisper to them.

"I can't hear anyone in Mr. Hall's office, so we have to be ready for anything." She looked into their eyes individually. They followed them out of the room. The offices seemed empty for a school. Sloane figured the teachers were in classes. Caroline stopped in front what must've been Mr. Hall's door. She reached her hand to turn the knob slowly. Jessie was perched on the balls of her feet.

When the door opened, Caroline's mouth dropped. Her daughter, Nicole was sitting atop the desk, arms crossed, grinning. Jessie raised her arms, but she didn't freeze. She smirked in Jessie's direction. Suddenly, Jessie turned and walked out of the room.

"What the hell?" She stopped Jessie before she got too far.

"Mom, it's so nice of you to bring some friends to play with me. I always wanted more friends." She smirked toward Mike and Sloane. Mike sat on the floor and began acting like he was playing with cars. Even adding, "vroom." Sloane stared down at him horrified. He had just been reduced to a child. She looked up at the girl. She didn't care if she was Caroline's daughter. She was going to kill her.

She cocked her head to the side and stared at Sloane. "Huh, it doesn't seem to work on you. Too bad, I thought you'd like to play with your little boyfriend there. Maybe, I'll have him play in other ways."

Sloane glared at the girl. Mike stood next to her and started dancing. When he lifted his shirt and began undressing, Sloane's eyes widened. "Oh, hell no." She pushed him out of the room and closed the door behind her, leaving Jessie and Mike in the hallway.

Caroline regained her composure. "Nicole, stop this." She attempted to be commanding, but her voice cracked at the end.

Nick took a step toward her. "Nicky, baby, this isn't you. You need to fight the demon. I know you're stronger than this." He said in a soothing voice.

Her eyes shifted to him. "Oh, am I daddy? Am I? I don't think so." She threw her head back and let out a villainous cackle. She narrowed her eyes, and he dropped to his knees.

"Nicole, stop!" he cried out. He tumbled to the floor, clutching at his chest.

"Nicole, I am your mother stop this nonsense, right now!" She took a step forward.

Nicole laughed. "Caroline, you think I'm going to listen to you? Nicole is gone. I have to tell you; she feels freer with me than she has in her whole life. That's why she's not fighting me. She doesn't want to be a boring student anymore. She wants to have fun. You both have stopped her from living her life. I set her free to be able to do whatever she wanted. You've kept her sheltered, caged. I set her free. There's nothing you can do about it." Nicole grinned as Nick gasped in breaths on the floor.

Sloane had crept around to the side of the room while Nicole had been focused on the other two. So, far she hadn't noticed. Sloane gave Caroline a knowing look, hoping she would keep her busy.

Caroline's eyes narrowed. "You are not my daughter. You don't know my baby. She'd fight. She'd never let a demon win against her. She's too strong for that. You're weak. The only reason she hasn't dispelled you is because of the amulet you wear around your neck."

Sloane had reached to stand behind the desk. She leaned forward, extending her hand. Trying to carefully grab the necklace before Nicole could realize she was there.

"Weak?" Nicole cackled. "I'm in your daughter, right now. I'm far from weak."

Sloane decided to just go for it. She reached her hand out to her neck. She gripped the necklace as well as her collar and yanked on them both. Her collar ripped, and the chain broke into pieces. Nicole whirled on her. Sloane ducked her first blow and landed one of her own to Nicole's gut. Her arms instinctively clutched her stomach. Sloane grabbed a paperweight from the desk and hit her in the side of the head with it. Her eyes went wide before she slumped to the side of the desk.

Sloane looked up, "Sorry Caroline, it had to be done." She shrugged. Sloane pulled the amulet the rest of the way off of her and slid it into her pocket. She strode to the hall to check on Mike and Jessie. They stood blinking on the other side of the doorway. Mike's clothes were next to him on the floor. He bent to retrieve them, holding the pile in front of him.

"What the hell just happened?" he asked, still blinking confusedly.

"Nicole thought it would be funny if you stripped for her." Sloane slid her gaze hungrily down his body. "I mean, I didn't mind except for all the other people around." She grinned wide at him. He rolled his eyes.

Sloane looked to Jessie, who looked stunned. Her eyes were wide, and she kept darting glances around the hallway. "That bitch could've gotten us killed," she said.

"I think that's what she was going for." Sloane looked back over her shoulder. Caroline was standing over her daughter. Sloane watched as she brushed a piece of hair back from over her eyes. She took a few steps and knelt next to Nick on the floor. He lay motionless. Sloane walked back in.

"Are there any other demons in the building?" she asked Caroline.

"I don't hear any, but that doesn't mean they're not here." She looked from Nick to her daughter. "Where the hell is Mr. Hall. I'd like to get my hands on him."

Sloane looked down to Nick. "Is he going to be okay?"

"I don't know what she did, exactly. He's breathing, but his pulse is faint. We need to get him to a hospital." She looked to Mike. "Do you think you can get him back down the stairs?" she asked.

"Yeah, I think I can carry him. What about Nicole?" he nodded toward Nicole who was still slumped on the desk.

"I'll take her," Caroline said.

"I'm going to check on the others." She reached her hand up to the Com in her ear. "Erik, you guys okay? We've got Nicole, but no Mr. Hall." She waited and listened. They didn't hear any response. "I thought we would be in communication with them?" She asked looking to Caroline.

"We're supposed to be. Let's get back down there to see what's going on." She lifted Nicole in her arms, and Mike took Nick. Jessie walked out front, and Sloane took up the rear. None of them wanted to be surprised by another demon. They'd dispossessed everyone they could find in the building, but Sloane wasn't sure how many of those damn amulets were out there.

Chapter 23

Erik had listened to thoughts as he led the group through the West building. The first floor was filled with classrooms. Erik frowned as they moved down the hall. It was the middle of the afternoon; classes should be going on. Many of the rooms they passed were shut and locked. They'd already walked by four rooms that were closed up.

Rachel walked up beside him. "Many of the students have gone home for break." She peered up at him.

He looked at her questioningly. "Reading thoughts isn't your gift. How did you know what I was thinking?" he asked.

She shrugged. "It was written all over your face. I'd love to play poker with you sometime. Your face is very transparent in your expressions. I could get a couple hundred off you easy." She raised a brow at him. He wasn't sure what it was about Rachel, but he liked her. Even though, when he'd first seen her, she'd sent him the worst image he could ever imagine.

"Sorry about earlier. I don't like my mind being intruded on." She kept following him. The first floor had been devoid of people so far.

"Yeah, I usually don't listen in on other Shikari members unless I have to. I don't like to invade others privacy. I only use my ability to hunt demons." He stopped as they approached the end of the hall. One room on the right had a light on. The hairs on the back of Erik's neck stood up. He knew there were demons nearby. He focused on listening for them. He held a hand out to stop Rachel from moving forward. He couldn't hear any thoughts which had him concerned. He knew there were demons, but he had no idea how many were in there.

He moved against the wall and bent to speak low to Rachel. "There are demons in the next room. I can't read their thoughts. They must be wearing amulets. With those on, our powers will be useless against them."

Ely took a step forward. "Not my power. I can astral project from here and distract them. You guys can then go through the door. Let's try not to hurt our own too badly though, aye?"

The others nodded. "Speaking of abilities, what can you guys do?" Erik looked from Peyton to Mya.

Mya bit the side of her lip. "Nothing much, just this." The knife Erik had drawn flew out of his hand and into Mya's.

"What the hell?" he'd blurted.

"Why didn't you say anything? You can just get the amulets off them." His eyes were alighted with anticipation. He couldn't believe he'd gotten so lucky.

"Well, I don't know if it will work on the amulets since they're meant to block our powers. I sure will try my darndest though." She smiled slightly.

"Okay, so Ely you go in and distract them. While you have them looking away from the door, we'll file in. Mya, you try to get the amulets off their neck. If you can't, we fight them. Only use knives though, we don't want to hurt any of them."

"Sounds like a plan. You ready?" Ely asked. They nodded. Ely closed his eyes and Erik watched as he seemed to shimmer momentarily, then he was utterly still. Erik sprang into the room, followed by Rachel and Mya. They were looking toward Ely. One had charged forward. His arms outstretched, ready to slam into him. A moment before the demon reached him; he shimmered and disappeared. The guy stumbled through where Ely had once been. Ely re-appeared next to one of the other demons. Erik was surprised; he didn't expect there to be four guys in here. All are wearing amulets around their necks.

Erik glanced to Mya, she had one finger pointed toward one of the men, and she flicked her finger. Erik whipped his head in the direction of her finger. The guy she was pointing at still had the chain fastened around his neck. Mya shook her head as he looked at her. He knew her power didn't work as long as they wore those chains. Erik rushed forward, his dagger in hand. He didn't want to injure them too badly, but he needed to stop them. They were Shikari, but they were also demons who would do whatever they could to try to kill him.

He rushed toward the brute before him. Erik knew his bulkiness would be to Erik's advantage as long as he didn't get any jabs in. He had a feeling one jab from this guy, and he'd be on his knees. The man charged. Erik ducked the blow and swung his knife out, grazing the man's abdomen. He sprung lightly around him, pivoting quickly before the man could grab at his clothes.

The man lunged for Erik again, and he somersaulted over the beast sweeping his blade across the man's shoulder. He heard Rachel behind him say, "Man, now you're just showing off."

Erik's grin grew wide as he turned to kick out at the man. He stumbled forward, and Erik reached to yank the chain from his neck. It gave easily, and Erik clutched the chain in his hand. The amulet had skidded across the floor. Mya saw the man was free of the chain, and she flung him against the wall. He hit with such force that he slumped to the floor. Erik whirled ready to take on the next attacker.

Rachel stood over one of the men. He was on his knees, his head in his hands, weeping. "Do you think you could just dispossess him instead of prolonging his suffering?" Erik shook his head at her.

"What? You were showing off your acrobatics. I think I can do the same." She smirked at him.

Erik rolled his eyes. "Come on, I know you don't know how traumatizing your power is, but I can say it's pretty traumatizing. Take care of the demon, already." Erik looked to Ely, Peyton and Mya had already taken care of the other two guys. They lay on the floor, unconscious. "Well, that wasn't too bad," Erik said, nodding as he assessed the four guys. "Have you dispossessed them?" Erik asked.

"Peyton just took care of one of them. We'll do the other guy next. You want to go take care of the guy Mya flew into the wall." Ely pointed to the guy Erik had been fighting.

"Yeah, I'll take care of him." Erik strode over to the brute. He said the incantation quickly and watched as the black smoke of the demon rose from the man, then dissipated into dust. "I love when they do that." He muttered, satisfied.

"Okay," Rachel sashayed up to Erik, one hand on her hip. "Where to next? I know those weren't the only demons in this building. We still have four more floors to go." She clapped her hands together once.

"Weren't you the one just saying that people were gone for a break? I'd prefer fewer demons, not more." He straightened his mouth into a hard line as he assessed her. She was standing on the balls of her feet, almost bouncing. He took a deep breath. "Alright, let's go to the second floor." He huffed. He scanned the others and trudged toward the door. He didn't mind fighting, but the way Rachel had hackled him about his fighting, he wasn't sure he wanted her around for their next fight. She relied on her abilities too much, and they may be useless if the demons all have amulets.

He took the lead again and motioned for them to follow him up the steps. He could hear more thoughts up here than before. He stopped before reaching the next room. There were two girls inside, neither of them was demons. He moved his finger to his lips to motion for them to be silent. He crept by their room without either girl noticing. It looked like a counselor's office or something. They made it past without being noticed. Erik concentrated as he moved forward.

Suddenly, Erik heard a thump. He turned, and Peyton had been struck. He was lying on the floor. Erik's eyes widened. "Look out," he said as a red-headed man lunged for Mya. She whirled and threw him down the hall. Erik smirked, damn that's an awesome power. Ely went to the guy who Mya flung. A moment later black smoke was evaporating into dust. He glanced to

Rachel, her eyes widened. Erik spun, ducking as he swept a foot out. The tall, bearded man fell backward, screaming. He looked back to Rachel.

She lifted her hands out, "What? He was coming after you." She stepped over him as he writhed on the floor, clutching his head.

Erik quickly said the incantation. He visibly relaxed when he was done. "At least you stop when they're no longer demons," he said catching up to Rachel as she continued down the hall.

"Aren't you supposed to be warning us when they're coming? Those two weren't even wearing amulets." Her tone was sarcastic as she continued forward without the others. Erik peered behind him, and Mya was crouched next to Peyton. Ely was hurrying to catch up to them.

"Hey, are we just going to leave them back there?" he asked.

"For now," Rachel said as she continued forward. She was glancing into the room as she passed. Erik couldn't hear anyone else on this floor. Rachel made it to the stairway and climbed up quickly. She stopped at the top. "Okay, mind reader, you want to let us know if there are any demons on this floor before we start walking down it this time." She crossed her arms over her chest and stared at him.

"Sure, princess." He watched as she scowled at him. He knew he'd struck a nerve. He made a mental note for later. He concentrated, there weren't any other people up here unless they had amulets.

"No one's up here," he said.

"Are you sure this time?" she glared.

"No, I can't hear demons if they are wearing an amulet. We should probably double check." He started down the empty hallway.

"Can we make this fast? I don't like the idea of leaving them two down there without us." Ely said as he followed them down the hall.

Rachel waved her hand, flicking it above her shoulder. "Mya can take care of herself. She'll watch over Peyton while we finish this. I'd like to go back to my life. I wasn't planning on spending all day in a stinking school."

Erik rolled his eyes and glanced toward Ely. He met his eyes, and they shared a meaningful look. Neither of them wanted to stick around Rachel much longer. When they got to the end of the hall, Rachel hurried up the last set of stairs. She began walking down the hall without stopping to ask him if anyone was there. So much for her being Erik's second. He had a feeling Rachel didn't take well to being ordered around. He was starting to think she was the one to typically do the ordering.

Ely stopped and reached out a hand to grab Erik's shirt. "I'm not a dumbass, do you hear any demons before we go charging in? My powers only effective if I can distract the demons while others take them by surprise. It'd be nice if we knew ahead of time if there were any demons to, you know, distract." He studied Erik.

"Yeah, I'll check, give me a second. It takes a minute to zero in on only this area. Otherwise, I can get bombarded with everyone's thoughts in all the buildings." He stopped and concentrated on the floor they were on. He heard at least three other demons up here, two male, one female. They were in one of the dorm rooms. He focused his energy on them, and he lifted the corner of his mouth. "Ah, there are three, two men, one woman. You're not going to believe what they're doing." Erik smiled.

Ely lifted a brow, "Oh yeah?"

"Um, let's just say, we won't need to distract them. They're a little busy, already." Erik began walking in the direction of the dorm room.

"Dude, are you telling me they're having sex? Two guys, one girl, seriously?" His eyes were wide as he jogged to catch up to Erik.

"Yeah, you want to fuck with them, anyway?" Erik raised his eyebrows suggestively.

"Shit, yeah, why not?" he smirked. Erik paused next to the door. Rachel had walked right past and was already four doors down. She hadn't slowed to even check any of the rooms.

"How about you project in there to surprise them? I'll burst in right after you and hit the guy nearest me. You come in after and go for the other. The girl won't be too hard because she's ah, in a compromising position, if you get my drift."

Ely smiled. "Sounds fun. Who knew Mike dragging my ass out of seclusion would be so much fun." He winked, then closed his eyes to project into the room. The girl let out a shriek, and Erik barged in the room, Hitting the guy nearest the door in the temple. He collapsed over the girl, taking her to the side with him as he fell.

The guy beneath her wore a look of utter shock. His eyes were wide as Erik lunged toward him, landing a quick jab to his face. His hand whipped up to his mouth, and he spat blood. Erik said the incantation and black smoke poured out of the man's nose and mouth. The man looked even more shocked in his state of undress. Ely had taken care of the girl. She was now gripping the sheet around herself. Erik finished with the last guy. He lay sideways on the bed.

Erik glanced at Ely, "Now that was fun." They both walked out of the room. Erik glanced back down the hall, but Rachel was gone. "Now where the hell did she go?" He muttered.

"No idea, but we better find her. I hate when people in fights split up. Something always goes wrong." Ely shook his head and started down the hall, leaving the three-some in their confused state.

Erik followed. Rachel was on her mission. She didn't think she needed them. Erik listened to the thoughts in the building. There were more demons here. He wasn't sure if they were on this floor or the next. He touched his hand to his ear. "Rachel, Mya, Ely, there are still demons here, four of them for sure. Keep your eyes peeled." Ely paused and waited for Erik.

"Where are they?" he asked.

"I think they're a floor above us. The upper floors are all dorms, right?"

"Yeah, so are they students? I thought most of the students were dispossessed by others before we got here?" Ely asked, hitching his thumb in his jean pocket as they continued to walk quietly down the hall.

"Sloane said they were trying to take care of most of the students. I don't know if they got all of them or not." They climbed the stairs, and Erik felt a shiver run down his spine, and he tensed.

"You feel that?" Ely asked.

"Yeah, demons," he said and pulled a dagger from his belt. Ely did the same.

"Do you hear Rachel?" Ely asked.

"No, oh hell no. I'm not trying that again. Her power sucks when used against you. I won't be that stupid ever again." He shuddered. He reached his hand to his ear. "Rachel? You still with us?" He waited, but there was no answer. "I thought we would have a connection to everyone using these coms. Why haven't we heard anything about what's happening in the other buildings?" Erik tightened his grip around the handle of the knife.

"I'm not sure. Maybe there's a glitch in them or something." Ely shrugged as they moved forward.

Erik kept listening for the demons. He heard four of them, and he was pretty sure they were up here. They'd been on every other floor unless some came in since they were downstairs. They walked passed a door to the right. Erik felt a chill again and froze. "We must be getting close," he whispered. Ely nodded toward him.

Erik heard the small creek behind him. He whirled but felt the sharp pain of a blow to the head before he fell to the ground. He wasn't knocked out, but when he tried to get up, he wobbled. Ely had pushed the guy away from him and was continuing to fight. Erik knew he needed to get up, now. There were three others somewhere. He used the wall for support and stood, shaking his head to clear it. The man fighting Ely was burley with a crook in his nose. He wasn't a student. He wore a flannel shirt and khakis. He reminded him of a shop teacher he once had. He heard another noise in the room behind him and saw Rachel lying on the floor. A woman kneeling next to her.

Erik listened and knew she was a demon immediately. He rushed her, landing a punch to the side of her face. He didn't like the idea of hitting a woman, but the occasion called for it. He learned long ago that when it came to demons, they would use any human weakness to get to you. The woman fell sideways, her maxi skirt falling around her. Erik spoke the incantation quickly before she had time to regain her composure. Erik turned, and Ely stood above the burly man. Black smoke rose from him, and Erik breathed a sigh of relief. Two down, two to go.

Ely walked over to them. Erik touched her neck, feeling for a pulse. "It looks like they just knocked her out. They were probably hoping to possess her." Erik brushed a piece of her hair back from her face and admired her feminine features. Her milky complexion was tinged with the slightest bit of pink in her cheeks. Her skin was silky soft, and she had a cute button nose. He smiled, she was really beautiful when she was unconscious. Her long blonde hair had been pulled up into a chignon, but pieces fell all around her head and face.

"She's nice when she's not talking," Ely observed.

Erik stood. "We need to find the last two. I think she'll be fine here until all this is over." Erik looked back out the door. The last two are women. I think they're in a room on the right at the end of the hall. They walked out of the room. Mya jogged up to them. She glanced to the guy laying on the floor.

"Hey, I moved Peyton into one of the dorm rooms. Where's Rachel?" Mya looked around.

"She's knocked out in there. She decided to venture off on her own, which as you can see is never a good idea." Ely was smug as he spoke.

"Alright, let's finish this so we can get them taken care of and check on the others," Mya said.

"There are two more girls down the hall on the right who are demons. After that, the buildings clear." Erik strode forward. He stopped before the open door. He could hear the girls talking in the room. They laughed out loud, and Erik took the opportunity to step into the room. Ely followed. Erik grabbed the girl from behind and restrained her arms. She kicked back wildly, but she didn't have the strength. She was a petite girl. Erik said the incantation quickly and watched the smoke dissipate into the air. Ely had done the same with the other small girl. They shook their heads and looked up to the two men.

"Oh my God, thank you. Being a demon was super lame." She reached her hand to pull the ponytail out of her hair. "I hate my hair up like this. It was driving me crazy."

Erik shook his head. "Glad to be of service ladies. Can I ask what you're still doing on campus? Isn't this a break or something?"

The girl who had just put down her hair nodded. "Yes, but some of us have shitty families we don't want to go home to. I would rather stay on campus alone, then meet my father's latest girlfriend. She's another leech. I prefer to spare myself the new mom routine when I can." She rolled her eyes.

"Okay, do you know if anyone else in the dorm stayed here?" he asked.

"No, only a few of us. Carly here is the only girl on this floor who stayed. Even if students did stay behind, they don't all stay here. Some drive to the city during the day to do stuff. I think there's maybe four or five who are in the city from this dorm." She looked up pointedly. "Anything else?"

Erik looked down at her cocked his head to the side. "No, I guess not." He could have just read her thoughts but didn't want to intrude. He also wasn't sure he wanted to hear what she was thinking. There were some things you didn't want to hear.

Erik turned and walked out of the room. He turned to look at Mya and Ely. "Do you mind taking care of Rachel and Peyton? I want to go find Jessie and Sloane and make sure everything went okay." His eyes filled with concern.

"Yeah man, no problem. We'll join you after we move them." Ely looked to Mya. "Can we move them into the same room? They'll probably wake up soon."

Mya nodded. "Sounds like a plan." They both walked into the room with Rachel.

Erik ran down the stairs taking two at a time. He began listening to the thoughts around him as he went. The people who they'd dispossessed were still a little dazed and confused, but Erik knew they'd be fine. They were Shikari, and they knew what had happened to them. Erik flew out of the door and raced toward the main offices. Jessie was rushing out the door by the dock when he got there.

"Oh good, you're okay," she breathed. Erik relaxed when he saw her. She walked into his arms, and he wrapped them around her, squeezing tightly. He needed to feel she was okay.

"We got Nicole, and everyone here is dispossessed. How about you guys?" she asked.

"Rachel and Peyton got knocked out. Otherwise, everyone is fine." He gazed down into her eyes. He dropped his mouth to hers, and a fire erupted throughout his body. His kiss was fierce. He felt her grip at his back, twisting one hand in his hair. He hitched his hand under her thighs and lifted her. She wrapped her legs around him, crossing her ankles just above his waist. He devoured her mouth. He couldn't get enough of the taste of her. She tasted of vanilla and mint.

"Ahem," Sloane cleared her throat behind them. "Do you mind?"

"Do you?" Erik glared at Sloane but dropped Jessie, tucking her against him. He wrapped his arms around her shoulders.

"It's good to see you're okay, too Erik," she smirked and walked around them. "So, did anyone plan on how we were getting home? I'm not keen on riding in the back of a semi-trailer again." She looked around the parking lot. "Has anyone checked on the other teams?" She turned back toward Erik and Jessie.

"We're done. The building is clear, but Rachel and Peyton were knocked out. Ely and Mya were helping them. They should be awake soon." He tightened his arms around Jessie, and she began rubbing the hairs on his arm.

Mike walked out. His eyes brightened when he saw Erik. "Hey, everything good?"

"Yep," Erik was tired of explaining what had happened. "Anyone see Magnus? Our coms weren't working. How about the last team?"

"I think Caroline was checking on them," Mike said.

"Should we head over to the other buildings? What if there were more demons in them?" Erik looked between them.

Caroline walked out the back door. "That won't be necessary, Erik. I've been in communication with everyone. There were only a few minor injuries sustained. It sounds like all the demons here have been taken care of, for now. I hear some of them went home for break. We'll need to address this when they get back." She turned her head to Sloane. "Where is Chloe? I'd like to thank her for her help. She took care of most of the students before we even arrived." Her voice was thoughtful as she spoke.

"Oh, I'm meeting her over in the library. They got everyone out of here that they could before we came. They wanted to make sure no other students got caught in the battle. The students did an excellent job. I'll make sure to pass on your appreciation." She reached out for Mike's hand. "We should head over there now." Mike followed as she pulled him toward her.

Jessie leaned back to look up at Erik. "Should we go with them?"

"Nah, I'm sure they got it," he shrugged.

Chapter 24

A black Tacoma pulled next to them in the parking lot. Bryant glided out of the front seat. "I see all is well here?" Erik shook his head thinking back to the conversation he'd had with Sloane. Maybe she was right; he showed up after all the fighting had ended. Bryant looked to Erik, concerned. "Is it not, my son?"

"No, Bryant, everything is fine. We took care of the demons here." He stroked his thumb over Jessie's abdomen.

"Good, good, where is Magnus? There is a matter of some urgency I must discuss with him?" He glanced toward Caroline.

"He should be here shortly." She muttered. "If you'll excuse me, I believe I will take my daughter home now." She turned and walked back into the building.

"Maybe we should go, too?" Jessie looked up to Erik.

"Yeah, hey Bryant can we catch a ride? Wait, where are we staying? Do you think Magnus will let us go back to his place? I think Caroline may want time with her family." Erik looked to Bryant.

"You will need to come with me to Magnus' we have much to discuss." Bryant got back in the sleek, black SUV. "Where is your sister? She'll need to join us, as well. We need to discuss what will happen, next. We need to address the issue of the order. Which building was Magnus in?" He asked, turning to Erik who'd gotten in next to him.

He's at the East building. Bryant nodded and drove toward the parking lot.

"I'll go check on what's taking them." He hopped out. Jessie jumped out, too.

"I'll come with you." She grabbed her phone from her pocket. "I'll call Sloane."

"No need, the library is in here. We can find her on the way." He opened the door for Jessie, and she walked passed into the building. "Library first? Maybe Sloane and Mike found Magnus."

"Okay, here, It's down this hall." He took a right and continued. Jessie hurried to catch him and took his hand.

Sloane was sitting atop a long wooden table in the reference section. Mike stood next to her and Chloe was sitting in a chair next to Katie. "Hey, you guys came over." Sloane put her hands together when she saw them.

"Yeah, Bryant drove us over. Have you seen Magnus? We need to find him. Bryant has something important to share with him, I guess." Erik rolled his eyes.

"Ahem," came from the doorway. "I have something to share with him, with all of you." A tall man with wavy blonde hair stood in the doorway. Magnus came up behind him.

"Ethan," Magnus held his hand out toward the man. Erik studied him. He wore khakis colored trousers and a navy sweater over his dark button-up and light blue tie.

"Magnus, it's good to see you." He clasped his hand and shook.

"So, what's the urgent matter?" Magnus asked. Bryant walked into the library.

"It's about the order. We've been attacked. I fled with many others, but we are in need of assistance. Demons, wearing the face of friends, have taken over the archive. We must not let them continue. It's imperative we dispense them at once, but we need your aid to do so. We need everyone. Many leaders have fled to various cities abandoning the archive. We need to take it back before the damage is irreparable." Ethan looked meaningfully around at the group.

"Oh my, they've taken over everything?" Magnus was in shock.

"Yes, this is why I rushed here. We need to get to Kansas City immediately. The future of the Shikari depends on it." Bryant looked to Sloane and Erik.

"I contacted those in Minneapolis, and they directed me here. I do hope you can assist us. You've been pivotal in all that has transpired, thus far." Ethan scanned the group again.

"I explained that it was your decision to make." Bryant gave Erik a meaningful look.

"Okay, onto our next adventure, then." Erik shrugged. "You guys game?" He met the eyes of Mike, Sloane, and Jessie.

"You know I'm always up for a good fight." Sloane smiled wide rubbing her hands together. "It's time we finally end this and find out who's behind the events which led to our mother's death."

Mike took a step toward Sloane, wrapping his arms around her and gazing into her eyes. "I go where she goes."

Jessie looked up to Erik. Her eyes glistened, and she squeezed his hand. "We need to talk."

I appreciate you reading my novel! I am a middle school teacher by day, writer by night. If you enjoyed reading this book please leave a review. It will be greatly appreciated. You're amazing! Thank You!

Here are some ways you can connect with me:

Fat Girl Problems blog and other writings are on my website:

https://dorablume.com/

Follow me on Facebook:

https://www.facebook.com/DoraBlumeAuthor

Follow me on Goodreads:

https://www.goodreads.com/**DoraBlume**

Follow me on Twitter

https://twitter.com/BlumeDora

Read on for the first chapter of Haunted by a Moment

Chapter 1

The hospital lights are blinding as I blink my eyes open once, quickly then shut again. I take a deep breath and the antiseptic smell is prevalent, the combination of alcohol and talcum powder sends my mind through a flash of memories. *What am I doing in the hospital?* I think. A shiver runs down my body and I open my eyes again, braving the fluorescents. I examine my surroundings, people are walking quickly around me. Few even notice my presence on the gurney. The hallway is filled with people; I am the only one on a gurney.

"Hello?" I call out.

A nurse points in my direction talking to a young man with a scruffy brown beard. "Go talk to her, keep her awake," the nurse demands as she hurries off to the next room.

"Hey, I'm Sam," the beard says. He smiles, and I couldn't help but return such a warm smile. Then I remember why I called out. I'm cold. I glance down and blush.

"Can I ask where my shirt is?" I'm lying on a gurney in the hallway, topless.

"Oh yeah, sorry. They had to cut it off of you in transit," he smiles again. At least he is looking at my eyes and not my chest.

"Do you think that I could get a blanket or something to cover up?"

"I'll check." He walks back to the nurse with the stern voice and finger.

"No, she can't have a blanket, she's in shock! Don't you know anything?" She scolds loudly and goes back to organizing the medical supplies in the cabinet.

He walks back over to me with slumped shoulders and rosy cheeks. "She said no, you were in shock earlier and so we can't change your body temperature, sorry." He looks down at the floor.

"Seriously, so I get to hang out in the hallway shirtless. There isn't anything you can do?" I am desperate, I don't like the idea of laying here shirtless.

"I will try to snatch you something as soon as she leaves." He winks and goes to check on another patient.

"Where is she? Where's Katherine?" I hear my mother, frantically calling down the hall.

"She's down here," a nurse says. I recognize the nurse who is holding my mom's hand. *Perfect, that's my old boss and here I am laying on a gurney without a shirt on.*

"Hey mom," I say, smiling weakly at her. I know I'm in big trouble because no one ever wants to greet any of their parents from a hospital gurney, especially after borrowing your father's brand-new convertible.

"Oh my God, Kat honey, are you okay?" She clasps my hand in an iron grip.

"Jeez, mom. Chill on the death grip would ya. I'm okay, really I'm fine." She loosens her grip on my hand. She takes my hand in both of hers and looks down at me.

"Really Kat, you're reassuring me? You're the one on the gurney." She shakes her head at me. "My girl, always taking care of me. I don't believe you're fine." I hear her near sob when she speaks, gripping my hand tighter in the process like she needs to feel I'm still here. "Where's her shirt?" she demands, glancing around. Carol, the nurse she approached with, hurries away.

She returns and lays a blanket over my bare chest. I breathe a sigh of relief.

"Thank you."

She smiles. "No problem." She looks to my mom. "Why don't we head over to the nurse's station. They're ready to take her into x-ray now. I'll bring you to see her as soon as she's done." The nurse takes my mom's hand and places a hand on her back guiding her away from me toward the other end of the hall. Another nurse comes and wheels me into an x-ray room. She starts with my neck while I'm still lying still. After she determines that I don't have a spinal injury, I can finally sit up to do the rest of the x-rays. I want to scream out at the slightest movement, but instead I bite my lip until I taste the familiar copper of my blood in my mouth.

Finally, I'm done taking x-rays, and I lay back on the gurney. The room spins, and I can hear the nurse say, "I'll take you to your room," before everything goes black.

Hours later, I open my eyes slowly expecting the glare from the fluorescent lights, but the room is dim. I hear the regular beat of the machine next to me and I glance to look at the monitor with numbers and lines that for the moment are inconceivable to me.

"Kat honey, are you awake, can you hear me?" My mom says quickly. There's panic in the swiftness of her words.

"Yeah," I croak.

My mom holds my hand, the warmth in contrast to the cold, sterile air around me. I try to think back to what happened, but my head throbs and the room spins. My head feels clouded. I have trouble focusing on any one thought as things flash through my mind one moment, and are a blur the next. I can't focus on one flash before it's gone, replaced by another. I look back to the monitor with the lines and numbers. *There are lines and regular beeps, that's good right?* I think as I try to focus my attention on something I can understand.

"What day is it?" I ask.

"Easter," my mom responds.

"Yes, but what day is it?" I ask again.

"Easter," she says again.

I blow out an exasperated breath. "That doesn't tell me what day it is."

"I'm going to get the doctor." She hurries out of the room.

I don't understand why she furrowed her brow when she left. The beeping is still normal, regular, like me. I'm fine; I'm sure I'm fine. I look down at myself. The IV line is running out of my hand and to the stand next to me. The drip is regular too, like my heartbeat. I scan the rest of my arm and notice blood on the sheet next to where my right elbow lay. I lift my arm tentatively and look at the spot just above my elbow. There's a gaping hole and these cords are hanging broken outside of the hole. It looks similar to what frayed electrical cords look like. I reach my left hand over to touch them. Instantly, I hear my mom's voice.

"Oh my God." she cries out. I jump in response and look to the door.

My mom is frozen with her mouth wide open. The doctor scurries quickly around her to examine my arm. I hold my arm suspended in the air. His hands are cold as he turns my inner arm toward him to look closely at the hole. He reaches for the call button and hits it to get the attention of the nurse.

"What's wrong?" I ask, looking at the doctor.

"We need to put a nerve block in your shoulder so you won't feel this," he says as he points to the hole in my arm.

"Is that bad?" I ask still in awe at the hole and the cords sticking out of it. I know I should be horrified but at the moment everything feels so surreal.

"No, we'll put in a block so we can repair the nerves here." He points to the wires coming from the inside of my arm.

"Oh, those are my nerves? They probably shouldn't be on the outside, should they?" I blink at him.

"No, they definitely shouldn't." He looks to the entering nurse. "We need to put in a nerve block and we may need to check her morphine levels." The nurse leaves the room. The doctor looks down to me, I smile at him. Within a few minutes several other people join the doctor next to my arm. The nurse grabs the tube that is coming out of my hand and carefully inserts a needle into the tube. I smile again and everything goes black.

Hours later, I can hear my cousin crying in the hallway. She sobs and asks, "Are you sure she's going to be okay?" I open my eyes and look around the room. It's dark and empty. The monitor beeps in a steady rhythm. I glance toward the sliver of light shining up from the bottom of the oversized wooden door. I look to my arm and notice that my arm has been wrapped in gauze. The tingling makes me reach to itch at it but I think twice before doing it. I sigh heavily as I listen again to the visitors in the hallway. I realize my mom never really answered when I asked what day it is. I look to the board across from my bed. Carol is written next to attending and 1730 is written below my name.

I take a deep breath and try again to remember what happened. I close my eyes to try to focus on the memories, but I only get flashes. I see myself laughing with my friend, then suddenly to another moment in a completely different car. As soon as that memory hits, like a flash, I'm in another place. Bellcreek, the skating rink that I've gone to every Friday for years. I can see the owner's face, frowning and I can feel her disappointment like a weight on my shoulders. I open my eyes. I can't take the random sudden flashes. I can't focus on any one thing for more than a few seconds and I don't want to see that woman's disapproving face again. I look back to the light, hoping that someone from out there will come in here to check on me.

It surprises me to hear my cousin crying, I know she loves me, but honestly, Melinda is the last person I thought I would hear crying outside my hospital room. I look around my bed to find the remote for the television. It registers for a moment that I should be feeling pain right now but I don't. My head feels cloudy and I know I've been drugged considering I don't feel any pain. I hit what I think is the power button on the remote and stare waiting for the ancient television to power up. When it does, I can barely register what the people on the screen are saying. I reach to turn up the volume, so I can actually hear what is going on before I start flipping quickly to find something bearable to watch. Infomercial after infomercial fills the screen. I realize it must be late. *Why is my cousin here if it's so late*, I think?

The light from the hall increases as the door opens. My mom looks to the television then to me in the bed. "How are you doing honey?" she asks as she reaches to grasp my hand.

"Fine," I answer automatically.

"You've been out for a long time," she says.

"Oh yeah, how long was I out for?" I ask, now curious about the voices I heard in the hall. Maybe there was a good reason for Melinda to be here so late. I glance down to examine my body. It's weird how I can see myself, move my limbs but still feel disconnected from myself. Like I'm both in my body and outside of my body at the same time. I look back to my mom and her brows are furrowed again and I know she is worried. The dark circles beneath her eyes let me know she hasn't left my side, no matter how long I slept.

"You've been sleeping for about two days now" she answers.

"Wow, I slept for two whole days," I say, unbelieving.

"Yeah, how are you feeling? Should I call the nurse? Are you in any pain?" Her questions come one right after the other with little breath between.

"No mom I'm fine," I respond. "What happened to my arm? The last thing I remember they were putting in some kind of block they said? Why did they need to do that?" I could remember what the doctor said but not much else.

"Oh, they needed to put in a nerve block. You had some nerve damage from the accident."

"Nerve damage? What does that mean?" I ask. I move my right arm up just to make sure I still can. I feel a shooting pain in my shoulder and cry out. It's not my arm that hurts but my shoulder is killing me.

My mom rushes into the hall. "I need someone in here," she calls down the hall and takes her place next to me.

The nurse comes in and goes immediately to the IV and monitors. She looks them over. The steady beat quickens as the pain increases. The nurse leaves and comes back with a bottle and a syringe. She plunges it into my IV and I look up to her.

"Seriously, my shoulder is killing me," I say before everything goes black again.

Hours later, I wake to hear my mother's subtle snoring from the chair next to my bed. I look to my arm again and it's still bandaged as before. A nurse wheels a cart to the door and I hear her trying to quietly get her supplies. She comes in and sets a container next to me on the bed. It has vials for blood, packages with needles, and tie off bands.

"Ah yes, the four am blood run, you must be my nightly vampire." I say. I'm not sure why I remember that they take blood every night at four but I do. They've done it at that same time every night I've been here. I don't remember much of my stay but for some reason I remember that.

"Ah yes, I love your sense of humor despite everything." She smiles at me. "Ready for a poke?"

"Yes, can't really feel anything, anyway." I look to her and laugh again. I can't help it, I laugh anytime I'm nervous.

"You might feel this," she says as she plunges the needle into my arm. The vial fills with blood and she pulls it out and inserts another.

"You must be good at this," I say.

"I have been taking your blood every morning," she replies.

"Normally, it takes several pokes before they find a vein." I look to her as she finishes and holds the cotton ball against the crook in my elbow.

"Hold this," she says and grabs the tape from the container. She wraps it quickly around my arm to keep the pressure.

"I have been doing this for a long time. You get good after years of practice." She leaves but before she closes the door she asks, "Is there anything else you need right now?"

"I could go for some ice cream. Can I get some or is the kitchen closed?"

"I think I can get that for you, even if it's closed." She smiles and this time it reaches her eyes.

"Thanks," I say and she closes the door. I try to recount how many days I've been in here but it's a blur. I've been sleeping most of the time. It's useless to try to think back to the accident. Every time I try, I get weird disjointed flashes that I can't quite put together. Everything is so jumbled so I don't bother. It might be awhile before I'm able to remember everything, if I ever really do. The brain has a strange way of making it difficult to remember certain things. I keep seeing my friend braced against the tree, the car on its side and I hear my own uncontrollable laughter. I'm not sure why those are the pieces I remember right now, but it's all I can put together. I wonder if I will ever remember more. For now, it feels too daunting a task to try.

Check out Haunted by a Moment Today!

www.ingramcontent.com/pod-product-compliance
Lightning Source LLC
Chambersburg PA
CBHW030559180626
46816CB00005B/1609